ABOUT US

LIZ EVERLY writes the sexy culinary-themed romantic suspense SAFFRON NIGHTS SERIES for e-Kensington. The SAFFRON NIGHTS series explores food and passion on an international scale. Think truffle hunting in Tuscany, exotic mushroom gathering in Hawaii, and open-air markets in Mexico. She also publishes her own erotic short stories on Amazon. Writing about Xander the sexy vampire in this collection gave her a chance to explore her dark side. In her other life, she pens a mystery series, has written cookbooks, and works as a freelance food writer. She's a member of RWA and of the Kiss of Death chapter. Contact her at Lizeverly@rocketmail.com; @lizeverly1, Facebook, or lizeverly.com.

MADELINE IVA enjoys writing and reading erotic romances with kinky-lite sex. Her books focus on whip-smart heroines, brooding heroes. Whether fantasy or paranormal, she always includes big whollop of comedy. She's a member of RWA, and Washington Romance Writers. She organizes romance panels for LOVE FEST at Virginia Festival of the Book. You can find out more about her, her books, and LOVE FEST by visiting her website at madelineiva.com. Follow her on Twitter: @madelineiva. Friend her on Facebook.

C. MARGERY KEMPE is a writer of erotic romance distinguished by its humour, intelligence and fearless sensual pleasures. Her stories range from contemporary thrillers to medieval era fairy tales. An English professor by day, she also writes on medieval literature, film, creative writing and New Media, as well as humor, drama, mainstream and genre fiction under her real name, noir as Graham Wynd and non-explicit romance as Kit Marlowe. Follow her on Twitter: @cmkempe or friend her on Facebook.

One of ELIZABETH SHORE'S great passions is writing historical and contemporary erotic romance - the hotter, the better. She's never met a bad boy she didn't love and she's swept off her feet by complex, tortured heroes, smart and sexy heroines, and conflicts that seem unresolvable. In addition to her zest for romance, she freely admits to being Stephen King's #1 fan (despite what Kathy Bates might have you think), is a devoted animal lover, and has never seen a bag of potato chips she couldn't conquer. In addition to Harper Impulse, she's published with the Wild Rose Press and Kensington. You can follow her comings and goings on Facebook, at her website, lizshore.com, via Twitter @ renaissance11, or contact her directly: elizabeth@lizshore.com.

The Lady Smut Book of Dark Desires, Anthology

LIZ EVERLY

MADELINE IVA

C. MARGERY KEMPE

ELIZABETH SHORE

Harper*Impulse* an imprint of
HarperCollins*Publishers* Ltd
77–85 Fulham Palace Road
Hammersmith, London W6 8JB

www.harpercollins.co.uk

A Paperback Original 2015

First published in Great Britain in ebook format by Harper*Impulse* 2014

A catalogue record for this book is
available from the British Library

ISBN: 978-0-00-812405-2

Automatically produced by Atomik ePublisher from Easypress

The Lying, The Witch & The Wardrobe

By

C. Margery Kempe

We must not look at goblin men,
We must not buy their fruits,
Who knows upon what soil they fed
Their hungry, thirsty roots?

~ Christina Rossetti, The Goblin Market

Jeanie looked up at the big rambling farmhouse with a mixture of happiness and misgiving. The worn clapboard had the comforting familiarity only your own childhood home could keep. But returning now just meant she had failed.

Again.

"This is the place?" The cab driver must have noticed her strange expression.

Jeanie flushed. "Yes, this is it. How much do I owe you?"

Before she even stepped out of the taxi, two figures appeared on the porch, waving eagerly. "Welcome home!"

Jeanie waved back as she and the driver walked to the back of the car to retrieve her bags. Her mother's cheery face lifted her spirits and her grandmother's cheeks glowed with a pleasure that was hard to resist. And why should she?

"It's so good to see you!"

"Is that all the bags you have?"

Jeanie hugged them both tightly, kissing one cheek and then the other. "Yes, a few more things coming by the shipping company later on, but these are the essentials." So little! It was a bit daunting to know how few belongings she had accumulated in her life so far.

Of course, it made moving that much easier.

The two women hustled her inside, chattering a mile a minute as she threw her bags down just inside the door, refusing any help. They were both strong women, but at twenty three Jeanie was more than fit enough to handle the weight of her own life, so to speak.

"Time for a cuppa?" Her grandmother bustled into the kitchen without waiting for an answer, knowing there would be no debate. Indeed the kettle already whistled in anticipation. Jeanie saw with a sudden surge of pleasure that the tea tray was already laid, the beautiful blue and white Staffordshire pot ready for the hot water and its snuggly cozy that looked like a rooster. The cups that surrounded it on the tray were mismatched, but she saw her favorite elegant gold filigree cup and saucer were there. They were an essential part of her mad childhood tea parties when she pretended to be queen for the day.

Her grandmother filled the teapot with boiling water and the exquisite aroma of Earl Grey filled the kitchen. "Biscuits? Or bread and butter?" Jeanie's mother asked.

"Oh, surely biscuits!" Beatrice might be a grandmother, but her tastes still reflected a girlish delight in sweets, something her trim figure belied. Jeanie always marveled at her.

"Well, it is a special occasion," her mother said with a smile. Gabriella didn't have her mother's lanky frame but she wasn't one to deny herself the little pleasures of life, particularly since her husband had died. Jeanie didn't remember him too well herself, but her mother's stories of his gentle humor and sweet romantic ways never failed to make her yearn for such happiness herself.

Jeanie pushed that thought away. She didn't need one more reason to feel depressed. "It's so good to get such a welcome home." She did her best to smile bravely and felt the better for it. Here in the kitchen of her childhood home everything seemed a little brighter after all.

"We're grateful to have you here, my dear." Beatrice kissed the top of her head as Jeanie took her seat at the big oak table.

"I hope you are happy to be here," Gabriella said with the slightest air of anxiety.

"I am," Jeanie said too quickly, then laughed half-heartedly. "There's nowhere I'd rather be licking my wounds than home."

Beatrice tutted. "Now, now, we'll have none of that. We all have our disappointments. It's part of life."

"If you're not failing, you're not trying," Gabriella said, laying a tender hand on her daughter's arm. "Take it from one who knows."

"Mother, you're not failing!"

"I'm not even trying," she said softly but firmly. "I'm proud of you for putting yourself out there and reaching for success. Sometimes it just eludes us."

"And it's not your fault the business folded." Beatrice poured the tea into their cups, bustling around the table.

"No, it wasn't my fault," Jeanie said. "But I should have realized it was happening. The signs were certainly there. I'm just not sure I cared to see them."

"You'll find something new," her mother encouraged. "Maybe something locally."

"It was such a long way away," Beatrice agreed.

Jeanie laughed. "I was less than a two hour drive! I don't think I missed a holiday here apart from that snowstorm that made me late for Easter."

"But we love having you here," Gabriella said, munching a chocolate biscuit. "You can rest up for a while before you look for a new job."

As Jeanie carried her bags up to her old room, she ruminated on her mother's words. The thought of looking for another job filled her with despair but she couldn't just sit here and hide from the world, although that plan had a lot of appeal just now.

She dropped her bags on the floor and looked around the room. It hadn't changed a jot since her last visit home, save for the little box of chocolates on her pillow. That brought a smile. *I love you, mom!* The view out the window toward the orchards also brought a poignant ache to her heart. There really was no place like home.

Jeanie sank onto the bed and let the tears welling in her eyes spill down her cheeks. Despite the kind words of her mother and grandmother, she felt very much like a failure.

Sure, it wasn't her fault that Morris, Hunt & Holman had collapsed taking a couple dozen jobs down with them. The signs had begun to appear six months ago. Her cubicle partner Liz took off soon after. "You should get out, too," she'd confided to Jeanie between sips of champagne at the going-away party. "The writing's on the wall."

She couldn't say she didn't know. So why hadn't she done anything to stave off the inevitable? It wasn't that she loved her job so much that she couldn't bear the thought of leaving. It was fun enough, but Jeanie had never really been passionate about marketing, not like Liz.

Face it, she was just lazy. Jeanie sighed. Look at this room! If she hadn't taken down the now-embarrassing posters of her teen pop star crushes, it would look little different from when she was in high school.

Maybe even junior high, Jeanie realized with a sinking feeling. She had to stop feeling sorry for herself and do something useful. Rubbing her eyes to dry them, she hopped up and went over to her altar. Clearly her mother had dusted it, but the half-burned candles had a neglected air so she stuck them in the cabinet below and got some fresh ones out. Crossing the room she opened her

4

red bag to remove the figures that had graced the altar in her flat in Springfield. Freya, Kali, Brigit and Bast looked much more at home here in her old room, circling around the Ganesh statue her father had bought for her birth. The elephant-headed god always remained here, a spiritual anchor to her home.

With a lifetime of practice, Jeanie cleared her mind and focused. *I am here, I am present, the magic is in me.* She lit a candle of welcome and thankfulness and prepared to set her intentions. For a moment she faltered, then fell back on her standard mantra: *I am ready for the opportunities the fates bring my way. Let me be open to the possibilities.*

That simple act of faith made Jeanie feel immensely better. She set about putting away the rest of her clothes and things with a pleasant song humming in her head. After all, she was home, the apples were ripening in the orchard, summer still held its golden sway. In fact as the morning wore on the room was beginning to feel a bit too warm.

Jeanie stepped out into the hall to open the door to the 'jumble room' as they always called it. Getting the stubborn window open in there would get a cross breeze going and cool things down much faster.

It took a few tries to get the sash up. The wood had swollen in the summer heat. Chances were no one had tried to open it yet that year. Her mother and grandmother both had rooms on the lower floors. Jeanie propped the window open with the little stick kept on the sill for that purpose and then looked around the jumble room. It hadn't changed much either. For years it had accumulated anything out of season or unused and on its way to being discarded.

Yet even here, the neatness of the house continued. Snow boots were lined up on racks. The various seasonal decorations were carefully stowed in neatly labeled boxes. Jeanie smiled. In any other house, this room would be an overstuffed chaos. The only discordant note came from the seemingly ancient mystery of her childhood: the antique wardrobe that stood like a sentinel between the two windows.

Jeanie approached it, feeling the anticipatory thrill of intrigue work its way up her spine. She knew the story well. It had belonged to her grandmother's grandmother, Lizzie, and was made from the oak of a single tree. In their family, oak and apple had always been intertwined with family legends. Their orchards were watched over by mighty oaks hundreds of years old. Jeanie had wandered among them since she could first walk.

But this wardrobe retained its eerie appeal. It had belonged to her grandmother's grandmother, but it had been sealed by that woman's best friend and sister, Laura. Jeanie traced the red wax seal that bound the ribbon around it. Although wax, it did not give way to knife or nail, which Jeanie and her friends had all tried at various times.

The blood red wax bore a hand print, Laura's she had been told. Jeanie traced it now. It very nearly matched her own hand's size. As familiar as the shape of it had been all her life, the mystery of it pricked her curiosity as much as ever. Not least because Laura had disappeared without a trace.

Old magic, powerful magic… what took her away? They only knew what Beatrice's grandmother had told her family, that the young woman had been taken by the goblin men. Jeanie shuddered. The goblin men had been part of her childish nightmares after she had begged to know the story. Jeanie memorized the animal-headed grotesques in Arthur Rackham's illustrations with a delighted horror then regretted as they tromped through her bedroom in the dark.

She looked up at the top of the wardrobe where the legend was carved. *There is no friend like a sister,* the carved letters announced, *in calm or stormy weather.* What secrets did the enchanted box hold? Why had the goblin men stolen Laura away? Even back in the nineteenth century such news would have brought out the doctors and skeptics. Goblins indeed! If Jeanie hadn't grown up in a family of witches, she supposed that it would be very hard to believe indeed.

Not that she had seen any goblin men. Her mother was of the opinion that the worlds that contained other beings like goblins and the fae no longer intersected with their own. "Technology and the hustle bustle of modern life," Gabriella said, when Jeanie had quizzed her for the umpteenth time. "Why, I expect that's what drove them away. Though now and then I almost think I can hear the bells of that other land in the distance."

"Do you ever seek it out?" Jeanie had asked, full of the boldness of the very young.

Her mother had laughed. "No, child. What would I find there that I don't already have here?" Then she'd enveloped her in a fierce hug until Jeanie wriggled free with a child's thoughtless impatience. Her father's death was still a raw wound then, Jeanie realized with a start. *Poor mama.*

Maybe that was why Jeanie dreamed of goblins that night despite the comfort of her familiar old bed. Just as the first light of dawn approached the unsettling images woke her, startled and at first uncertain of her location. Jeanie rolled away from the sunlight's persistence and tried to organize her thoughts.

It was times like this she missed her old cat, Boo. The fluffy black cat with the white patch on her chest would sleep at the foot of her bed and when Jeanie wrestled with nightmares, Boo would wake her with a paw to the face as if to say, "Stop that!"

Maybe she should get a kitten, Jeanie thought, then felt a stab of despair. Did that mean she was giving up and staying? She sat up, determined to push defeat away. Besides, there was something else. Jeanie frowned. There was something almost sensual in the dream, but the memory eluded her. She felt aroused, which reminded her how long it had been since she'd felt that way.

As she got up and dressed, Jeanie contemplated the depressing fact of her sex life. It had been months without a good workout: she had been dating Bill for a while and Stan before that. Neither too exciting, but she had been concentrating on work going south. Jeanie made a face at her reflection. Was there some rule about not having a good job, home and relationship all at the same time?

She trotted downstairs to find her mother up and making zucchini bread. "What else are we going to do with all of them," Gabriella groaned, gesturing at the basket full of green.

"Do you need some help?"

"What I need is some more sugar. Would you mind running to the store? There are a couple other things on the list on the fridge."

Jeanie tore the list off the pumpkin magnet pad and scribbled 'sugar' at the bottom of the list. "Shall I take your car or gran's?"

"Take mine dear. It's easier to park."

Jeanie hopped in her mother's compact car and pulled out onto the main road. Something from her dreams still haunted the back of her mind, a tune perhaps. It proved elusive, but it was almost as if her tongue remembered it. But there was something dark as well, a shadow that made her shiver despite the warm morning sun.

By the time she pulled into the supermarket parking lot, Jeanie found it had all slipped away. No matter. It was just a dream. But as she stood in the produce section by the heaps of berries, the tune very nearly returned. *Come by*, was it? Or *come buy*? Same thing, or different?

"Well, look who's back," an overly cheery voice broke in. It was accompanied by the garishly made-up face of Loretta Wanger behind an oversized shopping cart with a squealing child perched in it.

Of all the gin joints in all the towns in all the world, Jeanie thought, trying to smother her desire to run screaming from the produce section. "Well, hello Loretta."

"I suppose you just got in," Loretta said, giving Jeanie the once over and taking in her t-shirt, jeans and hastily pinned up hair. "How long are you in town? Get that out of your mouth!" The latter comment was directed at her small child, who had taken advantage of her mother's momentary inattention to stuff a large onion into her mouth and hum around it.

"Oh, not sure at the moment," Jeanie said with as much evasiveness as she could manage while she watched Loretta try to remove the onion from the mouth of her toddler, who had apparently bit into it and was now simultaneously shrieking albeit in a muffled way as tears ran down her cheeks.

"So help me Hannah," Loretta sputtered as she wrestled with the child, "if she's not into one thing then it's another. Spit it out!"

"Well, I should probably leave you—"

"There!" Loretta held up the onion in triumph while her spawn proceeded to scream at top volume. "How long did you say you'd be around?"

"Oh, not sure, it might be a couple weeks…" Why couldn't she just lie? Or shove an onion into Loretta's mouth. If there was one thing everyone could agree with about Loretta, it was that she was an incorrigible blabbermouth.

"Oh no," Loretta said with exaggerated alarm, "You didn't lose your job did you?"

No, I just mislaid it. "The whole firm went under, alas." Jeanie gave her best I'm-taking-it-on-the-chin look and tried to smile in a way that ought to seem brave.

"I'm so sorry," Loretta said, as if she had just received news of a terrible bereavement. "How awful for you. I suppose it's lucky you can always run home to your mother."

Jeanie tried to release an avalanche of potatoes onto Loretta using only the power of her mind without success. "I didn't 'run home'," she said as evenly as possible.

"Oh, you know what I mean. It's good to have *family*," Loretta said, grabbing her spawn's hand before she grabbed another onion. "For when you fail. They're ready to pick you up."

"Well, I should really be getting on with—"

"Oh, don't let me keep you," Loretta said, wheeling her cart around and slapping her daughter's hand, which set off another volley of shrieks. "I'm sure we'll be running into each other all the time now!"

Jeanie turned abruptly the other way, vowing to grab the sugar and hightail it out of the store, when another voice hailed her as she turned the end of the aisle.

"You survived the Gorgon."

It was another familiar voice, but not one that made her cringe. Jeanie turned to see Darren Flint looking a lot more grown up than he had when they last dated in high school. "Next time I'll get the mirror out of my bag first. Turning her to stone should have been my first step."

His smile immediately reminded her why she had said yes when the quiet guy who sat behind her finally asked her out. It looked even more comfortable on his face now.

"At least she only had one of the Gorgonettes with her."

"You mean she's got more? The horror, the horror."

"Rumor has it she's pregnant again." His whole demeanor had so much more confidence, too. He had turned into a rather attractive man, Jeanie noted.

"I was surprised she graduated without a bun in the oven. And how are you?"

"Well. Sorry to hear about the company going under. That's a shame."

"Indeed it is. But I have a number of irons in the fire, so I'm sure something will come up soon." Could he tell she was lying? Jeanie didn't want to think about it too much.

"I've no doubt. Anyone would be glad to have you." The warmth of his expression persuaded her to take more meaning from his words than he might have intended.

Or did he?

"Did your wife send you out for some milk?" Jeanie said. Wow, that was subtle!

"I'm not married." The amusement showed plainly on his face. "You?"

"No." Jeanie tried to think of something clever to say. She had to resist going through her pockets in hopes of finding something worthwhile.

"So, that's good to hear. I mean—" He winced. "Not that it's good, but you know."

"Yeah." Jeanie laughed and the tension she had felt melted away. "I'm after sugar for my mom's baking. You?"

"Just odds and ends and something for dinner tonight. You free?" he added carelessly, his tone suggesting it didn't really matter one way or the other.

"I, uh, I better check with my mother and grandmother. I think they may have something planned. But if not, perhaps tomorrow night?" Jeanie thought she had recovered well from her initial surprise. She was also grateful that she'd have a respite before the thought of a dinner date with someone she knew in high school.

Knew? Dated, groped, explored a little fondling with—it all came back with surprising clarity. On top of the half-remembered dreams it gave her a strange flush of arousal that Jeanie hoped looked like nothing more than garden-variety embarrassment.

They exchanged numbers and Jeanie trotted off to get the sugar, hoping it could be achieved without any further emotional rollercoasters. She managed to buy her groceries without more than a quick hello to a couple of people whose names lay in the furthest recesses of her brain.

"Remind me not to venture out in public at this time of the morning," Jeanie said as she dropped the bag of groceries on the kitchen counter.

"Oh dear," Beatrice said, relighting the burner under the kettle. "Who did you run into?"

"Well, first Loretta Wanger."

Her mother laughed. "Steele now, of course."

"Oh yes, of course. One of her little darlings was trying to suck down a few extra onions while she badgered me."

"Sorry to hear it, but at least that makes it a little easier now for you."

11

"Easier?" Jeanie considered this as her mother nodded. "Oh, duh. Everyone's going to know now." She sat down at the table and covered her face in her hands. "Loretta's probably started the nosy parker phone tree and got the chatter covering half the county. 'Jeanie is a failure; news at eleven'."

"You're not a failure," Gabriella scolded. "The company going under isn't your doing. You did nothing wrong."

"Quite right," Beatrice agreed, setting a mug before her granddaughter. "You've landed on your feet right enough and you'll find a new path."

"I am open to the possibilities," Jeanie said, her smile returning.

"That's my girl," Gabriella said, laying a hand on her daughter's arm. "Walk among the trees, remember the old magic. Ground yourself well and then you'll be ready to fly again."

"I know you're right," Jeanie said. "I forget how wonderful it is to be among people who know the magic. It's hard sometimes living in a mundane world."

"Why do you think we're both so happy here?" Beatrice said, pouring the hot water over her teabag. "Our magic has its roots here. Generations back—and before that in the trees they brought from the old country."

That reminded Jeanie of her strange dreams. "I was looking at the old wardrobe last night."

"What brought that up?" Beatrice frowned.

"I was opening the window in the jumble room to get a cross-breeze. I had strange dreams, too. Of goblin men. I think."

Her mother shuddered. "I can't even think about them. They always give me such an unpleasant turn."

"You were always fascinated by that story," her grandmother said with a hint of disapproval. "I know I must have told it to you a dozen times or more over the years. The terrible goblin men."

"The lure of the forbidden? Though I find it strange that Laura would disappear after locking tight the wardrobe with such an impregnable seal. Strange magic."

"I think she was protecting her sister. Old magic," Gabriella said, echoing Jeanie's thoughts from the night before. "Whatever awful thing happened to her, she didn't want her sister to share the same fate."

"Laura's handprint is the same size as mine," Jeanie said absently, blowing on her too-hot tea.

"You didn't—try anything?" Her mother's eyes widened. "I don't think that would be a good idea."

"No, nothing like that. But I was wondering why you didn't just get rid of the wardrobe if it's got something bad inside it."

Beatrice shook her head. "We don't know that there's anything bad inside it. It may be the charm that holds them at bay, that keeps things away."

Jeanie considered this. "An inconvenient charm! You can't really put it on a bracelet, now can you?"

They all sipped in silence for a while, each woman lost in her thoughts. "So who else did you run into?" Gabriella finally asked at last as she got up to check on the zucchini bread.

"Darren Flint," Jeanie said and then immediately wished she hadn't because both her mother and grandmother got that zealous match-making light in their eyes. "Now, don't go getting ideas!"

"Who's getting ideas?" Her mother said, batting her eyes with an air of supreme innocence.

"You know his photography business is the talk of the town," Beatrice added. "Not to influence you in anyway, but it's well known he's quite a catch. I hear," she added hastily.

"Well, then you'll probably want to know we're having dinner tomorrow night," Jeanie said with a sigh as the two of them squealed in girlish delight. "Now I don't want to hear a thing about it, especially this 'good catch' nonsense."

"We'll be good," Gabriella said meekly and the two older women tactfully changed the subject to zucchini recipes to deal with the garden bonanza.

Later as Jeanie walked out the back she saw even more of the green torpedoes ripening. Usually they had tapered off by this end of the season, but it looked like no respite was in sight. She inhaled the aroma of the herbs in the kitchen garden where the two venerable rosemary bushes stood sentinels, then struck off across the paddock toward the orchards.

Jeanie felt another stab of grief; how often Boo had followed her steps out this way, stopping to chase butterflies or poke a paw into a promising burrow. She strode between the trees admiring the green apples. They were a few weeks away from ripeness but she had eaten more than a few over the years, enjoying their tart taste.

Today though she found her steps leading to the woods beyond the near orchard. Its cool darkness called to her and when Jeanie stepped into its quiet, she felt a part of herself go, "ahhh!" She turned to look back at the house and thought how comforting its shape was. As a child she had often hidden in the woods, imagining herself well into the wilds. Never mind that the county road leading back into town lay less than half a mile beyond.

The stillness of the deep green filled her senses with calm. Jeanie realized that she still carried a great deal of stress from her failure, as she continued to see it. Let it go, let it go, she told herself as she walked along, open yourself up to new possibilities. With each step a little more of the tightness left her shoulders and by the time she came to the clearing by the stream, Jeanie was smiling.

As she stepped into the clearing, she made a little gasp of surprise. It was still there.

The fairy ring!

She hadn't thought of it in years and yet there it was, as fresh as always. Jeanie knew the organic explanation for a fairy ring—after all mushrooms weren't single plants but parts of a whole system—but the delight this natural circle gave her never changed.

Jeanie stepped into the ring. She closed her eyes for a moment, grounding and centering, then walked around the edge of the circle using her finger to cast a magical circle to match the fungi. "The circle is cast, I am between worlds." She sat cross-legged at the center of the circle, closed her eyes and reached for a magic she had not communed with for some time.

"Come, Cerridwen, share a drop from your cauldron with me. I seek wisdom and inspiration and I will offer you apples from our orchard when they are ripe." Jeanie conjured the image of the bubbling cauldron, full of power and magic, and hoped for a taste. Her intense concentration made the forest around her disappear and only gradually did Jeanie realize that she heard a strange step in the silence and a song that grew audible bit by bit.

Come buy! Come buy!

The voices had an otherworldly tone that made her shiver. Jeanie opened her eyes but there was no song, only the silence of the trees around her. Reluctantly she got to her feet and opened the circle, feeling unsettled and a little disappointed. "I'll bring you apples anyway, Cerridwen," she called out. Never break your word with the ancients, and the Welsh witch goddess had a powerful reputation of settling scores.

The phrase she had heard in her dreams! It was familiar somehow, and not just from that. It niggled at her memory like a toothache but by the time she had walked back to the house, Jeanie remembered what it was. She dug through the books on the bottom shelf of her red bookcase and found it.

The Goblin Market. The cover had an illustration of a young girl being attacked by the goblin men. Jeanie shivered again. That's where her nightmares had come from. As a girl she had read and reread the poem, glorying in the terror provided by Arthur Rackham's illustrations as much as by Christina Rossetti's poem about the two sisters. She flipped open the book and felt a fresh sting of uncanny fear at the pictures.

Two girls, Lizzie and Laura, just like great-great-great-grand-mother and her sister. Jeanie turned the book over, frowning. Was it coincidence or connection? Did Rossetti know the same tragic story?

She began to read the poem again, seeing it with the fresh eyes of an adult. It startled her to find the lines etched on the wardrobe, *There is no friend like a sister in calm or stormy weather.* Jeanie took the book in hand and went to look at the big oak wardrobe again. The other lines after it made her thoughtful, especially the exhortation *to fetch one if one goes astray, To lift one if one totters down.*

Was Laura trying to keep her own sister from going astray?

We must not look at goblin men, we must not buy their fruits. Jeanie found it easy to imagine not looking at the goblin men when she considered the horrid little men Rackham drew. Why would one want to look at them? She realized there was a lot she had missed in the poem as a child. There was a sensuality between the lines that seemed to be the real treat on offer. The sister who gives in to the desire to taste the sensual fruit pined away and nearly died.

Their offers should not charm us,
Their evil gifts would harm us.

Talk about your forbidden fruit!

Sweet to tongue and sound to eye, come buy, come buy! Was there something more appealing about these strange goblin men than the poem betrayed? Jeanie looked at the bound wardrobe and wondered yet again at the secrets it contained. With a thrill of fear, she reached up to fit her hand into the print made so many years before.

Nothing happened.

Jeanie smiled ruefully. What had she really expected? What price had Laura paid for her taste of the fruit? The goblin men had not accepted filthy lucre, but only a lock of her golden hair and a tear round as a pearl.

When her mother called her down to lunch Jeanie was still immersed in the world of *The Goblin Market*. As they sat down to their fresh spinach salads, she opened her mouth to say something about the poem, but checked herself at the last moment, uncertain why.

That night she dreamed of the goblin men again and awoke in

the dark gasping for breath as she felt tight little hands around her neck. Jeanie got out of bed and stood by the cool air of the window until her heart had stopped racing. *Come buy! Come buy!* She shivered as the word echoed in her ears.

In the moonlight the orchard swayed in a late night breeze. Normally the familiar surroundings soothed her thoughts like a soft blanket wrapped around her shoulders. Tonight the trees seemed to whisper with an uncanny menace as if they knew secrets Jeanie could not begin to guess.

She told herself she was being silly with a shake, but she went over to her altar and took a pinch of salt from the oyster shell and sprinkled it at the window, reciting a charm of protection as she did.

Jeanie got back in bed, but it seemed a very long time before her troubled thoughts let her ease back into slumber.

In the morning she tucked her copy of Rossetti's poem under the stack of personnel folders she had carried away in hopes of constructing a stronger résumé. Out of sight, out of mind. Jeanie busied herself with homey tasks around the house, helping her mother beat the carpets and working with her grandmother to clear out the pantry of mystery jars half empty, filled with who knew what.

"Smells kind of like mushrooms," Jeanie said sniffing gingerly at one such jar.

"It shouldn't," Beatrice said with a frown. "I think it was some kind of fruit paste."

"Eww!" On the plus side, they had a lot more clean jars to reuse.

"What time is your date, err, dinner?" Gabriella asked as she poured some fresh lemonade out for all three of them.

"Not until six," Jeanie said with reluctance.

"Six?! You should be getting ready." Beatrice looked at her with alarm.

Jeanie laughed. "It's not a date. It's just dinner with an old friend." But after her shower she chose the red silk blouse to wear with her jeans because she knew it flattered her skin tone, and she took a little extra time pinning up her hair so it looked casual but also more sophisticated than she normally had it. Might as well put her best foot forward. Who knew what gossip was already out there?

Jeanie arrived at Darren's house with a bottle of wine and a few misgivings, which she tried to quash at once. It wasn't really a date, she reminded herself as she rang the bell.

Or was it?

Darren answered the door with a big grin, a touch too much aftershave and a bear hug. "Sorry! Hope I didn't crush you. I'm just so pleased you decided to come." He showed her around the neat little house quickly, steering her to the patio out back. "I spend most of my time here anyway." The wooden deck featured a few chairs, a big glass table and a gigantic grill. "This is the Behemoth," Darren explained, blushing a little. "I know it's a cliché but I do love my manly barbecue machine."

Jeanie laughed and took the glass of wine he poured for her. "I enjoy having other people cook for me, so I will make no smart ass remarks of any kind. Unless the food is bad," she added with an arched eyebrow.

She had no complaints about the plump shrimp cocktail he plunked down in front of her while he busied himself with the chicken and corn. The scent of barbecue filled the air as Jeanie chomped on the shrimp. The view wasn't much; the suburbia in town held few charms for her, but Darren had made his little patch of it quite nice. He had avoided the regimented look of most of the yards and gone with a softer, more natural look with clumps of bushes and little decorative trees here and there.

They chatted about people they knew, about his photography business, about her work. He set the piping hot chicken barbecue before her then handed her a plate with a roasted ear of corn on it. Jeanie slathered it with butter and savored the creamy taste.

18

"Fresh always tastes better," she murmured.

"The right seasoning brings out the best flavor," Darren said with a strange smile that made her look down at her plate a little too quickly. "Eat all you want, there's plenty."

Jeanie took him at his word. She had never been one of those dainty eaters. Life on the orchard was enough to keep her fit and when she went away to college disappointment in the taste of the food there had been enough to keep her from developing the freshman fifteen.

"That was fantastic," Jeanie said as she wiped the last of the butter and barbecue sauce from her mouth. "Thank you so much."

"It's a pleasure to cook for an appreciative guest. Another glass of wine?" Darren poured more into her glass then put his feet up and sighed happily as he sipped his. "It's great to have you back in town. Even if you're only visiting…"

Was he fishing for more details? Jeanie found herself flattered that he was so interested and considered the question with genuine thoughtfulness. "I really don't know. I think I need to completely transform my life. I was happy enough with my job, but it wasn't something I felt a real passion for, I must admit."

"You picked the right place to regroup. I've always envied your orchard. Such a paradise."

Jeanie laughed. "You wouldn't say that if you were picking apples for hours on end. The way your shoulders ache!"

Darren grinned. "I suppose it's just the romanticism of a city boy. Suburbia seems like the wilds to me," he said, gesturing at the backyard.

"And the orchards don't seem wild enough to me," Jeanie mused, feeling a strange thrill of something run up her spine as she thought of the fairy ring. "Maybe I should take off for a year in the wilds."

"I'd rather you didn't. Not just yet anyway," Darren said in a soft voice. "I'm enjoying meeting you again as an adult."

"We have changed so much." Jeanie tried not to worry that

she hadn't changed at all. Saying good night made her feel little different from a teenager.

"Do you really have to go?" Darren smiled as they lingered at the door.

"I do, I was up early and am falling asleep even now. Probably due to you stuffing me with so much food. Thank you. It was a lovely dinner." Jeanie leaned in to kiss his cheek, but Darren moved in to kiss her on the lips. She let it happen, enjoying the warm contact of their lips.

Taking courage from her acquiescence, Darren wrapped his arms around her shoulders and the kiss grew more intense. His tongue probed between her lips and explored deeper. He was much more confident than when they had been awkward teenagers. No surprise, eh? But Jeanie found herself pleasantly impressed at the passion he showed.

She found herself responding, enjoying the press of their bodies together and the heat in the exchange. Yet she broke the kiss first, looking up at his face experiencing a mixture of eagerness and puzzlement. "Good night, Darren."

"Would it cause too much talk if I had you over for dinner tomorrow, too?"

"Probably."

"Seven?" He grinned, his eyes bright.

"I…let me think it over, okay?" Jeanie smiled nonetheless. "I'm not sure how much controversy I want to start in the first week."

"Call me. Or just come. I'll be here."

Jeanie drove home with those words echoing in her head. Certainly the buzz of the kiss filled her with a warm sense of arousal. It must have showed on her face when she walked in the house.

"Are you two waiting up for me?" Jeanie said, not a bit fooled by the detective novels her mother and grandmother held in their laps.

"No, no, we're just reading as we often do this time of night—ooh, is that the time?" Beatrice yawned.

20

"Looks like it was a good kiss," Gabriella said, rising and stretching, a finger keeping her place in the latest Val McDermid novel.

"Hush, mother! I don't want to have to think about you thinking about me having a good kiss." Jeanie made a face and they all laughed.

"But was it?" her mother persisted.

"Surprisingly good," Jeanie affirmed and then kissed the two of them good night before heading up the stairs. She thought of the kiss again as she brushed her teeth, but her dreams that night also reached back to the fairy ring and the book she had so carefully concealed.

Jeanie danced naked around the fairy ring, a blue circle of light protecting her. Around the circle the fae folk sang and frolicked. Darren appeared wearing an animal mask—badger? Or maybe it was a wolverine—and he used a knife to cut an entrance to the circle. He danced along behind her, closer and closer until he was right up against her, his erection nestling in the cleft of her cheeks as his arms wrapped around her. Jeanie leaned back against him, turning her head for a deep kiss. Another man appeared before her and pressed against her eagerly. She turned back to kiss him, unaffected by the wolf's mask he wore. "Never mind the teeth," he whispered, and as they kissed he slipped his rigid cock between her thighs and all at once she was on the ground and the music swelled as he ploughed deep within her. Jeanie arched her back with pleasure and felt many hands upon her, stroking her skin, pinching her nipples and biting the soft skin of her shoulders and neck. So many hands, so many mouths, and she cried out with pleasure as she came again and again.

"Come buy, come buy—"

Jeanie awoke with a start, the reverberations of her orgasm still echoing through her limbs. She reached between her legs to find herself very wet, a touch bringing another spasm of pleasure. Accustomed to trusting her body's responses, Jeanie nonetheless felt a bit betrayed by her body's wild pleasures in the dream.

Jeanie lay awake for a time, wondering if she should blame the book, the fairy ring or Darren for the uncanny dream. She smiled ruefully. She didn't mind an orgy dream, but the animal masks had to go. The cold air made her shiver and she slipped out of bed to lower the window. As she did so, a light drew her eyes. She squinted. It might have been a reflection—no. There was a light in the woods. Or was it *lights*—

—right about where the fairy ring lay.

Maybe she was still dreaming. But Jeanie didn't need to pinch herself to be sure that she was not. The chill of the night air on her skin was real enough, the goosebumps it caused were, too. In vain she tried to see more clearly. Where were her birdwatching binoculars? Jeanie glanced over her shoulder trying to remember the last time she had seen them. Then she looked back out the window.

If she got dressed and went to investigate, would she be like the stupid heroine of a horror film just before she gets killed by the monster? Or would she find a bunch of kids drinking beer and put an end to the silly idea of goblin men?

Before she could make a decision the lights winked out and there was only darkness and her own ghostly reflection on the window pane left. "I'm going back to bed," Jeanie announced to no one in particular and crawled back under the covers. She figured her troubled thoughts would keep her awake tossing and turning, but almost at once she fell asleep again and did not wake until the bright sun announced it was day. Jeanie stretched and hopped out of bed.

A sun salutation later, Jeanie stood before her altar. Grounding and centering came easy enough, but then she paused. What was it she wanted to do? Her altar was a workspace as well as a sacred one. It kept her honest as well as offering comfort and guidance. Usually when she found herself uncertain the magic of her communions with spirit renewed her resolve and showed her the path waiting to unfurl before her.

But now she paused because she didn't even know what to ask. Jeanie had asked to be open to opportunity but now she didn't know which way to turn. She looked at her goddesses: Brigit, Kali, Freya and Bast. Such fierce women! Jeanie felt a flush of embarrassment. Had she ever lived up to the models they offered?

She lit a red candle. "I ask to be worthy of your worship, great ladies. I ask to find my resolve as fiercely as your own. Where I waver, may I find certainty. Where I am wandering, may I find the path. Let me not drift, but find purpose. As you will it, so mote it be." Jeanie meditated on the flickering candle's flame as it burned and felt her spirits rise once more. She left the altar with a renewed sense of purpose.

Downstairs she found her mother and grandmother gathering baskets and buckets. "Ready to pick blackberries?" Beatrice greeted her, handing her a mug of tea.

"You betcha!"

They finished their tea and then trooped out to the rows of bushes that had been growing for decades. The plump ripeness of the heavy black treats was unparalleled in Jeanie's experience. As a child she assumed blackberries everywhere were just as flavorful and juicy. Experience had showed her wrong. Even in this region Jeanie had been surprised to find out how much better their patch was than any of the neighbors she had visited.

Though they had started early enough, the sun beat down before long with a considerable weight. Jeanie was grateful for the Red Sox cap she'd grabbed as they were heading out but looked with envy at her mother's broad-brimmed sun hat. "I should get a new hat for the garden," she called over to her.

Beatrice stood us, a hand to her back. "If you're buying, can I also get a new and far less creaky spine?"

"Sorry, I believe they're sold out on spines. I'll let you know when they're back in stock." Jeanie wiped the sweat out of her eyes.

"Well, we're almost to the end of the row. I say we reward ourselves with berries on ice cream with chocolate sauce," Gabriella

23

said.

"Hear hear!" Jeanie cheered.

Lunch was a noisy if not especially healthy repast, with much laughter. Jeanie felt refilled with joy and confidence. The uncanny unease from her dreams had evaporated at last, though her curiosity about the lights resurfaced.

"There's a fairy ring in the forest, near the stream in the clearing," Jeanie said, not quite sure how she expected her mother and grandmother to react. They exchanged glances and in the look Jeanie saw something pass that made her uncertainty return. "What?"

"You always come back to that," her mother said, shaking her head and picking up the dishes to take to the sink.

"Back to what?"

"The story, the girls."

"What? I don't know what you mean." Jeanie wrinkled her brow.

"Lizzie and Laura," her grandmother said softly.

The surprise on her face must have been clear. "But I thought that happened back in the old country. Didn't it?"

"Indeed," Gabriella said, her face uncharacteristically serious. "By a fairy ring near a stream in a clearing."

"Oh." Jeanie stared down at her hands. "Is there something more about the story you didn't tell me as a child?"

It was her mother's turn to look surprised. "What do you mean?"

"I—I don't know, I just wondered." Jeanie felt herself flushing a little. "I've had some strange dreams..."

"Strange?"

"Well, if you must know, sort of um, sexy." She could feel her cheeks turn pink.

"About the goblins?" Gabriella clearly looked surprised.

"Sort of. I think." Jeanie began to feel doubtful.

"Maybe it was influenced your date last night," Beatrice suggested. "And you just don't want to make the connection."

"I'm sure that's all it is," Gabriella agreed, though there was

24

something in her face that looked troubled.

Jeanie shrugged. "I suppose."

But later, as she went up the stairs, her steps drew her back to the jumble room and the big oak wardrobe. She'd forgotten to mention the lights, Jeanie realized as she stared at the red wax seal, frowning. While good at her job, Janie had never really had a passion for the work. She did it well and took pleasure in her accomplishments, but there was no zeal.

She felt a passion stirring inside her and somehow it was connected to the secrets inside the wardrobe.

Jeanie stared at the wax. Magic 101, she thought. What would Bast do? Suddenly inspired, she trotted back to her altar and hunted out the ceremonial dagger, the athame, from the cupboard beneath it. Blood was the oldest seal there was. Jeanie stood before the wardrobe, athame uplifted, its blade reflecting the bright sunlight.

"Blood calls to blood. Let the seal be opened."

She brought down the blade and winced as it struck her palm. Just a small cut, but enough to bleed. She let a few drops form, then put her palm to the imprint on the seal. It loosed a small vibration. Jeanie could feel it through the wood.

But it was no more than a shudder.

Jeanie frowned at the wood, disappointed. Then with a sigh she walked back to her room, intending to do some research on seals and locking charms, but on inspiration dug the Rossetti poem out from under the stack of folders and flipped through it again. There had to be a clue in there, she was sure of it.

She was still reading it when her phone rang. It always startled her. Most of Jeanie's friends texted back and forth, so an actual call was a rarity. Of course it was Darren.

"Are we on for dinner tonight?"

"I feel like I owe it to every chick flick ever made to play harder to get, but all right."

"See you at seven."

Jeanie laughed and agreed.

Yet when she pulled up at his house later a sense of misgiving rose in her thoughts. Maybe it was just the fact she was seeing him two nights in a row. Tongues would be wagging for sure, Jeanie thought as she looked at the neighboring houses, imagining she saw twitching curtains everywhere.

She was being contrary. She'd had a lovely time last night, the conversation had come easily and the kiss... Well, the kiss was entirely satisfactory. So what was wrong?

"Nothing, nothing at all," she muttered.

Darren opened the door before she rang the bell. "Hello!" A quick kiss as she stepped inside, then he was running back to the kitchen. "I just have to make sure the timer's set," Darren called over his shoulder.

"What's on offer tonight," Jeanie said, sniffing curiously. "I smell cilantro!"

"I hope you like Mexican," Darren said, making a face as she followed him into the kitchen.

"Love it, provided it's not New England Mexican."

Darren crooked an eyebrow at her. "New England Mexican?"

"I know too many people around here who think horseradish is too spicy!"

"Look," Darren said with a comically serious expression, holding out a spoon. "Not only jalapeños but also serranos."

Jeanie tasted the salsa. "Mmmm, delicious and with a good bite. I approve. Not New Englandish at all."

Darren marched Jeanie out onto the patio again with a pitcher of margaritas, bidding her wait to be served. She let herself be cajoled along and sat on the lounge with her feet crossed watching the late day sun descend. It was nice enough here, but she could never reconcile herself to suburbia.

Darren came out bearing chips and salsa, a fresh garnish of cilantro making the bowl look festive. "Pour me one of those, would you?"

They toasted over the chips. "To possibilities," Darren said with a mischievous air.

The food was good and Darren modest about his skills. Though Jeanie teased, "I'm a sucker for a guy who cooks well," she could tell the compliment pleased him. It had been some time since she had had a meal with as much flavor, although the simple freshness of the food prepared by her mother and grandmother had great power.

"Ow." Some of the sauce from the enchilada got into the fresh cut on her palm and stung. Jeanie put her hand to her mouth and licked it, hoping that would ease the pain.

"What did you do to yourself?" Darren took her hand to look at the cut. "Let me get a sticky bandage for it."

"Oh, it's nothing much. It just stings a little." Jeanie shook her hand a little. "I was just doing a ritual that didn't go anywhere."

"Ritual?" Darren frowned. "You're not still into that, are you?"

"Into *that*?" Jeanie looked at him with surprise.

"That witch stuff." He made a face. "I thought that was just your teen angst."

Jeanie laughed. "Teen angst? This is a tradition passed down through my family for generations."

"Aw, but it isn't."

"Oh, yes it is." Jeanie looked at him with confusion. "Didn't you believe me when I told you?"

Darren shrugged and sipped his margarita. "I just thought it a phase. Girls do that. Imagination."

Jeanie felt a heat in her belly that had nothing to do with peppers. "My family tradition you dismissed as 'a phase' that 'imaginative' teen girls go through." Her words rang with sarcasm.

"Hey, I didn't mean anything by it." Darren looked at her, a mixture of hurt and surprise in his eyes.

"It was very hard for me to tell you that when I did," Jeanie said, remembering all too keenly the terror she had felt at confessing

27

her family's true history to the boy she really liked. And he'd been sneering at her the whole time! She felt a flush of chagrin for her teen self.

"I just didn't—well, you could hardly expect me to take it seriously, could you?" It was his turn to look irritated.

"I opened my heart to you about the most important thing in my life and you dismissed it?" She was flabbergasted. A painfully truthful child, she had always been expected to be believed. It was the worst sort of betrayal—even if it was years in the past.

"I know now, there's a name for it—Wicca. I do read the newspapers." He poured another margarita for himself and held out the pitcher, ready to refill hers.

Jeanie ignored that. "I'm not talking about Wicca. I'm talking about my family's heritage, an art that's been passed down for generations, innovated by each practitioner, adapted to her own life but with the same skills. Not something learned from a book, a living tradition."

"But you don't believe in *magic,* do you?" He looked up at her for she had risen to her feet, passion tensing her limbs.

"It's the only thing I believe in." Jeanie turned on her heel and left, striding through his house out the door and into her mother's car. Her heart pounded a drumming sound in her ears.

When she pulled up to the house, her pulse had calmed somewhat. She felt a bit abashed at blowing up at Darren, but there was also something in her heart that seemed to have fallen into place and despite everything she felt good. As she walked to the house her spirits lifted.

Then she heard a sound behind her. Jeanie turned around, expecting to see a deer bounding away. They often did their best to raid the kitchen garden. Scanning the twilit grounds she saw nothing. Walking again toward the door, she heard a strange susurration behind her, turned and squinted.

Nothing.

A raccoon, probably—or maybe even a possum. Again she

28

turned toward the door and refused to turn around again until she felt a small hand brush against her leg and leapt into the air. "What?!"

And there was nothing. Nothing anyway that she could see, though once again her heart beat a staccato tune. Jeanie stared into the darkness and then turned once more and hastily trotted up onto the porch without looking back, muttering to herself *a plant, a long blade of grass, nothing, a bug, a moth, nothing at all, I'm sure of it*. Yet she stopped at the porch to look back one final time. There were a few lightning bugs in the air, lazily blinking along, nothing more to be seen. *You're being silly*, she scolded herself and stepped inside. "I'm home."

"You're early," her mother called from the kitchen. Jeanie followed the sound of her voice and found the two women cooking jam and making preserves of the huge harvest of blackberries. Jeanie took a handful from the nearest basket and started eating them.

"I had an argument with Darren," she said with a sigh equal parts annoyance and regret. "Do you know, I screwed up my courage to tell him about our tradition of magic when we were going out in high school and he thought I was just pretending."

"Most people don't believe it, dear," her mother said with equanimity as she stirred the bubbling pot of berries.

"Your grandfather pretended never to see it." Beatrice smiled over the jar she was drying. "He didn't mind benefiting from it but I think he lived in terror of being asked about it by the minister. What was his name? Father Stephens or was it Stephen?"

"You didn't tell him?" Jeanie sat at the table, munching on the sweet berries.

"It was a different time," her grandmother said, laughing a little at the thought. "People would have wanted me locked up as a crazy woman."

"I told your father, but he never spoke of it. It was like he thought it 'women's work' somehow. Not shameful exactly," she said with a smile, "but not really his business."

Jeanie frowned. "Have there ever been men who practiced the art?"

"Oh definitely. My cousin Collinson, he did for sure. He had a big revival tent business, curing people and whatnot. Until he was jailed for seducing a sheriff's daughter somewhere in the Carolinas."

"Revival tent? Like a Christian thing?"

Beatrice laughed. "Well, you aren't going to get southerners to go to a witch tent, now are you? And this was what? The nineteen-thirties? Oh, well back in the day."

Jeanie shook her head. "Curiouser and curiouser, as Alice would say. There's a lot of family history I don't know."

"Someone should write it down," Gabriella agreed.

"But you should cut Darren some slack," Beatrice said. "As the kids say, it's a lot to process. We've the advantage of being to the 'manner' born, so to speak."

"Listen to grandmother and her slang," Jeanie said with a grin. "I'll think about it." She grabbed a handful more of berries and headed upstairs, turning their words over in her mind. As she passed the jumble room door, Jeanie reflexively glanced at the wardrobe. All kinds of family history to record.

The book of the goblins lay on her bed where she had left it. Turning it over she found herself back in the scene where Lizzie rescues Laura with the fruit juices smeared on her face by the angry goblins. For a modern reader the sensuality of the lines was plain and somewhat unsettling:

Hug me, kiss me, suck my juices
Squeez'd from goblin fruits for you.

Jeanie looked with dismay at the blackberry stains her fingers had left on the margin of the page. Like a tiny bell ringing in the back of her mind and gradually gaining strength, an idea occurred as she stared at the blood-like prints.

Jumping up Jeanie strode across the hall to the wardrobe with a hope in her heart. "Let your secrets be revealed to me," she said with great solemnity and pressed her berry-stained hand to the seal. The vibration she had heard before intensified and without much fanfare the seal cracked in half and fell to the floor, taking its ribbon with it.

Jeanie clapped her hands together then opened the doors with a creak. Her face fell. The wardrobe was full of clothes. *Not so odd that*, she thought crossly. But that couldn't be all. She pushed aside the dresses and found there were three drawers at the bottom of the wardrobe. She rifled through the hand-sewn silk undergarments in the first without an appreciation for their beauty.

The second contained ribbons, stockings and garters, and the third cotton chemises, but under them lay the reason for the seal. Two rough artist notebooks lay hidden, untouched since the night the young woman had disappeared. Jeanie sat down on the floor and opened the first with eager hands.

It was a sketchbook. The initial pages were filled with familiar orchard lanes, this house and people who bore the stamp of family resemblance—the wide mouth, the sharp cheeks and the nose that was just a little too pointy. Jeanie felt a flush of familiarity to see such faces capture here by an amazingly assured hand. What an incredible artist she'd been!

As she flipped through there were more pictures of a similar nature but gradually the sketched turned to wilder fare. With a start Jeanie recognized the massive oak at the forest's edge—huge even a hundred or more years ago. The sleepy glades and the stream and yes—there!

A fairy ring. A shiver of recognition went down her spine. It was the very same location, the *very* same. How long did mushrooms live? Jeanie shook her head. Surely they didn't live past the season. It was a bit of a shock to see the same ring, but there was bound to be a reasonable cause in the lay of the land.

Turning the page she got a bigger shock… goblin men. And goblin women! And they were nothing like the hideous trolls of

Rackham's illustrations. They were beautiful, though they were certainly odd, too. Many did have animal heads—or were they animal masks?

They definitely had human bodies. Jeanie felt her face grow warm as she gazed on the very frank life studies of the naked goblin men. The first few were detailed and clearly caressing in their attention, but modestly incomplete. As the pages continued the artist focused on a pair of goblin men, one with a bear face and the other with a stag's.

And they were not modest at all.

She had drawn the two side by side, naked and smiling. Then she had drawn first one then the other, rigid cocks in hand and devilish gleams in their eyes, as if daring her to take part. The eroticism was undeniable. Jeanie shared their arousal and gasped with surprise as she turned to a page where the two men, masks up, caressed a young woman between them.

She could have been Jeanie's double.

Her dream the other night returned to her with sudden force. It made her wet. Her lips parted as she traced the lines of the sketch, admiring its erotic power. Taken by the goblin men, indeed!

The pages after that were blank. With an effort, she tore her eyes away from the alluring sketch and opened the other book. She experienced a shock of recognition: it was Laura's book of shadows. Jeanie had one of her own, a dog-eared red journal. She had bought a special blank book with a fancy cover that had medieval script on it, but it had always seemed too nice. She had always intended to copy over the rituals and charms she had scribbled down in the red book, but somehow it never happened.

Laura's book looked the same. Words were crossed out, pages had been ripped out, various things had been spilled on the pages. Jeanie flipped through the leaves seeing many a familiar ritual and charm, but not what she was looking for. Did she really think Laura was going to have a page entitled 'Summoning the Goblin Men'?

Of course not, but then she spotted the much-blotted page that bore the legend, "Opening the fairy ring". Jeanie felt her breath stop.

Come buy, come buy!

It was a simple enough ritual, little different from any another opening ritual—apart from the location. She had most of the required items already. But she wouldn't do it, would she? Jeanie looked over at the sketchbook, lying open to the erotic trio. Although rendered with quick strokes rather than fine detail, the figures had been made so vivid they seemed to writhe on the page.

Jeanie felt an electric urge to join their sensual feast. A warning sense of caution itched at the back of her mind.

We must not look at goblin men,

We must not buy their fruits

Yet an excitement bloomed inside her that she had never known before. With a start Jeanie realized, *this is what passion is.* And to her shame, she knew that she had never really felt it before. Not for a person, not for her work, not even for any of her hobbies. It was as if something lay unawakened in her all this time.

Jeanie picked up the books and went to her room, sitting on the bed but staring out the window as she tried to make sense of things. She couldn't really be contemplating this, could she? Her eyes watched the dance of the fireflies outside her window and pretended she had not already answered her own question. Suddenly she gasped.

Fireflies only shone in midsummer; it was nearly autumn.

Were they trying to lure her outside? Was this the goblin men? Did they put on a pretty show then lure the enchanted away? She looked at the poem and remembered how they pinched and scratched and mauled poor Lizzie.

Jeanie frowned. She opened the sketchbook again and saw the ecstasy on Laura's face as the two goblin men took her, her leg wrapped around him as the one drove into her, his body straining against her and his fellow behind her, sharp-nailed hands on her breasts as he leaned in to kiss or bite her neck.

It made her so wet; she could almost feel the warmth of their

33

bodies—longed to feel them wrapped around her flesh, thrusting inside her. Unconsciously her own hands had sought her breasts and she wanted them, the goblin men, and she knew it, and knew she would do it.

Swift fire spread through her veins, knock'd at her heart,
Met the fire smouldering there...

When she knew her mother and grandmother had gone to bed, Jeanie took the canvas bag she'd stuffed with the needed items and struck out the back through the orchard. No fireflies now met her, just a soft breeze that whispered summer's abandonment.

Treading the path she knew so well, she found the clearing at once. The fairy ring shone white in the starlit night and Jeanie walked around it to set her candles at each of the cardinal points, lighting each one and invoking its guardian as she cast the circle. As she stood at the center, she remembered her promise to Cerridwen and smiled. "So you did give me a drop of wisdom after all."

She set the bag at her feet and lay the sketchbook open to the erotic illustration. With Laura's book of shadows in hand, she raised her athame and read aloud the summons.

"I open the ring to the goblin trade;
My purse but a golden curl.
Be merry in the dance,
For your pleasures take a chance
Let the fairy folk caper and whirl."

Jeanie knelt down and thrust her athame in the ground and waited, her heart beating fast. At first there was nothing, and then the tinkling of a tiny bell, something so small and so fine that she wondered if she had been mistaken.

Then a hubbub began and she opened her eyes and all around her the dancers twirled unmindful of her presence as she gaped. They were of all shapes and sizes, some with gossamer wings, some with gorgeous hulks, but all a wonder to her startled gaze. Over there the band played—small green figures blew on living snakes, a drum seemed to be a turtle played by a woodland sprite, unconcerned by the position of his shell, watching the dancers cavort.

Jeanie stumbled away from the center of the dance to see the other world spread out beyond. The market indeed sprawled beside the ring, stands and little barrows filled to the brim with goblin fruit: pellucid grapes and rosy apples, lush strawberries and rounded pears, peaches ripe as breasts begging to be caressed.

And everywhere the cry, "Come buy! Come buy!"

Jeanie pressed forward and there by a cart full of tart green apples stood a pair of goblin men who seemed more alive to her eyes than anyone in that magical place. They were not the men in the sketchbook which lay forgotten behind her, but they had something of the same lively sensuality that drew her to them like a strange magnet.

"What have we here?" The one said, his goat mask pushed back to reveal dancing black eyes.

"Looks like an eager customer," his fellow said, moving the stag mask away from his face to get a better look at Jeanie. His smile showed bright white, even teeth as he held an apple out to her. "Have you ever seen anything so tasty?"

Jeanie grinned, but the goat man said, "I sure haven't." His look was frankly lascivious as he ran it admiringly up and down her form.

"She may only be interested in apples," the one in the stag mask said, though he continued to smile.

"I live on an orchard," Janie said at last, feeling her tongue loosen as she gave rein to her feelings and let go her fear. "I have apples every day."

"No sale for us," the goat one said with mock sadness, stepping closer to Jeanie to take her hand. "What a shame."

"Perhaps she has other tastes," said the one like a stag. "My name's Cervus."

"And mine's Hircus," the goat boy said, kissing her hand. His lips warmed her skin with a touch that was nearly electric.

"My name's Jeanie," she managed at last as Cervus took her other hand and kissed it too, provoking a similar heat.

"Such an unusual name," Hircus said. "Why don't we take this skin of wine and get to know a little more about you, Jeanie."

It didn't seem strange at all to be walking away into the woods with two goblin men. Nor when Hircus kissed her lips was she at all surprised to feel Cervus start kissing the back of her neck.

"You've not come to the market before," Hircus said when he finally let the kiss end, leaving Jeanie dizzy with delight.

"No," Cervus murmured in her ear. "We would have certainly remembered you." His teeth gently nipped her skin and she gasped with pleasure.

Hircus grinned and let his hands slide down to her hips. "Are you sure you wouldn't rather have some apples?"

"No," Jeanie said, surprised to hear how husky her voice had become. "I want you. Both of you."

"Well, that's easily arranged," Hircus said laughing. Cervus' hands moved to her breasts as Hircus began unbuttoning her blouse. "You're pretty as a fairy witch, but you don't live in these realms."

"I'm a mortal witch," Jeanie said, then gasped as Cervus pinched her nipples.

"How exotic," Hircus murmured as he kissed her belly and undid her jeans with some difficulty. "Mmmm, you smell as good as a fairy queen." His long tongue felt warm against her clit.

Cervus had slipped his trousers off for she felt his erect cock against ass as she squirmed. His fingers squeezed her breasts tightly, flicking her nipples while he bit her shoulders and neck with increased vigor.

Hircus swirled his tongue around her clit then surprised her as he thrust two thick fingers inside her. "Oh, look at her dance," he crooned. His fingers slipped in and out, coated in her juices, while Jeanie shuddered with pleasure.

Cervus groaned. "I want to feel that warm, wet hollow."

Hircus withdrew his fingers and stuck them in his mouth. "Mmmm, you're going to want to taste it, too. Here, you sit down." He waited for his friend to sit then helped Jeanie ease back onto his waving cock. Hircus watched her face closely as she squatted down upon him and her face dissolved in pleasure.

"Oh, gods. I think I'm going to come!" Cervus thrust up into her with groan as she continued to cry aloud. No doubt about it; the orgasm built up and exploded as he continued to thrust up.

"Oh, you should feel this!" Cervus called to his friend. "Ecstasy! All those stories of mortals—they're true." He closed his eyes and tried not to come.

Hircus grinned down at her as she panted with the effort. He held his stiff cock out before her and Janie took it in without a word, gobbling greedily at the length of it. Hircus' eyes rolled back as he moaned. Jeanie sucked the plump head as if it were a plum and felt him shudder. Gradually she found herself matching the thrusts of Cervus below her as she took Hircus cock deep in her mouth.

"I think I'm about to spend," Cervus croaked, his hips speeding up as he shook with the passion about to release. Jeanie sped up her own movements, grabbing both cheeks of Hircus' bottom as she heard him begin to cry out. The two of them came, one after the other and all three moved with sweaty passion as one.

Hircus collapsed beside them when he stopped spasming with pleasure. The two of them squeezed Jeanie between them. "You're amazing," Hircus said, looking at her intensely.

"Yeah, what he said," Cervus agreed, turning her head so he could finally kiss her on the lips too. "And when I've had a chance to recover, I am going to show you what a goblin man can do to please a woman."

"No less will I!" Hircus cried, wiggling against her ass as if to urge his own body on to recovery.

Jeanie laughed. "I have been pleased so far."

"Oh, but there's so much more we will do." Cervus brought his mouth down to her breast and began to suck.

"Eat me, drink me, love, goblins make much of me," Jeanie chanted as they did just that. An idea struck her. "You two don't know of a mortal woman named Laura do you?"

Hircus lifted his head from her other breast as his hand drifted down to her mound. "Laura? You mean Arthus' woman? She came from the orchards too. Do you know her?"

Jeanie moaned as Cervus' teeth teased her nipple. "Sort of." Laura had given herself to sensual delights. Lizzie had lied—or convinced herself that Laura was wrong. It was another time; women weren't supposed to enjoy sex.

I wonder if I can go back? Jeanie wondered, then surrendered herself to the hands and tongues of the goblin men. Tonight would be a feast she had never known possible. Suddenly her confidence surged along with her pleasure. *I can do anything!*

The Immortal Longing of Brenna Bang

By

Liz Everly

Xander drew back his lips, savoring this moment, baring his teeth. He drew in the scent of her, gazed at her long tender neck, savoring, savoring the moment before penetration.

"Xander," she said breathily, her eyes glistening with longing. "Please."

He took her neck, her vein, her blood so tenderly that she swooned from the pleasure of it. As he bit and sucked her life force she writhed from the exploding passion. As he had told her, submitting to him would bring her the most intense passion and orgasm she'd ever known.

And that was just the beginning—for he'd yet to give her the "love bite" between her thighs. But she wasn't ready for that.

He pulled his teeth from her neck, just in time, of course. She wouldn't die—he'd see to that. She'd just crave him above all others, and he would oblige.

He'd keep this one safe.

He sat back on his haunches and watched the woman as she bucked and moaned. He held her naked body and sunk two fingers into her moist center. Her life force was still boiling within her—now was the time to take her.

As her blood entered him, his erection grew stronger and harder. He plunged into her…

Plunged? How many times have I used plunged in this book? How about thrust? Or pressed? No, not pressed. It's not forceful enough.

Thrust it is.

As her blood entered him, his erection grew stronger and harder. He thrust into her, making her scream with pleasure, him moan with fevered curiosity. He'd taken countless women like this and each one felt different. He enjoyed this one's legs as she wrapped them onto his shoulders, and moved deeper within her. The throbbing of her blood and the throbbing of her sex surged through him.

Her hips met his in opposite reaction.

Oooo. He liked this one. She was strong, with hips that moved him, lifted him; hips that made him remember what it was like to be a man, not immortal. And yet so tight, so smooth and grasping at his cock. He would give her all he could in one explosive moment.

When he came in her, the orgasmic rush was as he expected. But there was more… The clapping of thunder. The rolling noise of heaven meeting hell, with earth couched somewhere in between.

He jerked away from her.

"Just who the fuck are you?"

Good question Xander. Who is she?

I took another sip of wine. Red mulled wine, thick with spices. I think it was my third of the day. And I left my mind to play with the idea of this woman bringing my Xander to his knees. So to speak.

This is what my writing life is like. I don't plan it. I don't plot it. I write where the feeling takes me and then sometimes I have to stop and figure out where exactly that is. Like who is this woman? As always, my hunk of a naughty vampire Xander and I would figure it out together.

In those days, I was writing in my basement. Dark, cool, and without distraction. Until the day he came to me. No. Not Xander. I know it's confusing, but bear with me.

Now, you will think I'm perfectly mad. And that's okay, because maybe I am. I've wondered if it never really happened at all, if it was nothing more than extended dream, a fantasy I created from too many hours alone.

We writers spin our tales, never imagining they will take form in quite this way. But really? Once you understand that not everything in life is explainable, what we do takes on a dangerous edge. Is it some form of dark magic? Can we tap into our subconscious in such a way that we create characters that become real not just on the page, but as sentient beings? Can we imagine our perfect lover into a reality of flesh and bones?

Because I think that's exactly where he came from.

After three glasses of wine and a long, intense writing session, I fell asleep at my computer.

After meeting one deadline and launching into my next vampire novel, I simply slumped down in my chair and drifted off. I awakened to an odd buzzing or humming. I jolted awake, blinking at my computer screen, which was snowy and vibrating. I sat up straighter. What the hell? I'd just bought the thing!

Suddenly the room bristled with energy, but my eyes didn't leave the screen. Something was forming. Its shape looked familiar. A cheekbone. The hollow between it and full, upturned lips, a long nose, eyes, and a forehead. Still blue and gray, the face lifted out of my computer screen and the air in my office crackled as I struggled for breath.

The room suddenly settled and I felt a soft, warm brush of breath on my neck. The reflection of a man stared back at me from my computer.

I don't know why I didn't scream or struggle, except that I felt an immediate sense of safety coupled with excruciating longing. Warmth emanated from his soft dark eyes when they met mine and he drew me in to a dreamlike space, where time didn't even seem to exist. He smiled. And it was all over for me.

He bent down and leaned into me, ever so softly kissing my neck sending prickly sensations up and down my spine. I was mesmerized. He was so beautifully put together that it reminded me of my vampire character, Xander, who had women swooning all over the planet in my books.

Was I dreaming? Was that it?

But when he kissed my neck, it felt real. His full lips pressing to my skin, sending tendrils of pleasure through me, down into my very center.

There was a man in my basement, kissing my neck.

I wilted beneath his expert touch. His hands ran along my arms as his tongue, then teeth, grazed along the nape of my neck. A small sound escaped from somewhere inside of me. Where did that come from? Was that sound coming from me?

He smelled spicy and musky, as delicious as he looked. His dark hair fell in waves framing his face, with cheekbones that stretched his skin taut and dimples framing either side of his mouth. His eyes were closed as I watched him. He was enraptured with me, attentive like I'd never experienced. With each kiss, each breath, a force traveled to my center, making my hips feel like they needed to move. It was a strong force, rippling, tingling, as my head rolled back and I drew in a breath… was I going to… yes, yes… From just his kisses on my neck and chin, now his mouth on mine, an orgasm ripped through me. I closed my eyes with each rocking, blasting pulse.

…And suddenly I felt cold. When I opened my eyes, he was gone and a deep sadness and overwhelming sense of loneliness came over me. I felt so incredibly empty.

My neck ached as I lifted my head. Damn. I'd fallen asleep at my monitor and had had the strongest, most realistic dream ever. And to top it all off, it was a wet dream. Interesting, as that had never happened to me before and I wasn't exactly the most orgasmic woman on the planet. In fact, Josh used to tease me about being an erotic romance writer and not really having many orgasms at all. I could describe them so well that you'd think I was having them all the time. Oh, I had them, just not every time I had sex. Not that I even had sex that much anymore. Face it, writing those incredible sex scenes was often more pleasurable than the real thing. There was just so much bad sex going on these days and I'd had more than my share of it.

So. Back to my story about him. The man who visited me in my dream. To say that he left an impression would be an understatement. I dreamed about him for three nights in a row. Each time, I woke up shuddering in orgasm. I was getting a little concerned about my trip to New York, hoping that I wouldn't have one of these wet dreams in the room with my roommate, who I was meeting for the first time at the national erotic romance conference. We'd hooked up just to share expenses. I didn't want her to think I was some freaky perv having wet dreams in the neighboring bed.

***

When I disembarked from my cab, I stood a moment on the New York street, as I always do. I love the city, love to soak up the energy I feel there. The doorman took my bag and I turned toward him to offer a tip… and I saw him.

The man from my dreams.

My heart lurched and everything around me hummed, vibrated with energy. He walked by me and winked as I stood with my mouth hanging open. *I should say something. Do something. But what? "Hey I saw you in my dreams, what gives?"*

"Excuse me, miss, are you alright?" The doorman politely

nudged me.

"Oh, yes," I said, shaking it off, telling myself that the man just looked the hunk in my dreams. I was staring at him like a star-struck schoolgirl. My face heated, as did the rest of me, right to the very tips of my nipples which poked hard at my cotton dress. Way to make an ass out of yourself, Brenna. As the hotel was taking care of my bags, I felt it entirely appropriate to head for the bar. Not just appropriate. Necessary. I needed something to clear my head—and fast.

Tomorrow I was scheduled to be on the "Sexy Vampire" panel. With all those young writers in the place, and the people I was on the panel with, it could get intense. I needed to be on top of my game. And there I was having hallucinations about that hot guy.

I ordered a JD on the rocks and the bartender raised an eyebrow. "Make that a double," I said.

"Are you sure about that? You're a tiny thing," he said.

"I'm certain and I can handle my liquor. Thank you very much," I said. The place was packed and I couldn't see two feet in front of me because people were packed so close together. I struggled to find my way through the crowd. Finally, I found a place at the bar so I sat and sipped my whiskey. I thought about seeing the face of the man in my dreams.

What kind of logical explanation could there be?

It could just be someone who *looked* like him, right? There are a lot of people that look like one another on this planet. But the resemblance was uncanny.

My hand trembled a little as I lifted the golden liquid to my lips.

"Brenna? Brenna Bang?"

Oh shit. Someone had recognized me.

It was a young woman who I guessed was a conference attendee, oh, about twenty-five. She was all coiffed to the hilt. Perfect blonde hair, thin, beautifully dressed in almost all black with a red velvet scarf around her neck. Ah yes, the red velvet around her neck. How blood-like. How vampirish. That's exactly what I'd thought

44

when I wrote my first vampire novel, Red Scarf. So now some fans wore red scarves. Wish I'd thought to license that—I might be a millionaire by now.

"Big fan, here," she said, almost bouncing with joy. I kid you not. This is what it's like for me as a successful author at the age of thirty-five, someone who never had the time or inclination for make-up, or the gym, or to even keep up with my haircuts. And it's kind of weird for me because most of my fans obviously do. They take obvious pains in creating the "look." You could call it goth. You could call it vampire. Whatever. I called it pretense.

"Thank you," I said.

"Red Scarf. Such a classic," she said, sliding her tight little body up to the bar next to me. Boobs all high and firm. Not an ounce of fat on her. Bet she didn't sit in front of the computer for hours on end. "I think it's my favorite."

I smiled and lifted my glass to her. Bet she wouldn't get a beer, or a whiskey, for that matter.

"Can I please have a diet coke?" she said to the bartender.

I rest my case.

"Although I do prefer the narrative structure in your third book," she went on, taking her coke from the bartender.

"MFA?" I caught myself saying with disdain. Until that point, I wasn't certain if she was a fan or a writer.

She nodded. "I'm studying at NYU."

"Good for you," I strained to say, then took a large drink of what was left of my whiskey, almost draining it.

So much for clearing my head.

"Nice chatting with you," I said, sliding down off the bar stool.

"See you tomorrow."

I barely heard as I bolted for the door.

The thing I've found about twenty-five-year-old writer-wannabes in the classes I've taught is that most of them really don't want to be writers. They think they do, but they don't want to sit in front of the computer all day every day, wrangling with words.

I do love to teach writers who want to learn the craft, who work hard and will write as many drafts as they need. There's nothing like witnessing a young writer learning their craft—and even helping them along.

And, of course, I do love my readers—most of them. Some of them have scared me from time to time. But that's another story.

I pushed the elevator button, noting the blurriness of the numbers on the panel. I hadn't had that much to drink, had I?

I was glad my roommate hadn't checked in yet. I was just going to hit the sack and hope she wouldn't arrive until the morning. After the elevator stopped at my floor I walked to my room, feeling a bit drunk. My legs were heavy and things spun every now and then. Like that pretty plant the hotel had in the corner.

Well, I guess I'd had more than I thought.

I slid the card key into the door, once, twice, no, three times before the damned light turned green. I opened the door and headed straight for the bed. Now, in the back of my mind I thought I'd rest a few minutes then get up and get ready for bed. I closed my eyes and heard my cell phone beeping. Fuck. Maybe it was my roommate. Maybe she needed help. Or something. I picked it up and pressed the screen to see who called.

My screen turned to gray-blue fuzz and, just like in my dream, the blur began to form into a face. The room began to crackle with energy and the next thing I knew he was standing in front of me.

I was not dreaming.

There was a man in my room.

A man that came through my iPhone?

My heart thumped in my chest. I looked around for a weapon and tried to pick up the lamp—bolted down.

He laughed.

"Brenna," he said my name so sweetly that it calmed me immediately.

"You know me?"

He laughed again. "Mortals can be so daft. I know you remember

46

me. You just don't want to acknowledge it."

I stood thinking for a moment. Okay so if this was the guy I thought he was, the man in my dreams at home, what was he doing here? And how did he get into my room? He surely didn't come through the phone like I thought he had. Maybe he was a magician, an illusionist like Houdini.

"How did you get here?" I asked.

"You saw how I got here. I came through the phone. You know, these new devices are wonderful for us. Cuts our travel time immensely," he said. He was wearing all black: black jeans, t-shirt, and a black leather jacket. I think that was the outfit he always wore. I think.

My mind was reeling with possibilities.

"What do you mean you came through the phone? Talk about daft," I said. My voice was quivering. It was betraying my tough, but totally fake, stance.

He leaned in and tilted toward me. "We used to fly, turn into bats or crows. Now that was time-consuming, and sometimes a bit tiring." His eyes widened.

He was fucking with me. Who was this guy?

"Who are you and what do you want with me?" I said after a few moments of eye contact.

"You don't recognize me? The great vampire-chick-lit author Brenna Bang doesn't recognize a vampire when she sees one? That's rich," he said, with more than a note of sarcasm and maybe a hint of anger in his voice. Something about him frightened me in that moment. Was it the menace in his voice? Or the firmness his jaw took on?

"Pshaw. I write about vampires, sure," I said. "But I don't believe in them. You can feed that line of BS to someone else. I'd thank you to leave." My voice was still betraying me. The more I tried to control it, the worse it seemed to shake.

He walked toward me, stepping out of the half-shadows, and he nearly took my breath away. He looked like my Xander, my imagined vampire, the fantasy man I wrote about. How could that be? A swirl of energy tore through my body as he approached me.

"Brenna," he said with a softer tone. "You and I have unfinished business."

"We do?"

"You know, our lovemaking has given me great joy. Most mortal women don't appeal to me anymore," he said, and reached for my hand. He was cool to the touch yet heat spread through my body.

"It was you. But I was dreaming," I said, tearing my hand away from him. "I'm dreaming now."

But I knew that I wasn't. I was wide awake. If I told myself that I was dreaming, it would make more sense. A man in my room. A man who claimed to be a vampire. A vampire! I touched my neck. The impulse caught me off guard—was he really a vampire?

"You are starting to believe me, then," he said.

"I'm not sure," I said. I'm a writer, more prone than most to good stories and, more than that, I was a woman, alone. And this man—vampire or not—made my pulse race, my knees weaken, and my center moisten. I hadn't felt so alive in years.

I leaned closer to him and took a good look. He was pale, with a strong jawline, and his chin was almost square with a dimple in the center of it. His cheekbones high and eyes deep set. It was in his eyes that I saw something—a brew of humanity and animal, tempered by tenderness. A feeling of sweetness overcame me and I touched his face. His full lips pulled back, as if to show me his reality, and there were his fangs, bright, white, menacing.

Fear shot through me and my body chilled as I trembled from head to toe. He was either a vampire or I was the butt of some very complex joke. But those teeth looked real.

"Brenna," he whispered my name. "I'm not here to kill you."

I just looked at him. I mean, what else could I do? I couldn't move if I wanted to.

"If I wanted to kill you, I'd have already done it. It would have been so easy to fuck you lifeless…" he said as if wistful and longing for the killing. "You are, as we say, ripe for the killing."

My eyebrows knit. I didn't like the sound of that.

"It's a pity. You barely have any friends. No love life to speak of. No family. You hide away in your basement creating stories all day, every day. Who'd miss you if you were gone?"

I blinked back a tear. "That's my job. I'm a writer."

He suddenly hissed at me. I fell back on to the bed.

"Writer!" he said. "Is that what you call yourself? You and the other vampire maligners have no idea the trouble you've created in my world!"

The room was thrumming with his anger. I felt the air pressing on my chest. Was I going to pass out?

"Young people walking around with red scarves is just a part of the problem," he said, calming down a bit. At least he wasn't hissing anymore. "Now everybody wants to be a vampire. People are seeking us out as if we are goddamned celebrities and not cold-hearted murderers. Make no mistake Brenna. That's what we are."

I swallowed hard. There was mad man in my room!

He sighed, visibly shifting mood. Now, he was thoughtful, if not serene. "Killing is nasty business. But one must survive."

I was still trembling. "If you're not here to kill me, then what do you want with me?"

"Besides the fucking?"

"That was real?" I said, feeling heat creep onto my face.

"Indeed," he said with a smirk. "And there's more of it... if you wish."

If I wished?

His grin widened. "You have everything wrong about us vampires, Brenna."

Suddenly, he was behind me on the bed, breathing on my neck. I twisted my head so that I could see his face.

"All but one thing," he kissed my neck, the tingle traveling from my nape to the center of me. Suddenly I was wet and longing for him. I shivered. "The one thing you have right is that we know

49

how to fuck."

I almost laughed. "Everybody knows how to do that..."

"Do they?" he said between nibbles and kisses at my collarbone. "But we vamps have a special skill. We are able to see into your deep, dark, lusty places and meet them, mold ourselves to meet your desires."

His hands wrapped around my waist and he pulled me underneath him. It happened so fast that I wasn't sure what was happening, but I knew what I wanted. A surge of desire swelled in me.

"Give in to it," he whispered. "Your passion is a gift."

Within minutes my skirt was wrapped around my waist and I don't know what happened to my panties. I just knew I had to arch against him as he entered me from behind. Just like that. It was as if his very presence was foreplay. I was ready for him, wanted him, ached for him. I knew for sure I wasn't dreaming then as he entered me. I felt every vein throb against my insides. He kept himself inside and stilled my hips.

"Luscious," he whispered.

The room stilled. My breath was hard to catch. He was almost too big for me, but my hips pressed harder against him and he began to rock in me so slowly, tantalizing me, while wrapping his hand around to work at me from the outside. When he touched my clit, it sent me further into an abyss—somewhere between passion and depravity. I lost all control of myself and became a mass of quivering energy. Exquisite pain and pleasure melded then erupted as I felt him coming at the same time. His seed deep in me... the thought of it made me want more.

"You will never get enough, now," he whispered. The truth of that statement hit me with a hard, cold, thud. Something in my universe had shifted. I felt him harden again. "Nor will I."

Suddenly, there was movement at my door and he disappeared. I sat up, tried to comport myself and picked up my cell phone—it burned my hand and sparked. I dropped it, just as my roommate walked in.

"Brenna? Hi, I'm Lexi. Man, I'm knackered," she said, and placed her suitcase on her bed.

"Hey," I managed to say. Wasn't it just a moment ago that he was inside me? Didn't I just have the most amazing orgasm ever? How was I even sitting up? Looking presentable?

"You okay?" Lexi said.

I laughed. "I think I had just bit too much to drink. I used to hold my liquor better. These days, I just don't know."

My cell phone alerted me to a text message.

Meet me tomorrow at 8 at Jeremy's Place, a bar just across the street from where you are.

It wasn't signed, but I knew who it was from. I bit my lip as I realized I hadn't even gotten his name.

***

The next day, the writer's conference dragged more than any other I'd attended. Were there more questions this time, or was I longing to see my "vampire" friend?

One question from the group freaked me out a bit.

"When writing vampire stories, some people claim writers are digging deep into the psyche and tapping into their own immortal longings. What do you think of that theory?"

Not your everyday question, and the man who asked it was not your everyday man. He was gorgeous, in exactly the opposite way to my "vampire" friend. He was light and tall, dressed in light brown slacks and a blue dress shirt—unusual for one of these conferences. His eyes were extraordinarily blue. I've never been attracted to a blonde before, especially one who obviously spent a lot of time at the gym.

After, he stood in line and asked for me to sign his books. His name was Micah. He had all five of my books. "Might I interest you in a drink?" he asked. Was this guy for real? Who talked like that?

"I'm sorry," I said. "I have plans."

"Oh, maybe tomorrow for breakfast?" He persisted.

"Okay," I smiled.

"Let's meet in the lobby at seven," he said.

I nodded.

"I just love the Red Scarf, but I think Red Ink might be my favorite," the next person in line said as she moved into the space in front of me.

I smiled, grateful that she was the last in line. Suddenly I was famished and grateful that I'd be meeting my mysterious friend at a place known for good food.

When I entered the bar, I was startled briefly. A variety of costumed vampires were sitting at the bar, eating in the restaurant. Then I remembered it was Halloween. Zombies, fairies, angels, and ballerinas were scattered everywhere and The Monster Mash played over the stereo system. Sheesh, how could I forget that it was Halloween? And what had I just stepped into, a huge Halloween party? I was exhausted and not up for that at all. I was thinking about leaving when I felt a warm tingle in my crotch. The next thing I knew, he was standing next to me.

"I'm really not up for—"

He grabbed me by the elbow and the maître de nodded. He led me into a snaking hallway that ended in old winding stairs. We walked up the stairs to a beautiful dining room that overlooked the festivities, but it was a quiet, private, and elegant space.

My favorite red wine awaited me, along with what looked like an Italian feast.

"I didn't want you to have to wait. I knew you'd be hungry," he said, as he placed a napkin on his lap and fiddled with his silver.

"You're going to join me?" I said, after sipping my wine. Fuck, he was so hot.

He chuckled. "Of course. We eat. In fact we enjoy food very

much, but we just don't get much nutrition from it," he said. "That's just one of the fallacies about us."

The wine was extraordinary. I enjoyed every nuanced flavor it left behind in my mouth and I felt my body slowly relaxing.

"You vampires, that is?" I said, smirking. I couldn't help it.

His mouth twisted. "Still don't believe me?"

"Does it matter?" I asked

"What do you think I am, then?" he asked with an incredulous look on his face.

"I think you're some kind of trickster or magician," I replied.

"Interesting deduction," he said, cutting into a rather bloody steak. "And in truth, I'm a little of both." His nostrils flared a bit when he brought the piece of steak, dripping with blood, to his lips.

"So what do you want from me?" I said, eyeing up my lasagna.

"Besides the hot sex?" he asked, sending my insides churning. The word sex on his lips was like a magnet to my pulsing center.

I felt my face redden. "Yes, besides that." The crowd below us was a distant murmur but I could see them in all their regalia. Witches, fairies, and so many vampires, several red scarves. Blech.

"We need your help Brenna," he said, as I bit into my lasagna. "There a couple of things I need to ask of you."

Okay, I'd play along. I'd hear him out, even as I was thinking of him deep inside me.

"Vampires have become quite the hot commodity because of writers like yourself. As I mentioned earlier, it's more than red scarves and sparkles," he said.

"That sparkling thing? That's not me. That's—"

"I know who it is," he said with a look of disgust. "I hate her, worse than I do Anne Rice."

"Now, wait a minute," I said. Anne Rice was a good writer. I wasn't going to listen to this shit.

He held up his hand. "We are not here to discuss literary tastes, Brenna." There was a frightening edge to his voice. How could I be so turned on one minute and so scared the next?

Once again I was reminded that I was probably in the presence of a mad man who thought he was really a vampire. My heart thumped in my chest. Hard.

His head twitched and he sighed. "Honestly, Brenna, you try my patience."

"Humph," I said. "Would you just get to the fucking point?"

"As you noted in your travels, your fans will wear scarves and so on," he said with a flourish.

"Yes, it's flattering and maddening all at once," I said and bit into my chunk of Italian heaven.

"The thing is, we are being hunted," he said.

"Hunted?" I said, dropping my fork.

"Due to this surge in our popularity, people are hunting us. Oh, we are used to that. Generations ago, when people really believed in us, they tried to find us and kill us. We can handle those hunters," he said.

Despite myself, I watched those beautiful lips glide over his teeth and longed for his kiss. He grinned, then looked away. Could he read my mind?

"This is very serious, Brenna," he said, and cleared his throat. Maybe he could.

"These hunters are seeking us out. They want to become vampires and it must stop."

"You think I can help you?" I said.

"Yes. There's a group of young men who have actually attacked several young women, killed one and made it look like a vampire attack," he said.

A chill traveled up my spine. I'd actually heard of the young woman who was killed. I get Google alerts about vampires and that story had been on my radar.

"Of course, it was a sloppy killing, and any vampire or vampire scholar would have known..." he said.

"What can I do to help?" I said. Vampire or not, he had my attention now.

54

"I have evidence that points directly to the killer," he said. "And I want you to deliver it to a certain detective."

"Why can't you?"

Loud music was beginning downstairs and thick red velvet curtain fell between us and the balcony. It was suddenly quiet.

"It's too dangerous for us to socialize much with mortals, particularly very smart detectives," he said.

That made a certain sense.

"If you are so certain who this man is, why don't you go after him yourself?" I said, realizing I'd just taken a last drink of my wine.

"This particular man has very strong guardians in place," he said.

"You mean bodyguards?"

"No. I mean guardians. Maybe you should think of them like guardian angels," he said.

I suddenly laughed. "Really? Not only are there vampires, but there are also guardian angels?"

He shot me a look that nearly froze me.

"Brenna, if only you knew what creatures there are in this world you mortals call your own," he said. He was deadly serious and deadly sexy. Why couldn't I keep my mind off sex? "So, you will take the evidence to the detective?"

"Of course, I will," I said. This had all just gotten more interesting. Maybe he was a poser, not a vampire, and he knew something I didn't about this murderer. "That's no problem. Can I ask you why me?"

"That's a very good question," he said. "Several reasons, actually. First, you are Brenna Bang, the upstart vampire romance novelist. The police will buy that a fan sent the information to you or put it in your hands at a book signing or something, yes?"

"I think so," I said.

"Also, you have some strong but reasonable guardians. They will protect you, if need be," he said. "As will I."

"I have guardians like the suspect has guardians?" I was confused. Guardians?

He nodded, impatiently. "All humans have them. Some guardians are stronger than others. Yours are strong."

"Good to know, I guess. But protect me?" I said. "From what? I'm just turning in some evidence."

"What will you do if this disturbed young man finds out who you are?"

My stomach twisted. Was I going to lose all the delicious food I'd just eaten? I hadn't thought about that.

"Humph," I said. So articulate.

"Brenna," he said, with such a comforting note that my fear vanished. "You are stronger than you think. You come from a long line of strength and passion. You will do fine."

Strength and passion? Me? My family? My mom and dad? I didn't think so—or at least what I could remember of them. They both died in a boating accident when I was about ten.

"How did you do that?" I asked. "Calm me like that?"

He shrugged. "I'm not sure how I do half of what I do. I don't pretend to know. None of us do."

"Us? How many of you are there?"

"I have no way of knowing," he said. "There's about eight hundred of us in New York City. Two hundred of those have banded together and formed a tribe, so to speak. We run a computer gaming software company, which is how we learned to use the Wi-Fi signals to travel. Quite ingenious, really."

"So there's a group of vampires who run a software company here in the city?"

He nodded. "We've taken to the new technology in remarkable ways. And our company is doing very well. Would you care for dessert?"

"Frankly," I said. "I need to get going. I have another long day tomorrow."

"You'll be fine, believe me. You need to stay with me longer tonight. I have a surprise for you," he said and lifted one dark eyebrow, which made me tingle.

Up until now, we had been on my turf. My house. My room. Was he talking about going to his place? I shuddered.

"There's a party I want to take to you to. It's Halloween, you know..."

I shrugged. What the hell?

***

With each step I took that night it felt more and more like a dream. And when I look back, I wonder if there was something in my drink, or if I simply drank more than I realized. Or maybe what he told me that night was true: that I have only begun to explore my true nature, that my dark, sexy writing was just the tip of my longings, my fantasies.

As we walked down another flight of twisty stairs, I felt a surge of sexiness.

"The only reason you can't find a human man is because you scare them. They don't know what to think of a woman like you," he whispered behind me.

I wanted to believe that.

And that night I did believe it.

When I walked into the club, where bongos were playing and semi-clad women and men were dancing, I was mesmerized. It smelled of cinnamon and alcohol and something even sweeter. He led me into the back room, where candles were lit among the red velvet couches and beds and bodies were writhing against each other. I bit my lip. It was so naughty. But I stood and watched with his arms around me. I could have reached out and touched them as they slid around on the beds.

I should have been disgusted but instead I was incredibly turned on. He knew it and kissed me—kissed me into oblivion. When his lips met mine that night, among the grunts and groans of pleasure, the smacking of flesh against flesh all around us, I gave in to my darker nature and knew I was his. I would comply with whatever he wanted from me.

But he let me know it wasn't about him. It was about me—exploring the depth of my desire.

He pulled me into a private room, where a masked man stood with a huge erection and handed him a mask, as well. Then he helped my vampire to undress. I noticed the furtive looks between them, but next their focus turned to me.

What was happening here, I asked myself. But only once, because I was too caught up to know or worry what came next. I just knew I was a raging fire and didn't care who entered me to put it out.

I wasn't tentative or unsure. I surprised myself. Maybe I was sexier than I thought, sexier than Josh thought. The two men surrounded me with their legs and arms and bodies, undressing me.

One of them lay on the bed. I thought it was the original masked man, though I couldn't be sure. The lights were dimmed. The men chuckled as I slipped into the bed. One behind me and one in front. Their bodies so similar that I couldn't feel the difference, both hard already. I sighed between them.

"Yes…" I said as one cupped my breasts from behind, the other sliding his fingers between my slippery folds, sending waves of pleasure through me. The one behind was gently kissing my neck, my shoulders, my back, his hot breath against my skin, while the other slid his tongue in my mouth and fingered my juicy mound.

"Let go, Brenna," one whispered. Not necessary, I was already gone.

Deep, heavy breathing and groans—almost guttural, almost animalistic— filled the air as I reached for one cock and rubbed it gently, and the other crept in between my ass cheeks. I pressed them together, squeezing it between them. The one in the front of me brought his cock to my mouth as the one behind moved to the bottom of the bed, spread me wide, and began to lick me just as I took the hard cock in my mouth. It sputtered salty juice into my throat as I came undone, bucking hard against the chin of one of my masked lovers.

This wasn't hard at all. It surprised me. I had always wondered how it would work. It was very Zen, once you gave in and let your body take over.

The cock was pulled from my mouth and he held my legs high and wide as the other man mounted me, filled me, pulsed within me, rocking and rocking, his hips grinding against mine.

The other man breathed hotly as he watched the pummeling until we came in crashing waves, with him spilling himself onto my stomach. One masked man cleaned the puddle from me as the other collapsed next to me. Soon, I was sandwiched between the two hard bodies, both sighing, cooing, one stroking my back, one my breasts. I couldn't tell them apart yet.

But one was ready for me again and pulled me to face him. He lifted my leg, holding it there, and slid into me. He entered me with a sharp pang. The other man was soon next to us and rubbed my mound. Feeling the large cock deep inside and a gentle finger stroking me on the outside, I felt poised on the cusp of eternity.

Was this the desire he told me about? The desire for more? Always more?

I was pulled on top as the man sucked in air, watching me grasp the other as he writhed beneath me. He came up behind me, draping himself along my back and jabbing his manhood between my ass cheeks. Everything was a wet, hot lather and soon he entered my ass. I gasped.

The man beneath me rolled over to the side, my legs were wrapped around his neck, his cock never leaving me. The other took his place on the other side of me and moved slowly, deep inside my ass.

"Relax," he whispered.

I felt as if I was being exquisitely torn apart, swallowed. We were nothing more than our body parts and an easy, natural rhythm between us. One in my center, the other in my ass. I shivered, then waves of sharp intense pleasure overcame me and I was Brenna

Bang no more but an animal, bucking, heaving, pulsing, sweating, moaning, exploding.

When I awoke sometime in the middle of the night, one of my masked lovers was awake and watching me. He kissed me tenderly and rolled on top of me. He slowly, tenderly entered me and I felt every vein in his throbbing cock. Our rhythm started slow and quiet. His cheeks twitching with passion, sweat beads on what I saw of his face. I met his hips with a slow grinding movement, his eyes never leaving mine, and I felt love, not just passion… even as my other masked man reached for me, kissed me, his tongue reaching far into my mouth, swirling deep as my other lover squirted hot juice deep inside.

I felt a complete unraveling against the man on top. He rolled off me and the other began to lick at my breast. I opened my mouth to his cock and tongued around the head, finally took it all in, in all of its beauty and glory. I wanted to taste it, couldn't wait for the spurt in my throat.

He groaned, growled, and gave me what I wanted.

The three of us collapsed onto one another again, a heap of sweat and salt and satiated cock and pussy. I knew it was more than I could ever ask for, but I prayed a night like this would come again.

***

When I woke up, I was back in the hotel room. I don't remember how that happened. Perhaps I traveled through Wi-Fi, too. I laughed out loud.

"Brenna? Are you up?"

Oh, my roomie.

"Yes," I said, amazed at how good I felt after last night's sex romp.

"Don't you have an appointment at seven?"

"Yes."

"It's six thirty, and I'm out of here. Have a good day," she said, and left me alone to gather my wits, shower, dress, and meet my reader for breakfast. Ugh, did I really want to do this?

I grabbed my phone, now completely charged, and the snow pattern I recognized as my "vampire" friend formed as the room sparked with energy.

His arms were around me and all over me.

I met his lips with passion and then pulled away. "I've got an appointment."

"I know," he said. "I felt I should warn you about him."

"He seemed like a nice man," I said, picking up my bag.

"Oh yes, he's very nice," he said with a salacious grin. "He's one of your guardians."

I kept my thoughts to myself.

"Brenna," he said, with a note of warning.

"Okay, if he's my guardian, why are you warning me? They're good guys, right?"

He hesitated. "It's complicated. He won't like that I've marked you."

"Marked me?" I raised my voice. "You what?" I had no idea what that meant, but I didn't like the sound of it.

"Relax," he said. "It just means that among immortal creatures, you are hands-off. You are mine." He said it almost with a growl and he bared his teeth slightly.

I wasn't sure how I felt about that, intellectually, but it made something deep inside me perk up and bloom. Was there time to—? No, I had five minutes to get to the lobby. I wrapped my arms around him. "In that case, you should at least tell me your name."

He gave me a sideways smile. "You can call me Xander."

Then he disappeared. Literally right in front of my eyes. He left behind a brown envelope that contained the evidence and research he told me about.

I marched down to the lobby where I was supposed to meet with the magnificent blonde, and was met by a member of the hotel staff.

61

"Ms. Bang?"

"Yes?" I said. She handed me a package.

"He sends his apologies," she told me with a pitying look.

I shrugged and made my way to the breakfast buffet, finding a corner to eat in. I was famished. I sifted through the last twenty-four hours and tried to make some sense of it all. Vampires. Sex. Murders. Now, my supposed guardian had just stood me up.

The package, wrapped in a brown paper, sat on the breakfast table. I decide to open it now rather than later. Inside was an old journal tied with a ribbon. On that ribbon was a necklace with a beautiful angel hanging on it. I'm not sure what kind of stones they were, but they were blue and dazzling, even though the piece looked very old. I placed it around my neck. Then I turned my attention to the book, which was a history of a family. Hmmm. Why would he give me this?

I opened the cover and read the inscription.

My dear Brenna,
This book is the history of an important family: yours. I'm giving it to you so that you might understand what happens next.
With all my love,
Micah

'What happens next?' What was that supposed to mean? I flipped through the pages and was dismayed. It was written in a strange language. I'd have to see about getting it translated.

Some mysteries remain unsolved, though.

I haven't been able to find someone to translate my book—not yet. Evidently it's in an ancient form of Aramaic. Which leads me to believe it's not really a history of my family. I've no idea what this person (or guardian) was trying to tell me.

I delivered the envelope with "Xander's" evidence to Detective Karen Stonefield, who took it without argument, said she was glad to meet me, and asked for an autograph. Least I could do.

"Where did you get this?" She asked, nonchalantly. "Or shouldn't I ask?"

"I have no idea how it came to me. I've tried to trace it," I said. "But it was on my door step one day. It looks legit."

She sized me up with a long stare. She was not at all what I expected a woman detective to look like. She was almost as short as me, but could have been a model with her glowing mocha skin and amazing physique. "I suppose you get a lot of troubled sorts attracted to you, with all of your vampire writing."

I nodded. "If you have any more questions, or if I can help you in any other way, please let me know." I handed her my card.

She seemed satisfied with that. As for me, I hoped this was the end of my involvement in any crime-fighting activities, even for my new vampire friends. I preferred the quiet life.

Just last week, I received an email from her, telling me that they apprehended the young man, along with a few cohorts. Good news. Exciting times for a woman who doesn't leave the basement much.

My part in the criminal apprehension was minimal. Xander and his crew had done all the leg work. But I felt good that I had a part in bringing justice to the killer, even though it was small. I wouldn't dwell on the possibility that he might figure out that I had a part in it. After all, Xander said my "guardians" were strong.

I had to laugh at myself. Before this all started, I hadn't even thought of the possibilities of real vampires, let alone guardians. Now here I was, feeling comforted by the thought of some kind of invisible force keeping me safe. A guardian.

I hadn't heard from my "Xander" since I've been home. But I knew I would. Still, I sit in front of my computer, sometimes willing myself to sleep in hope that he will visit my dreams. Often I just plunk away at my keyboard, feeling the cool metal and stones from my new "guardian" necklace dangling between my breasts.

Yesterday, I woke up and decided to move my office the dining room on a lark. It was the most light-filled room in the house, full of plants and good energy. I had been working on my blog and some short stories, but figured it was time to get back to the novel. It felt like a fresh start as I clicked on the file and read over the last bit, as I always do.

As her blood entered him, his erection grew stronger and harder. He thrust into her, making her scream with pleasure, him moan with fevered curiosity. He'd taken countless women like this and each one felt different to him. He enjoyed this one's legs as she wrapped them onto his shoulder and moved deeper within her. The throbbing of her blood and the throbbing of her sex spun around in him.

Her hips met his in opposite reaction.

Oooo. He liked this one. She was strong with hips that move him, lift him, hips that made him remember what it was like to be a man, not immortal. And yet, so tight, so smooth and grasping at his cock. He would give her all he could in one explosive moment.

When he came into her, the orgasmic rush came as he expected. But there was more. The clapping of thunder. The rolling noise of heaven meeting hell. With earth couched somewhere in between.

He moved off of her, jerked away.

"Just who the fuck are you?"

Now at least, I had my answer.

Sexsomnia

By

Madeline Iva

Chapter 1

Her dreams were scalding hot and shameless, leaving her limp and listless by day.

"I'm sorry, what?" Jenny asked the poor woman for the third time.

"I said the machine revealed he kicked his leg sixty times in one hour."

"In his sleep you said?" Jenny tried to remember the woman's name. Nadia. Jenny had spilled soup all over her in the lunch line, and they'd ended up eating together. Nadia was a sleep researcher.

"Like a dog trying to run in its sleep. Like that."

Jenny swallowed. "So how do you get to be a sleep subject for one of these studies?"

"Sure, sure, I get that all the time." Nadia said, waving her fork. "Everyone's like, 'you mean I get paid to sleep fourteen hours a day? Sign me up!' It's the secret fantasy of half the adults I meet."

Jenny was aware she should be putting in face time with her own group, the behavior economics crowd, sitting way at the back of the lunch room. Only, she'd started to develop a secret revulsion towards them. The tone they used when saying her name creeped her out, for instance. Not to mention the touching. There was a lot of touching for such a professional setting.

Nadia was saying her love life was in the toilet. She was stuck in the research lab all night, every night.

"And I was thought there would be men here," she added. "I mean, single men." She chewed a sandwich. "You know, waiting on the park benches. And you could pick them up, like fruit in the grocery market." She smiled around her sandwich, eyes twinkling.

Jenny listened sympathetically. Most of the econ guys were single, but she'd rather poke a fork in her eye than suggest Nadia get close to one of them. On the other hand, she refused to look off to her left where the biology folk sat.

Where Turner sat.

"You've got salad dressing on the end of your braid," Nadia told her.

Jenny wiped it off with trembling hands, her eyes focused on the end of her orange tray. She was not going to look at where Turner was sitting. The effect was too overpowering. She could feel his eyes, sure that he looked all easy-going. His faded maroon T-shirt, complete with a constellation of moth holes in the back, screamed laid back. She both envied the way he wore his own skin and half-hated him for being so completely free from self-consciousness. She was stuck in a body that recoiled from any kind of scrutiny, and when he'd caught her watching him in the lunch line it was bad. It'd made her crash into Nadia, spilling hot soup and wet salad all over her. Her face boiled in a blush as she remembered.

"Have you tried the gym?" Jenny suggested. "I think a lot of the guys go over and work out before dinner." She could have reported that the biologist Turner, for example, ran three miles on the track every other day and then did sit ups and tummy crunches. Not that Jenny was stalking him or anything.

"Ah, that must be it," Nadia said, unenthusiastically.

"So Nadia," Jenny said twisting up her napkin in her hands. "After hearing you talk I've been wondering…if I've got a sleeping disorder of some kind."

"Ah." Nadia put the tips of her fingers together, her light Eastern-European accent thickening a tad. "The doctor is in. What seems to be the problem?"

"I'm sleepwalking maybe? I'm not sure. It's probably no big deal, right?"

"No, no, now you've made me curious. Sleepwalking is rare in adults, actually."

Jenny launched into her symptoms. She was beyond tired every morning, and it was only getting worse.

"How long has it been going on?" Jenny told Nadia that it had been really bad at the institute, but she'd been having problems with sleep since spring break.

"So, it's June, but you've been having problems since…April?"

Jenny nodded. "It's getting worse. A lot worse. I mean, I was just tired before, but now I'm waking up and I'm not in my bed. Also I've got rashes or bruises and other marks and I don't know how to account for them." Often she woke with a stiff neck, aching back, sore hips or all three.

Nadia raised her eyebrows. Jenny skipped over some of the other soreness she occasionally felt. Mostly, she confessed, she worried about the abrupt shift in demeanor that her colleagues had shown after a few weeks at the institute. They were all in the same dorm, and she wondered if they were…noticing things.

"What do you mean?" Nadia asked.

"I don't know. Maybe if I'm sleepwalking they see me? Maybe they're just weird." Jenny was reluctant to go on, but Nadia pressed her.

They were supposed to be writing a group paper, and at the start Jenny had been rather intimidated. Two senior professors bullied the rest of them—but that was par for the course. In return for lending their illustrious names to the paper, the senior professors made everyone else do most of the work, while they went off to play golf. They were not the problem.

"It's the five other men who make me profoundly uncomfortable," Jenny confessed.

In the beginning they were dismissive of all her suggestions. They also made it clear that due to her lack of seniority, her name was going last and she was going to do all the number crunching.

"Basic academic pecking order stuff, whatever."

Nadia made sympathetic noises.

"That was until two weeks ago. But since then…"

"What happened since then?" Nadia asked.

Suddenly the econ guys all seemed interested in her in a whole new way.

"It's like they're being nice, but it's too nice. It's creepy. A few of them have started touching me."

"Touching you!"

"Nothing too gross—it's like little pats on the arm. Or even grabbing me around the waist to hug me." Jenny wanted to crawl out of her skin simply describing it to Nadia.

"They sound fond of you, friendly," Nadia said. Jenny shook her head. She couldn't express that it wasn't what they did, it was the way they did it… their eyes cold, lips smirking.

"And I'm so tired all the time," Jenny added. "I'm at the end of my rope Nadia. I told them I used to sleepwalk and asked if they ever noticed me wandering around at night. This one guy gave me the strangest look. Then they all started laughing but wouldn't tell me why."

"That," Nadia said, wrinkling her nose, "sounds obnoxious. You think you're sleepwalking and they're all laughing behind your back or something?"

"Yes." Jenny remembered how furious she was when she tried to ask Bonifellow straight out if they were laughing at her for some reason.

What do you mean, Jenny? *Why would we do that* Jenny? Even the way they said her name seemed overly significant and full of secret meaning.

"Well, I could put you in the lab overnight and we could see," Nadia said, taking the last bite of her sandwich and wiping her hands. "How old are you?"

"Twenty-seven."

Nadia nodded, dimpling. "You've got such a baby face, I wouldn't be too surprised by the guys treating you like a student. You said you have a history of sleepwalking?"

"Yeah. Could that be why I feel so tired?" Jenny explained that on her return from Thailand she'd started feeling exhausted every day and had gone to the doctor—who hadn't found anything.

"Hmph." Nadia was looking more like a scientist by the second, Jenny thought, her dimples and smiles replaced by a look of no-nonsense clinical analysis.

"Wouldn't want to say until I saw your stats. But these colleagues are causing you a lot of stress."

"Yes."

"Well, stress can disturb your sleep."

"I guess." Jenny said, rolling her cherry tomatoes around with her fork. "It's just..."

Jenny wasn't going to share the dreams she was having. Erotically-charged dreams of a certain biologist stretched out on a narrow twin bed, gripping his magnificent member in his hand. No shame on his face, just a low lidded stare of promise.

A tap on the shoulder interrupted her thought. The ringleader of their economics group, Bonifellow, stood before them. He had the dark good looks of Italian heritage meeting Eastern Indian, with a generous splash of super-geek. Jenny saw Nadia was suddenly sitting up a little straighter and crossing her legs.

She wanted to tell Nadia he was an arrogant dipstick. He always wore wrinkled white dress shirts and a loosened tie. The heavy smell of Drakkar Noir cologne announced his presence about a minute or two before he arrived.

"Introduce me to your friend," he said.

"Bonifellow," she said, stabbing her cherry tomato with her fork, not looking up, "this is Nadia."

She saw from beneath her lashes the smirking leer he gave to Nadia, as if he was God's gift. His hand on the back of her chair moved to walk his fingers up her back. Jenny sat up suddenly, her back arching, and the desire to stab him viciously with her fork almost overcame her.

"Bring her to our table next time, Jenny."

He smiled and, tipping a mocking salute, he moved on.

"He's cute," Nadia said. Jenny sat in shock at her sudden feelings of snarling impotence.

"I can't stand him," Jenny spat. "That way he smirked at you." She gave an involuntary shiver again.

"It's called flirting," Nadia said. "Maybe you're being a little paranoid, yes? Myself, I'm still looking for likely prospects this summer. What about you? How's your love life?"

"I don't know," Jenny said, bending low over the table, playing with her food. The lunchroom was emptying out. She hung her head even lower over her salad, looking off under her bangs towards the biology table. *Don't do it.* But she did. Turner and some guy with glasses and a round tender baby face were leaning forward in heavy conversation. Even so, Turner looked over and stared. It was not a friendly stare. You didn't stare intensely like that at friends. It was clearly an *I want to fuck you* stare—one she had no idea how to communicate with. She looked away, craning her neck in the other direction.

"So tell me more about that econ guy." Nadia said. "Single?"

"He's an asshat, Nadia."

"Or he's interested in you. Clearly you're a hot prospect."

Jenny shook her head. "Ugh."

"Come on," Nadia cajoled. "You're tall, skinny, blonde, and, well..." Nadia waved a hand, as if to indicate that they weren't in the same league.

That morning Jenny had emerged from the dorm room in white cigarette jeans and a cute little teaching blouse. While she was crossing the lounge someone gave a highly inappropriate wolf whistle. She looked down the hall. The guys were all there—she couldn't spot who had whistled, but they were *all* staring at her.

So she dived back into her room, only to emerge a minute later with a boxy lemon yellow cardigan, a real granny sweater. It was even embroidered with goldfish.

"So are there?"

"What?"

"Any likely prospects in your group?" Nadia pointed her chin at Bonifellow.

"Bonifellow? Ew. No. Anyway, I'm here to work. This is not economics sex-camp, Nadia."

Nadia sprayed her milk. Laughing, she wiped her chin.

"Well…actually, there's this one guy…" Jenny started to confess, slowly. "We met in the elevator the first day."

Turner, of course. He'd been carrying a duffle over his shoulder and a messenger bag slung across his back. She'd been trying to hold a box of academic files under one arm, along with her suitcase handle, but somehow she kept losing the box as it slipped out from under her arm. Turner took it from her without asking. He held it for the rest of the elevator ride.

I'm Turner, he'd said.

It could have been a nice beginning. She could have said *I'm Jenny, thanks for the help*. But no. She'd spent the rest of the ride on the world's slowest elevator her hands sweating, her mind a complete blank. Then she'd decided to be all feminist and insist she have the box back, that she could carry it and *should* carry it. She still cringed at the memory, her hands tightening on the lip of the table as she related it to Nadia.

He'd given her a look like she was weird.

Then the elevator door had opened, they both stepped out onto a mezzanine floor, and he gave her the box back. She'd taken it with one arm and promptly spilled it all over the entire mezzanine area. He'd helped her clean it up, looking bored.

"Then he asked me if I'd be at the faculty mixer after dinner."

Jenny had choked out some totally incoherent reply, crammed the papers back in the box, swept it up with her suitcase, and strode away over the bridge that separated his dorm from hers. But she'd been looking back at him as she did so, so she hadn't seen the glass door that separated the dorms.

"I walked right into it. Wham! Bruised my nose and everything," she confessed.

"Oh no!" Nadia laughed.

After bouncing off the door and spilling the files *again*, she'd heard him call out that he'd see her that night. At the mixer. If she got over her concussion. Finding her assigned room, she lay down and grabbed a pillow. After putting it over her face, she'd pounded her head through it for a few minutes.

When self-asphyxia hadn't helped, she'd gotten up, washed her face, changed her attire, and went to the mixer. The room had been incredibly loud with conversation. Turner had come over to her within ten minutes, and she'd asked him about his research. She'd only heard about every three words of what he was saying and had tried to fake her way through her replies, acting all nonchalant like everyone else.

He'd leaned his head in towards her every time she talked, sort of a pecking motion, to try to catch her words over the noise.

"What?" he'd asked several times.

"I hate this, it's so loud," she'd said.

"Sorry," he'd said. "Didn't quite catch that."

Into a sudden lull in the conversation she'd yelled, "I said I *hate* this place, don't you?"

He'd given her an odd look, "Yes, I gave up twelve weeks of my summer to come here. Because I hate it so much."

After that no one could get a peep out of her. She'd been on the verge of tears.

"So what happened?" Nadia asked.

"Nothing."

"No, I mean after."

"The thing is Nadia, I've got no game." Jenny slapped her hands down on her white jeans, which had an oily soup stain across them now, and stood up. "I admit it, I accept it, and I've resigned myself to the fact that I am probably further ahead in my career than most of my peers—because let's face it, you can get a lot of work done if you never have a social life. Fun is a massive time suck."

"I smell a summer fling," Nadia said.

"She who smelt it, dealt it," Jenny said. "I don't do flings, I'm no good at them."

"How can you not be good at a fling? That's ridiculous. I think you're over-thinking this stuff."

"You're right, I do over-think. Always. I think if I get involved with Turner I'll probably want it to go on. Meanwhile, he lives on the other side of the entire country from me. So how's that going to work?"

"You don't know where he lives."

"He said at the mixer he spends a few months each summer up in Alaska doing field research."

"What does Turner study?"

"It's on the tip of my tongue. It's a high school mascot."

"Bears? Eagles?"

"No."

"Cougars? Wild cats?"

"Some kind of varmint."

"Wolves? Beavers?"

"Like a muskrat."

"What sad little high school in America," Nadia asked, tossing down her crumpled napkin, "has a muskrat for its mascot?"

"My point is, do you realize how expensive airfare to Alaska is these days?"

Nadia crossed her arms to lean in. "Okay, fine. But what about the guy that's been staring at you for the last five minutes across the cafeteria?"

Jenny looked over, and instantly squinched down in her seat, one hand covering that side of her face.

"That's him," she hissed.

Nadia made a purring noise. "The biologist? You didn't say he was tall and hot. I thought you meant one of those other geeks." Dropping her voice she said, "You're crazy not to jump his bones."

Jenny kept her face hidden. "It's not that I don't want to, it's that I don't know *how*. I couldn't get from hello to the bed without making a total ass of myself."

"It's sex, Jenny. If you have to talk your way through it, you're not doing it right."

"You make it sound easy, but he's a strange man, and I absolutely suck at talking to strange men."

"He's coming this way."

"Oh god."

It was too late to get up and flee.

"Ladies."

They murmured in response. Jenny found the pattern on her orange cafeteria tray completely absorbing.

"Jenny." She was level with his pelvis and swallowed hard, feeling acutely self-conscious. She knew what his face looked like, but could not seem to force her eyes upwards to meet his.

"Want to introduce me to your friend?"

"This is Nadia. Sleep disorders."

"Hello, Nadia Sleep Disorders," he said, and then looked at Jenny again. She felt his eyes studying her, waiting. His hair always seemed to need brushing, but the clean, strong lines of a Greek warrior offset his messy hair, just as his broken Roman nose set off the sculpted perfection of the rest of his face. Together his face and body sent her into a deep primal frenzy.

74

He was sex on a stick and there she was fizzling and popping in his presence,

That stare she'd received before was now slightly masked, but only slightly. If he could stare at her like that, why couldn't he take over the situation and move them along to the post-talking stage so they could enjoy the next part of the adventure? The part that would involve kissing and silence. And fucking. She'd lied to Nadia. She'd take a fling with him any day.

She realized she was frowning in alarm as she looked up at him, and made herself stop it and look down again.

"So, Jenny," Nadia said. "Introduce me."

"This is…"

She turned away, only to look back up at him completely stricken.

His name had fled her brain.

"This is—?"

He turned to Nadia, obviously pissed. "Turner Michael. Biology."

"His name is backwards," Jenny said to Nadia. "I told Nadia that you studied varmints." She wanted to slap herself. Idiot. Idiot.

"Love these institutes. Smart ladies everywhere you look. Yes, I study varmints." Then he looked down again. "What are *you* researching this summer Jenny?"

The paper had been her idea, in fact. "Five crucial aspects of social reality for the continuance of consumer goods spending."

A conversation-killing silence met that announcement.

"It's behavior economics," she explained slowly, wishing she could crawl under the table and die.

"Sounds fascinating," Turner said. Nadia choked a little. Jenny blushed hard.

Then she swallowed. No one said anything.

"So," Nadia said. A pause hung in the air. Jenny studied her empty juice glass like it was a precious cultural object in her hand. Turner seemed to notice her indifference.

"Didn't mean to interrupt you. I'll be on my way then," he

said. "Just wanted to say hi."

"Hi," Nadia said.

"Maybe I'll see you later," he said to Jenny softly. Her guts churned over at those words.

He was gone.

Jenny hid her face behind her hand, a fit of fatigue overwhelming her now that all the adrenaline had poured out into her system.

Nadia threw her balled-up napkin into Jenny's face.

"He is so into you. And trying so hard to be nice to you."

"I don't want nice. I want to do him."

"Jenny! Now that's more like it."

"I'd also like him to bring up something we both have in common so we can actually have a conversation."

"Ask him about varmints again." Nadia giggled.

Jenny smacked her glass on the table. "I suck." She tapped her glass in time with her words. "I. Just. Suck." She stood up. "Moving on."

"Maybe being over-tired is making it hard for you to think on your feet. I'll help you with that."

Jenny tilted her head. "I wish, but no, I'm always this pathetic around guys. I tried blaming it on going to an all girl's school for years, but…"

"I can help you." Nadia grabbed her arm and began walking with her out into the steamy green campus. "This guy I know is bugging me to try a new sleep recording device he's created. Let's do an intake on you at the lab and then we can try it out tonight."

"Yeah? Oh Nadia—"

"We'll see what's going on. If the device works."

Of course, she saw Turner in the elevator coming back from Nadia's intake at the lab. Before the doors closed he stepped on. She nodded and then looked ahead and up because her palms were sweating hard and she was squeezing her mind for what the name of the varmint was that he studied. Badgers? There weren't badgers on this continent were there?

He said nothing either and, in the long silence it took before the doors finally closed, she reflected on her acute consciousness of his body.

He suddenly turned towards her and stood much closer in a way that stunned her with its familiarity.

That body. His shirt rode on top of it, like it was too muscled and curved and unreal for the shirt to know how to sit on it the normal way.

"So you're not going to say anything? Even when we're alone, you're just going to stand there and pretend like you can't even remember my name?"

Her mouth opened slightly as a voltage of shock from his words stabbed like an arrow into the center of her brain. Absolutely not one word—not one iota of English came forth from her gasping mouth. The door opened, he got off, and those shoulders were gone.

The doors closed, only to open again. He got back on the elevator and was kissing her, hot and demanding, spreading her against the cold steel wall until the bones of her pelvis were crying out with tingling nerves in response.

The door opened. "Fine." He strode off the elevator, as she blinked at the unreality of what had just happened.

Chapter 2

"Any family history of sleep walking? Other than you?" Nadia asked.

"I was adopted."

Nadia filled in notes as Jenny provided details.

"Any sleep talking?"

"When I was little. My mother said I would scream and shout like I was fighting something. My dad was in the state department in Morocco. The locals said I was, um, possessed by an evil genie." Jenny gave a small smile.

No smile from Nadia. "That's superstition."

"Right. Sorry. I suppose you can't publish findings on an evil genie." Jenny had signed a waiver allowing Nadia to use her findings for her research. Jenny ducked her head. Nadia was going to help her. The happy fact lifted up her spirits through the thick mud of her brain.

"The housekeeper in Morocco quit because of it, so finally my mother hired an exorcist to treat me."

"Did she really?" Nadia's cute nose wrinkled.

"Oh, she didn't believe it would help. She just wanted the maid to come back."

"What happened?"

"Nothing. I mean, I guess I fell asleep, I don't remember. He spit some chewed up tea leaves in my face. My father said it was a total waste of money, but the serving staff came back to work and I stopped sleep walking."

"The power of suggestion. How old were you?"

"Ten?"

"That's about the time kids usually stop sleepwalking anyway."

"Oh, okay."

Nadia smiled. "Aside from being possessed by an evil genie, did you have any other symptoms?"

"Like what."

"Snoring?"

"No. No, I don't think so."

"Do you live alone?" Nadia asked and Jenny nodded. "So how do you know if you snore or not?"

"Okay, I get your point."

"Last spring, were you under a lot of stress then?"

Thinking back on her first year of teaching, Jenny responded, "Definitely."

"Going through a lot of sleep deprivation then?"

"Yes. Then I went to Thailand. I had some serious jet lag there and when I came back, and... it just never seemed to go away."

"So it's fair to say you're operating under a substantial sleep deficit?"

"Definitely." Tears welled up in her eyes and she struggled to control her voice. It was more emotional answering the questions than Jenny expected. Or maybe she was so weepy because she was so sleep deprived. Her nerves were frayed. She felt like she was underwater and moving slowly, but jumpy at the same time.

"What? I'm sorry."

"I was asking if you suffered from any other major health disorders. Any epilepsy?"

She shook her head.

"Are you on any medication?"

"No."

"Do you take any sleeping pills?"

"Actually, I did this spring. After Thailand I was taking Ambien for a while."

"Oh, Ambien is the *worst*. So, here's a calendar. I want you to show me how long you've been experiencing poor sleep."

"I also, well, sometimes I smell sort of funny in the morning."

"What do you mean funny?"

"I don't know. Sweaty? Musky? Like I a need a shower. Badly."

Nadia pushed out her lower lip as she considered this. "Are you having night sweats?"

"I have no idea."

"Are your pajamas drenched with sweat?"

"Yeah..." Suddenly her heart was beating fast....

Before falling asleep each night, the string of awkward moments with Turner came back to life before her eyes unbidden. It was like she opened up the box of all the embarrassing things she'd ever said or done throughout her entire life—not just with Turner. Soon she was writhing in self-loathing. The next morning she'd wake up on the floor, sweaty, sticky, and with some completely

79

hot forbidden image of Turner seared into her brain. It always made her heart beat out a heavy staccato rhythm. By the time she crawled off the floor and into the shower she was so exhausted she wanted to go to sleep all over again.

They agreed to meet again at her room at ten-thirty that night.

***

Nadia took out a white plastic tray and rolled back a black nylon cover. Across the white tray was an array of felt pastel stick-um dots. "This device allows us to do a polysomnograph."

One large felt patch was the size of a half dollar. It was tan and would go on the inside of her arm, down near her armpit and to the side, like a nicotine patch. It was a micro-transponder, Nadia explained. It was bigger and heavier than the rest of the dots, collecting their information and transmitting them wirelessly to Nadia's iPad. The rest of the dots were electrodes that transmitted their info to the transponder.

"Okay, let's do it," Jenny said.

She got up and removed her pj top. It was her favorite, with slices of cake on a pink background. Underneath was a white cami. She sat on the bed while Nadia dragged a chair over from the desk. Like a beautician, Nadia took out the tray from her bag, rolled back the cover and began to apply the felt pads all over Jenny.

The smallest light pink dots went right on her eyelids. They felt like wearing false eyelashes and were the size of a pea. Nadia placed them in the corner of each eye as well. Some light purple dots went up along her hairline under her bangs, and on the side of her face. One came with a tiny needle that stuck into her ankle—"Ouch!" Nadia said it measured oxygen levels in her blood. There was one behind her ear. Nadia told her it measured audio vibrations to see if she was snoring, or gasping, etc. A few went on her back near her ribs and others dotted down her sternum and under her breasts—they measured heart beat and respiration.

Jenny put back on her cami top and then her pj top. She walked Nadia out to the elevator. She was happy, and it felt almost cozy walking around in her pj's in the dorm. She took the elevator down with Nadia and said goodnight. Outside fireflies were all across the campus lawn. Another reassuring sign that everything was good in her life, and it was going to be okay. She stayed there next to the elevator for a second. The pads felt light; she was already forgetting them. She wanted to run outside and catch the fireflies, it was that kind of summer night. Then the elevator door opened.

Of course *he* was inside. She stepped in barefoot, trembling head to toe, her hands clenched at her sides. Had she been waiting because she was hoping to see him? The world stopped whenever he was around. In fact, she felt sort of terrified of him. Why? She didn't know why, but she couldn't help it. She just was.

There was another long tense silence.

"*Fine,*" he said. "We don't have to talk. If that's what you want. Whatever."

Then he stopped the elevator, which made the alarm go off.

She froze. Clearly the problem wasn't just that she was ridiculously shy, clearly she also had a crush on a madman. That didn't help matters though, when her heart was going berserk and she could barely catch her breath from some mix of fear and longing. She was looking down at his jeans, and he was forcing her face up, which just made her eyes try to stick even harder to his jeans. But he was having none of it. A pulse beat in his tan neck. In her dreams he had a kind of farmer's tan, his arms dark but his chest pale, with a thin T shape of darker hair than the light brown stuff on his head.

She couldn't think about that when he took her face into his hands, his thumb near the side of her mouth, which somehow made her whole body pulse and throb. Now her pelvis was acting up again. It was alive, and seemed to have a mind of its own. It throbbed hard, speaking clearly about what it wanted, which was to grind against him.

Her resistance shattered. The atoms of her body bunched up to explode into a million pieces. She felt herself squish against him, her eyelids closed as she waited for what seemed like a crazy long time before he finally kissed her up-tilted lips. He captured first the lower one, then the upper one, taking his time, using firm pressure. Then his lips spread hers and his tongue moved slowly, slowly into her mouth, feeling along.

It was like being kissed for the first time. The trail his tongue explored brought into being hundreds of nerve endings she'd never felt before. While the nerve endings sang out their glory at being alive, her head felt like the world was tilting on its side. She was feeling the heavy little tabs of felt on her eyelids as they fluttered closed. Her hands was gripping those pliant, firm muscles in his shoulders and biceps.

Her arms barely had time to wrap around the strong slope of his shoulders and dig in, really feel the muscles under her hands bunching, before he was drawing away. Which was unfair, and mean, and evil. But he was too tall and too big for her to make his head come back down to her mouth. She wanted it to, so she could feel all those nerve endings come to life once more.

She tilted her head up, her lips eager to taste him again, her pelvis eager to feel the hot thick bar under his fly. He was already stepping back like she'd done something wrong.

He gave her a look of utter betrayal, mixed with some utter puzzlement and combined with a little disgust, before turning away.

What did *she* do? She didn't understand. She wanted to protest, but he was already pressing the emergency button back in, the elevator did a little jump up to their floor, and the door was open. One last moment was left hanging in the air between them. He walked out to the left, then gave her one last look of frowning puzzlement and was gone.

It was *him* this time, not her, she thought. Walking rapidly up the bridge, she went through the glass door and back to her room.

It was *him*. He was weird, he was inexplicable, he was playing games. A secret part of her brain said, *oh and wouldn't you like to believe that?* But wasn't it more likely that *she* was a horrible kisser, *she* was not the hotty-patotti he'd thought? Her self-esteem was about two inches high by the time she reached her room.

Her cell phone was ringing as she opened the door to her room. It was Nadia.

"What was going on? I went to check the monitor to get some base levels and your heart rate suddenly went through the roof."

"I saw Turner in the elevator." Jenny explained.

Nadia's laugh was cruel and indifferent. "As long as the device is working," she said, before turning to leave. "See you tomorrow morning. Don't touch those dots or else."

Jenny worked on typing up her notes from the morning session on her laptop. After emailing them out to everyone she climbed into bed, the happy feeling she had just a few hours earlier eroded. It was *him*.

At the same time a part of her brain thought it not at all unusual that someone seeking her out would be some kind of freak. Or, the devil in her head suggested, what if he was responding to her so oddly because he thought she was stalking him?

She also worried she should have mentioned Johannes to Nadia. She met him on the plane over to Thailand. He was so gorgeous, a model from Budapest. She'd been nervous about traveling alone for the first time. By the time they'd gotten through the airport they'd decided to hang out. They both spoke a little German, so their time together had involved a lot of pointing or shrugging. Soon somehow they were holding hands, embracing, and such was Johannes's skill that, almost without words, he got her into bed that night.

He was *so* handsome, and she kept thinking she should feel ridiculously lucky. Yet it all felt a little unreal—just like with Turner—though Turner was far beyond Johannes in that respect. The fumbling amongst clammy sheets in the cheap poorly air-conditioned Thai hotel had left her feeling more than usually pathetic the next morning.

But Johannes had crazy dark bedroom eyes—or was she simply sick of being so lonely? Once his clothes had come off, it was disturbing to see how thin he was. She slept very poorly afterwards with rotten nightmares all night. The next morning when she woke Johannes looked positively unwell, with raw purpleish pink hollows around his eyes and even thinner ribs. But even though he looked like the walking dead, he'd been full of pure good cheer and held her hand even more tightly as they walked around all day and explored.

He'd even tried to give her his necklace at the end of the vacation. It was a metal coin slightly larger than a half dollar with a square opening in the center. She fingered it, feeling the lines etched onto the surface in the shape of a maze, and then fingered the slender notch going through the side.

"Doesn't it fall off?" she'd asked. He'd smiled and shook his head, showing her how the frayed white thread he had strung it on was fatter than the open notch so the coin couldn't fall off. She wouldn't take it, and all his cheer had faded. He'd looked at her with some kind of alarm registering in the back of his eyes. Or maybe it had been guilt?

She'd worried from that moment on that something was wrong. That even though they used protection she'd somehow picked up something from him during their encounter. *Sie ist crank?* She'd asked over and over. *Nein*, he'd said, denying he was sick. So she'd put on the necklace to appease him and he'd been satisfied. He'd left before she woke the next day, and she'd left the necklace behind on the bureau. Let a maid have it… the feeling of the two-night stand had made her want to scrub herself clean and forget the whole thing had ever happened.

Once she'd gotten home she became convinced he'd somehow given her AIDS. Her doctor gave her an AIDS test, and then every other test in the book. He'd finally told her she was fine, and prescribed the Ambien. But what if she had some kind of sleeping sickness? Wasn't there a disease *called* sleeping sickness? Could she have picked it up while traveling in tropical Thailand?

Her thoughts slipped from Johannes over to Turner again and she felt that forbidden wet little clench down low. Yes, the dreams she'd had about him—shockingly filthy—left her writhing. He evoked a primitive stabbing sensation right behind her pubic bone, a sensation as alarming as it was pleasurable. So alarming, so overwhelming, it was as if she would die of happiness in finally having him.

Chapter 3

The next thing Jenny knew, someone was knocking on her door. She blinked, her eyelids feeling gummy and strange. She opened them and found she was sprawled across the carpet with her head under her desk. Feeling shaky and exhausted, she pulled herself up onto the bed. The knocking continued. She wondered where her pj top had gone—she was in her white cami and aqua blue boy shorts, but that was all. She looked at her bed. The sheets were peeled back to one side, but no pj top was to be seen.

She stared at the sheets until she heard "Jenny? It's me Nadia," through the door and went to open it.

"You were a busy girl last night," Nadia said, sweeping into the room. Ignoring the stripped bed, she pulled the tipped over chair upright and sat down on it. Then she dug around in her bag with an air of suppressed excitement.

"You've got the spike marks of sexual arousal with autonomic activation."

Jenny had no idea what that meant. "My head hurts."

She felt like someone had removed her blood and replaced it with neon green radiator fluid.

"Of course it does. You didn't get any sleep. Come here," Nadia said. Jenny moved towards her. Nadia sniffed at her delicately and then took out two swabs. "Lift up your ponytail please."

"Pony—my hair wasn't in a ponytail when I went to sleep last night." Jenny patted the high ponytail spouting at the top of her head delicately while Nadia stood behind her and ran two swabs across her neck.

"That tickles," Jenny said. "What's it for?"

"You, um, stink a little, like you've been perspiring heavily. These measure the salts on your skin." She popped the swabs in a small paper bag and then tucked that into her larger bag.

Jenny sniffed under her arm. "I need a shower."

"Did you feel warm when you went to bed?"

"No. I was cold. They turn the a/c up so high at night and I was under the all covers." Jenny plucked at her white cami and looked around again for her pj top. It was over on the other side of her bed. She went and put it on. "I was almost shivering."

"Well your heart rate was sky high around, oh, two or so, then again off and on for three hours. Maybe you were doing jumping jacks in your sleep to stay warm."

Jenny sniffed at herself again. That musky stank was about her again. Almost as if someone else inhabited her body at night and was marking their territory. She looked around.

It wasn't unusual for her to wake up and find the place messier than when she last remembered it. She didn't want to believe in monsters, but deep down she felt like *it* had been in her room again. *It* had been blindly trying to escape the room, destroying the place in the process. Though whether in panic or anger she didn't know.

She sat down in her undies on the naked bed. Her knees and elbows felt sore, raw and sore, and her back had a kink in it... She tried to stretch, but that only made her head hurt.

"Last night you had several abrupt spontaneous arousals from SWS."

"What's S-W-S?"

"Slow-wave sleep." Chuckling to herself, Nadia pecked at her iPad then looked up. "Let me get those little electrodes off you. They're quite expensive little buggers so we don't want to lose any."

She brought forth from her bag the white plastic board where the little felt pads went. She began peeling them off Jenny—first the ankle one with the needle.

"Ow."

Amazingly they were all still in place. They did not peel off easily, but Nadia distracted her by saying, "I was worried this equipment wouldn't work at all, but it did. My friend Karl is modifying the lab equipment we usually have to use in order to eliminate all the crazy wires. He said you could be up to five miles away and I could still take readings on my laptop. From here to the lab is probably less than a half mile, but he was right—I got an excellent readings all night long, clear as a bell."

She seemed to hardly notice Jenny's state of dejection, but when Jenny didn't respond she patted her shoulder and said, "Cheer up. Figuring out what's wrong with you is the first step to curing it."

"Then there *is* something wrong with me." Jenny knew it. It just felt different to hear someone say so out loud.

Nadia used the edge of her fingernail to scrape off a purple dot. "Yup. It could have taken us much long longer to see these findings in the lab. You understand most people don't display their symptoms in the lab like they do when they're at home."

"So what did you find?"

"I think you've got NREM Arousal Parasomnia. In fact, it's so evident, I can even write you a script for it, if you like."

"You can?" Jenny felt a wave of relief break over her, like sweat. It was that easy—less than a day after meeting Nadia, her problem was fixed.

"Sure. I'm a doctor, why not? The common prescription is Clonazepam. What's this?" she asked, stroking Jenny's neck on the left side.

"What?"

"On your neck, a bruise here."

"I have no idea." Jenny stroked her neck. "I can't feel anything."

Nadia shot her a look then went back to removing the dots, almost humming with pleasure.

"I forgot to ask you," Nadia said, keeping her eyes on her work. "What's your alcohol intake like these days?"

Jenny confessed that back at her college the other faculty were heavy drinkers. She had upped her intake of alcohol a lot in an attempt to fit in, but now that she was at the institute for the summer, she wasn't drinking at all.

"Stress, sleep deprivation, and alcohol. The magic three." Nadia pursed her lips, and focused on the dots again. "Classic," she muttered to herself.

"I still don't understand. Why are you so excited? Am I sleepwalking?"

"Oh yeah."

Jenny felt her sense of desperation hike up a few notches while Nadia continued removing dots.

"Hey," Nadia said, putting the black cover over the white board. "At least it is not one of the other autonomic disorders—like bedwetting. Be grateful for small favors."

After all the dots were removed and she'd showered and dressed, Nadia wanted her back at the lab. She asked if she could draw some blood to compare to the sample taken during the night. Then she asked if she could take a vaginal swab.

Jenny inwardly balked, but finally agreed. After all, Nadia was doing a full work up on her free of charge—no insurance deductible, no nothing. She had Jenny sign a release form so that Nadia could request her medical history and use the medical intake and history for publication, if the findings were relevant and worthy of study. "You'd be anonymous, of course," Nadia assured her.

Lovely. After having her feet up in stirrups, Jenny went back to her room and showered again until the hot water ran out. She missed breakfast and couldn't face up to the morning session with Bonifellow, Rick, and the rest of the econ fellows, so she played hooky instead. She felt guilty about it, but she went over to the library trying to stuff the feelings down.

She dived into her email on her laptop to get caught up on some departmental work back at the college, feeling her tummy rumble, and her head hurt. She was a mess. She reminded herself there was a plan. She was merely following the plan.

The plan was for her to stay out of the way until after lunch. Nadia was going to try to reach out to the guys. "I'll flirt with them a little, then ask them if they noticed anything strange about your behavior at night," Nadia said.

She'd waited for Nadia to get back to the part about sexual arousal. She hadn't, but said she thought the guys would have observed something but that they might be more candid without Jenny around... especially if it was something embarrassing.

After a few hours' work, Jenny felt her tail was dragging so low she finally put her head down on a table in the periodical room and took a cat nap.

Her phone woke her an hour later.

"Those guys," Nadia huffed, "are total assholes."

"Welcome to my world."

"I thought they'd downplay things in front of you, but they are *foul*." Nadia said some bad words in a foreign language. "They wouldn't mention anything specific, but obviously they know something."

"How can we make them talk?" Jenny was surprised at how ruthless she felt. "Screw them. I'm going to rig your room and the floor with cameras so we can watch for ourselves. You said there's an afternoon session? So they'll all be together somewhere this afternoon right?"

Jenny tried again. "So I *am* sleepwalking?"

"Jenny, the way the guys are acting, I think you may be doing more than sleepwalking."

Jenny's stomach lurched and she bent over, holding onto herself with her free arm. "Like what? What do you mean?"

"We'll observe tonight and see."

"Nadia. Tell me."

"You showed several sexual arousal spikes. Most of us dream we're running from monsters or being naughty with the man we desire and our body remains asleep, paralyzed. Rarely is an individual actually out there running around or …doing other things. You may be one of the exceptions."

"What other kinds of things?" Jenny felt her windpipe closing, her heart jackhammering.

Jenny could hear Nadia typing out a note on her iPad. "A few years ago a man got in his car while asleep, drove to his in-laws and killed them."

Jenny frowned at her phone. "What are you saying? I'm a potential homicidal maniac?"

"I don't think you're dreaming about killing people, though the way those idiot colleagues of yours act, I'm surprised you're not tempted."

"Murdering people. God, I hope not."

"I think you're dreaming about having sex."

Gulp.

"That, or you're possibly masturbating… that's commonly what we see with in patients who have readings like yours."

It was like horror movie. It kept getting worse and worse.

Nadia was saying something about the psychological underpinnings that led to sleep disturbances, but Jenny's head filled with the buzzing of a thousand bees. She thought she was going to pass out. She tried taking a big deep breath but couldn't manage to fill her lungs.

"You're saying I'm some kind of sexual deviant?"

She felt suddenly clammy all over, her skin wanting to creep and crawl. She had an overpowering urge to go back to her room and hide under the covers. But who knew what that could lead to?

That's why… Jenny licked her lips. They felt sore and puffy, which took on a whole new context.

"What can I do?" Jenny asked, her voice a hoarse whisper. She'd just spotted someone lurking at the back of the library. Someone tall with messy hair. Automatically she started packing up her computer into her bag. The need to run and hide became paramount. "Didn't you say there was some drug I could take?"

"Before we start taking drugs, let's see if we can catch you in the act, as it were. We'll stick to the plan for now. I'll meet you at your room around ten pm tonight," Nadia said. "I'm running over there right now to get the hidden cameras in place. In the meantime, feel better."

"Why should I feel better?"

"You're not wetting the bed and you're probably not a murderer."

"Nadia, your bedside manner stinks."

Suddenly the tall messy hair moved from out of the reference section.

It *was* Turner.

"Nadia, I have to go." She hung up and headed for the exit. She got there and put her head up to find he was blocking the way. They stared at each other across the atrium for a long time.

"What?" she finally said.

He turned away.

The econ guys were one kind of horrible, but Turner was another horrible all together. She would rather die—just die—than have him find out about her little problem. He kept expecting some her to understand some mutual hipster code and respond accordingly to his silences and significant glances. She didn't speak one word of hipster.

With a deep, twisting feeling of agony, she fled past him out the door and headed off towards the café to mainline some coffee into her system so she could stay awake until night.

The econ guys were all in line at the café, getting gassed up on caffeine before settling in for the long afternoon session. She was angry when she saw them, but didn't feel she could blast them with her condemnation. The last thing she wanted to do was tip them off. She wanted Nadia to get the cameras up. She wanted to see for herself. So she got in line behind them and greeted everyone in a soft voice. They greeted her back warily, no one asking why she'd been missing that morning.

"So what did you guys do last night?" she found herself saying, her tone a little artificial and a little defensive.

Rick finally said, "You know, hanging out in the lounge. With everyone." No one looked at her directly.

She turned to Bonifellow. "What did you do?" she asked.

"I was hanging with Rick. Had some *popcorn*." The word popcorn seemed to have special significance for him. A leer quickly faded from his face. "Why you asking? What did *you* do last night Jennifer? I mean, Jenny."

A quick glance that went down the line at the word. *Jennifer.* Jenny knew they all played poker sometimes, but their poker faces needed work. They knew something they weren't telling.

Oh I was walking around and then suddenly decided to get myself off. In front of you all…

What if she really was masturbating in front of them at night? No wonder they gathered around the lounge with popcorn. Jesus!

Jenny went back to library, forced herself through a ton of database research, printed up her articles, and fell asleep with her head on the desk. She woke up to a puddle of drool and a cold Red Bull someone had left for her on the table. Did Turner leave it for her? She sucked it down and made her way back to the dorm while everyone was at dinner. Looking left and right on her way to her room, she marveled at Nadia. If there were hidden cameras about, she couldn't see them.

Nadia showed up at ten pm exactly.

"The natives are restless," Nadia said, bustling in. Nighttime seemed to be when everyone talked over their work from the day. Late night was when everyone did their work for the next day.

"I don't think I'll be able to sleep tonight," Jenny confessed.

"You didn't nap today did you?" Nadia asked. Jenny knew

her face revealed her guilt. Nadia chided her with one finger. "Remember, no naps."

"No naps," Jenny echoed contritely. She started emptying out the cans she had gone through that day into her recycling wastebasket.

Nadia looked at the over-flowing receptacle. "I can see you're fighting the impulse. That's a lot of Red Bull."

"You're telling me."

"Jenny, how many cans did you drink today?"

"All day? Only four. I also had maybe two quattra-venti's at the café as well but that's all. I don't do more than that," Jenny added, trying to be helpful, "because it makes my heart beat too fast."

Nadia sat in the chair. "I crunched the data and you're definitely having what we call confusional arousals in your sleep." She pulled out the white tray from her bag.

"What's that mean?"

"It means you're having periods where you're awake and asleep at the same time. Because you're awake, you can get up and perform activities, unlike someone who normally can't move in their sleep. But because you're also asleep," Nadia said, placing the first felt dot, "you have amnesia, and you can't remember any of it."

"Awake and asleep at the same time? Isn't that an oxymoron?"

"Not really. Sleep isn't an off on switch. You're coming out of your different phases of sleep, but you're not staying out long enough to wake up. Basically it's a classic marker for sleepwalking."

"So I am definitely sleepwalking." Please let it be sleepwalking, please, please, please.

"Yes. But let's see what else."

Jenny didn't like the sound of that.

Fifteen minutes later, the dots were in place. "Okay, my work here is done," Nadia said, yawning. "Back to the lab for me. I'll finish examining the samples I took this morning while checking on the monitors. Goodnight." Another jaw cracking yawn followed the first one.

"Geez Nadia. Are you getting any sleep yourself?"

"As they say in my profession, I'll sleep when I'm dead."

***

By eight am the next morning, Jenny was hunched over Nadia, seated at the desk with an open laptop in front of her.

The room, so neat the night before, was once again trashed. Jenny watched a bleary-eyed Nadia get her laptop configuration all set. Jenny felt like someone had removed her brain through her nose, crapped on it, and then shoved it right back up into her cranium. Maybe it was all the Red Bull from the night before.

On the computer screen there were videos divided into four quadrants. They were labeled *Nanny Cam 1, 2, 3,* and *4.*

"I used these at home," Nadia said.

"I didn't know you had a kid."

"Two."

The cameras showed the current scene—which was people slowly wandering down the halls towards the bridge on their way to breakfast. Then Nadia called up the saved file and all the people disappeared. The time stamp at the bottom of each mini-screen lit up in green numbers and the rooms seemed different because it was night and they were darker. The bottom left corner was grey. Jenny's bed was black her sleeping figure white.

"That's infrared," Nadia said tapping the screen. "Your light is out but we can still see you.

The other three cameras covered the hall, the lounge and the elevator.

Nadia looking tapped out. She was wearing glasses today her curls bunched into a hasty rubber band knot as she silently tapped away.

"You ready for this?" she said. "Here, you sit. I'll stand."

Jenny sat down in front of the screen. She didn't like the tone in Nadia's voice. This wasn't going to be good.

The first part of the screens showed the guys gathering in the

94

lounge. There was a time stamp at the bottom, one-thirty-five. It was distracting watching four screens at once, but Jenny found she quickly got used to it.

Rick came with a big bowl of popcorn, and the guys gave each other bullshit greetings and fist pumps.

"They're excited," Jenny said.

"Yup," Nadia nodded back at the screen. "Just watch." Jenny started feeling the anxiety inside her ratchet up.

"This time," Bonifellow said to Rick, "She wants your fucking kettle corn, you give it to her, asshole."

"Don't worry about it," Rick told him, grinning around the mouthfuls he munched on.

Meanwhile, the bottom left corner the white figure was up.

"Hey, that's me!" Jenny said.

"Wait," Nadia said. "Watch."

Jenny in the bedroom was throwing off her shirt, and then she was fumbling around the room in the dark. Jenny looked over her shoulder for the actual camera. There it was, stuck right next to the outlet that rested next to her the bureau. Nadia was good at this.

Jenny watched herself stretch, then pace more swiftly about the room, head down. It was weird watching herself like this. On screen the white figure pulled her hair up into the high pony tail, looked at herself sidewise in the mirror, put on some make-up, and then pulled down her pj's to a few inches down to her hip bones and folded them over the waist, revealing the flat space of her belly, making the pj bottoms sag over the tops of her feet.

Nadia reached forward and punched a button. Everything went fast forward until about 1:47am. At that point Jenny watched herself on camera going out into the lounge area. By now the halls were empty, but the six guys were still waiting in the lounge. Four from her group and—her stomach started to shrivel up—two guys she didn't even know.

"Is she going to do it – is tonight the night?" Bonifellow whispered. They talked about her like wasn't even there, but she was standing right in front of them.

"Who are those two other guys?" Jenny pointed.

Nadia pointed at one with her pinkie. "He sits at the psychology table, I think."

"You've watched this already?" Jenny asked Nadia, who didn't answer. She was watching the screen and had taken out her iPad to take notes.

"I'm feeling lucky," Rick said to the other guys. "Hey, hey! Jennifer, come sit on my lap."

Rick put his bowl of popcorn on the fat arm of the chair and patted his lap invitingly.

"Jennifer?" Jenny asked, her voice pitching up an octave. Nadia shrugged. Suddenly Jenny couldn't sit still anymore. She stood up as well next to Nadia and folded her arms across her chest.

Meanwhile, on-screen Jennifer went over and straddled Rick where he sat in the overstuffed beige chair. She covered his eyes, playing guess who. Jenny covered her own eyes.

"Oh, I like that," Rick said. "Now what?"

"Why is she wearing so many clothes? That's not our Jennifer," Bonifellow said.

Rick leaned back to avoid her breasts in his face, and said "Jennifer, aren't you hot?"

"Of course she is," the psychology guy said.

Jenny shuddered and continued peeking through her fingers while on the camera her parasomnia self slowly pulled down her pj bottoms as the guys ooh'd appreciatively, and skipped out of them all together. Suddenly Jenny felt cold. She went over and got her pj bottoms and put them on.

Oh, taking off her bottoms, yes, that's better, that's more like it, the guys all crooned.

Great. She was their own personal strip show every night.

At least she didn't have on a thong. Instead she was in aqua boy shorts with thin lace insets on the sides. On-screen ponytail Jennifer got up from Rick and bent over straight-legged to pick up the bottoms. She started to gently beat Rick across the face with them, which he didn't seem to mind at all. He grabbed them and, *ew!*, smelled the crotch. He slumped a little lower in his chair pumping his pelvis towards her. Jennifer then leaned forward and this time rubbed her breasts into Rick's face.

"Motorboat, motorboat," the psych guy chanted.

"She's going to suffocate him," Bonifellow said.

"Yeah, but he'll die happy," psychology guy said.

Jenny thought she was going to throw up. Nadia tapped out more notes.

On-screen Jennifer stood upright again, rubbed Rick's hair—or what was left of it—and dumped the big bowl of his popcorn all over his lap. She walked away while the guys cat-called, and Rick remained sitting where he was, his body stiffening up, a stunned expression on his face. Well, the one good thing about all this is I really have a pretty good looking tush, Jenny thought, stunned.

"I think he just came in his pants," Nadia said.

"Probably the closest he's been to having a lap dance… Wait, where'd I go?" Jenny asked. She looked at all four cameras, but her nighttime doppelganger was gone from the screen.

Nadia pointed with her pinkie nail to the screen again.

"They watch you go out that way and then there," She moved her finger right. "They're looking out that window. I think they can see you through the window, so I went this morning and looked. There are about five dorms you can see from the window."

And the bridge, Jenny thought. That connects through the mezzanine to the other dorm.

But that wasn't all. Nadia fast-forwarded the footage, until Jennifer came slinking back.

"There—you're back." Jenny watched herself collapse across the bed, unconscious. Nadia stopped the recording.

"And that's that." She tapped the time marker: 4:45.

"So where did you go for almost three hours?" Nadia asked.

"Where do I go?"

"And what did you do when you got there?"

"I don't know, I don't remember." But she could guess, couldn't she?

Jenny looked at the clock. She was due at the morning session in half an hour.

"I will find out. I have ways," Nadia said, sounding more than ever like a high voiced gypsy. "I'd like to follow you tonight—then the mystery will be solved." Something about Jenny's face made her lean in. "Is that okay?"

"How am I going to face them?"

"Listen, the men seem to think you do this regularly, so there's a good chance we can capture it on tape tonight."

"You know what I'm doing, don't you?"

"This is a huge *huge* advance for my research project. You're saving me two years—maybe five years, or ten."

"Then I'd better get a big thank you in your paper."

"Sure, that and my first born child." Nadia turned around suddenly and faced her directly.

"Look, I've got something else to tell you. I studied your vaginal sample under a microscope."

Jenny's stomach hit the floor.

"Jenny, did you have sex with someone last night?"

Jenny could only manage to raise her voice to a hushed whisper. "No."

"I think you did," Nadia said. "I think you don't remember because you did it in your sleep."

Which one? Jenny spent the morning session looking from one member of the group to the other. Rick. *Please god, no. Please.* Bonifellow. *Not him – not him either –or him...* she wouldn't have shown up to the session, only she was waiting for one sign, one slip or tell that would reveal who it was.

She heard nothing, took no notes. The distant drone of the older professors was mere background noise.

What if it was more than one of them? At one time? What if there was a broom closet or something somewhere—or not even that. The place was full of deserted dorm rooms—.

She groaned, covering her eyes, trying not to notice as several pairs of eyes turned her way.

At lunchtime Nadia dragged her along to the cafeteria. "You have to eat."

But Nadia didn't really care if she ate. Nadia just wanted to grill her.

"Did you have any sexual dreams that you can recall last night? Or did any sexual fantasies go through your head?"

Jenny ducked her head in shame. "Yes."

Out came a notebook, her pen poised above the blank page. "Tell me."

"...about *him*." Jenny's voice was a whisper.

" H i m   w h o ? "

"Mr. Stares-a-lot from the other side of the cafeteria." She hiked a thumb behind her towards Turner.

"The varmint guy?"

"The varmint guy."

Nadia wrote it all down on her notebook.

"What happened to your iPad?" Jenny asked.

"I forgot to charge it." There was a stain down the front of Nadia's shirt and she smelled like someone who hadn't showered for a day or two.

Jennifer gulped down her cereal, which was all her stomach could handle. She felt nauseated. What if she was pregnant? The closer she got to having a definitive answer for what the fuck was going on, the worse everything was getting.

Meanwhile, sleepwalking, shedding her clothing about the dorm, practically giving lap dances to the guys she wanted to respect her intellectually—and let's not forget the all-too-common masturbating that might be going on. Gee, she was just her own little porn channel, wasn't she?

"So we lost you at the bridge," Nadia was saying.

Yes it could. Hands over her eyes, she said, "I want to die."

"Tonight I'm going to put a tracking sensor in your hair. Just a little thing, it clips on. Then I'm going to follow you, and record your behavior. From a distance. You won't know I'm even there." Nadia gave a big yawn. "Well, of course you won't know anything—"

Jenny stood.

"But I'll hang back so I don't scare anyone off."

Jenny imagined herself as an evil twin. She imagined her evil twin rolling around with one of the guys—probably Bonifellow—in another dorm. He was handsome, but a true slug on the inside. She pushed away the cereal.

Nadia eyed her distaste for food. "Hey, you're not having stomach pains, or burping or anything are you?" They tossed things back and forth until Nadia decided Jenny was probably not going off and eating in the night.

She saw Bonifellow across the room. God please no. He was not worthy of the tiniest, most forbidden sexual fantasy. Not like— She stiffened. She knew where she'd been last night.

Chapter 4

She didn't bother saying anything more. She got up and left Nadia, went back to her room, and napped uneasily with horrible dreams during the rest of the day. Jennifer came out in the dream. Jennifer was a mean sorority girl and was laughing at her. Jennifer morphed into Johannes and grew teeth all over his/her body and then—Jenny woke up with a scream.

That night it was easier to let Nadia came by and do her dot thing. Jenny pulled on another cami, this one pinkish, put her hair up in something that looked a little like the sexy ponytail *Jennifer* had worn the night before. She changed into a pair of slinky silk pj bottoms with pale peach stripes and, with the uniform on, she

100

was ready to go.

She'd sipped so many Red Bulls that evening she felt on the verge of tachycardia while she practiced *Jennifer's* slinky walk and hooded stare in front of the mirror. *More like she doesn't give a damn. Eyes lower, chin up. More like everyone else is cow shit.*

When she mastered the trick of moving about like she owned the goddamn place it was time to roll. The first steps outside her room were the hardest. She strode down the hall, swishing her hips, feeling the wide legs of her slinky pjs slap at her ankles.

She could bypass the lounge, but she wanted a little practice. She wanted everyone to think she was Jennifer that night, *everyone.*

Bonifellow was eating ice cream. She sat on the arm of his chair, tucked her leg over her knee, and grabbed his hair in one hand, pulling it back. With the other hand she took a spoonful of his ice cream and licked at it like she was making love to the spoon. Bonifellow swallowed hard, but seemed to enjoy himself.

She passed.

She stared through them all one by one, letting go of Bonifellow's hair, and going over to Tucker who was sitting on the edge of the back of the couch.

"She's up," Rick said.

She turned around and drifted up against Tucker. His arms tentatively wrapped around her waist. She pulled away, worried that she'd gag or actually feel the boner he probably sporting.

As one, the guys turned on Tucker chiding him. *No touching Tucker*, they said in unison.

"And she's off," Rick said, as she headed toward the bridge, trying to keep the sway going. That particular stomp stomp Jennifer had, along with the dead eyes.

As she went through the door she heard Bonifellow. "Tucker, Jesus, you ruined it again."

The door closed on Tucker's feeble apologies to the others.

Even through the door she could hear the psychology guy calling *come back*. She floated down the stairs off to the right of

101

the elevator. Down to the mezzanine floor, down another short set of stairs on the right and towards the lounge.

Once she was in the open lounge, she stopped. Which way to go? The path of least resistance led her into a cluster of furniture. There were four hallways going off in each direction from the lounge, but she didn't know which one to take. Her eyes darted to the hallway on the right but the darkness was overwhelming.

She could smell microwave popcorn off to her left. So she opted to go right, thinking that Jennifer on the prowl probably would avoid the friendly female voices echoing from the far end of the hall from whence popcorn smells were emanating.

Just then something tugged her ponytail. She let out a short scream and practically levitated as she turned around.

"*Nadia!*"

Nadia dropped her camcorder.

"Why are you awake?" Nadia said, picking up her camcorder. "And if you're awake, why aren't you in your room?"

"I had to know, I couldn't wait another night."

"What? You mean you—" Nadia understood her look. "No. Jenny, you're ruining everything for me. I kept watching the monitor thinking what the hell…"

Two or three women came into the lounge from the hall on the right.

"You hear someone scream?" they asked. Nadia and Jenny shook their heads.

"I think they're making popcorn down there," Nadia offered, pointing to the smells of popcorn. The women drifted off in that direction.

It had to be the dark hallway. Had to be. Her gut told her that's where he was.

"Look, this is the way I think I went."

"But you're not asleep."

"But I have to know. How did you find me? What are you doing here?"

102

"I saw you go past the cameras in the lounge. I've been running around the whole building trying to find you. What am I doing here? What are you doing here? You're ruining our plan. I was hoping to record this."

"It was your plan, Nadia, not mine. And I'll tell you what happens. Probably. But I don't feel comfortable with you following right behind me."

"I don't feel comfortable leaving you alone! Please go back to bed. Let's do this the right way. Please."

"You're groveling. I can't tell if you're really worried or you just want the research statistics."

Nadia looked guilty. "A little of both," she admitted.

"Look, it might not be anything, right? It could just be empty rooms down that hallway."

Nadia opened her mouth to argue, but Jenny gave her the Jennifer look.

"That's creepy, don't do that," Nadia said.

A door opened down the dark hall. Jenny heard male voices. She gave Nadia the look again.

"Go."

"Fine." Nadia flipped shut the camcorder and put it in her big bag. She turned and retreated to the mezzanine and behind the bank of elevators. "I'll stay here."

Jenny braced herself. She knew Nadia wasn't gone for good, but she opened the glass door to the far right hallway and started her slink-stomp down the corridor.

The hall was dark. They were doing some maintenance or painting on the floor. There were no florescent lights overhead, and she passed a stack of long light bulbs propped under the red glow of an exit light. About half way down the corridor was a big rectangle of golden light. Two rooms were open, the men in them talking across the hall to each other.

She could hear one better than the other. Abandoning her Jennifer stride, she crept up closer then stopped

One had a low rumbling voice. Turner. The other voice alternated between a radio-slick baritone and a protesting pitch that cracked like a teenage boy whose voice was changing.

"So you've settled for being her man-meat," the silky radio voice said.

"She doesn't want to play in public it seems."

"That's cold, bro. I guess I can see why she'd just want to use you for sex though. Probably already has a boyfriend back at home. She dresses all granny-like but her body is slammin'."

Turner's low rumble was indistinguishable.

"Probably they have some kind of agreement—like sex with someone else is fine, but nothing emotional. You know?"

Another rumble.

"Yeah, but you're hung up on her. You gotta be cold dude. Don't succumb to the mind games."

She tried to call to mind the baritone. Had to be the pale-faced guy with glasses.

Turner's voice rang out clear and strong this time. "I didn't say I was hung up on her. I said we're very sexually compatible."

Where were all the other biology people? Her floor had the econ people everywhere you looked. Maybe the biology people had enough numbers that they were spread out across the other halls. Maybe no one else wanted the dark hallway.

"Look at you, trying to play it all cool. I see right through you. You're totally obsessing."

"Because —"

She couldn't hear and tried to creep closer. Turner was deep in his room. The other guy had his desk near the door; his voice was as clear as a bell and she was afraid he'd see her if she got too close.

"That isn't a deal breaker for you?" the baritone was asking. "Sounds freaky to me."

"Takes all kinds, Harrison," Turner said. Harrison was Turner's lunch buddy.

"Obviously she's not *such* a good girl. I've seen good girls—they don't pounce on guys like you. And don't think I can't hear what you're doing in there, because I can. It's indecent."

"Because you're not allowed to join in."

"Exactly. Why you can't just accept that you're dating a sexual predator? So what if she doesn't want to talk to you during the day? That's not the important part anyway. Who cares?"

There was another rumble from Turner's room. What was he doing? Changing his clothes? She couldn't make out a word he was saying. "Did she really?" Turner's sidekick laughed. "What did you do?"

"Let's just say I'm not going to let her tie me up again anytime real soon."

"But you *did* let her tie you up."

There was a pause. "Yeah. Once."

"Oh man, I am *so* living vicariously through you right now."

Jenny felt her face go deep red, and fanned herself rapidly. *Jennifer* was not a blusher.

"Hey, I'm going to hit the hay," Harrison said. "If the senorita wants to have a threesome, I'm here for you."

"Thanks."

She stomped into the lit carpet. The men were instantly silent. Turner stood with his hands on his hips just taking her in.

The other guy talked like she couldn't hear him. "Speak of the devil."

Turner gave her the same look from the lunchroom. It was like a punch to the stomach, because here they were, in a place and time where he could put the actions to what that look promised her. He came up to her and put her hand on the side of his jaw. She smoothed his skin there, feeling the difference in texture between his stubble and his skin.

"Dude, she's asleep isn't she?" Harrison was behind her, his voice hitching higher.

She made her eyelids heavy, but she was a thousand points of radiant energy throughout her body when she heard this comment. How could he not notice that she was so awake, so alive?

"That's the current theory."

"Dude, that is so wrong." Harrison's voice, on the other hand, was all admiration.

Because she felt that Jennifer would do such a thing, she stopped stroking Turner's end of the day bristle and gave him a smart little slap. The grin he gave back made her melt and froze her organs simultaneously. He reached for the door.

"So, if you need anything, h—"

The door slammed shut and they were alone.

He locked the door without looking, his eyes still tracked right into hers. They were tired eyes, pinkish-red lids bracketed by deep shadows. He took the hand that had given him the playful slap and nibbled on the sensitive center of her palm. She felt it all the way down to the throbbing ache centered right behind her pubic bone. Her pelvis, her womb, they wanted to have a talk with him. She might not have much to say, but they had plenty they wanted to communicate. She saw that his eyes were lit in a mocking way.

"Jennifer," he said.

The realization hit her like a crazy rollercoaster ride. Jennifer didn't talk. She realized she could touch him wherever she wanted. Jennifer was not shy.

Turner was not shy either. He started taking off her clothes, plucking the silky bottoms from her.

Moving mighty fast, mister. She would have stiffened normally, but Jennifer wouldn't mind. Jennifer would be a heat-seeking missile. She sucked in her breath as her cami was shucked instantly. She dragged her hand across his naked abs, savoring their heat, and he sucked in his belly, as if her fingertips made him shiver with sensation.

She plunged her hand into the gap between the light furring of his stomach and his jeans. That quick fraught look in his eyes gave her a feeling of sudden power as she grabbed his silky hard length.

106

At that moment she could have him, she realized. She could have the boy across the hall—or both of them together. She could have any man on the campus, in twos or threes, or crawling before her on the ground. It was so odd, but she never realized the power within her before.

He skinned off her undies and her heart began racing as he shucked his jeans. She wanted to cross her hands in front of her sparse strip of pubic hair, but Jennifer wouldn't cover up.

Wombats, weasels, martins, minks—why couldn't she remember what he studied? It didn't matter. They reached the point of no words, and to her it was like a sanctuary. Not to talk but to feel. Not to think but to touch. She worked with her brain until her body became a stranger.

She watched him spring free from the jeans, and she forgot her own name. His entire pubic region was shaved, and his cock was naked, enormous. He pressed up against her, his fingers stroking upward from her outer thigh and then fanning out in a mesmerizing fashion across her hips before sliding down and in between her legs. She tightened, but felt how much more wet she got as his fingers remained there. She wasn't going to remember how to breathe soon, especially if he kept dragging his fingers in from the tender flesh of her inner thighs to plunge back into the wet spot between her legs.

His mouth took over hers, his tongue exploring while his fingers slid around below. Their naked bodies began sliding against each other in sensuous greeting. He felt that delight too, she saw, his brow furrowed with the sharp pleasure of it. She didn't, couldn't, wouldn't be embarrassed by the searing kiss he was giving her. Or the way his fingers plunged sure and hard into her wet pink shell once more. All slippery, his fingers curving inward, stabbing her g-spot as she opened herself to the tingling slightly numb sensation they left behind. His hand cupped her there, spreading her inner thighs apart more firmly as she gave an involuntary wiggle. Her pelvis was speaking again, the very bones throbbing for him.

She was surprised when he suddenly turned and tossed her over onto the bed. Catching herself with her hands, she held her position, on hands and knees on the edge of the mattress. She felt her feet pushed apart from behind, then wider still. Now her hands were on the bed, her head low her backside up, legs spread very far apart.

Her head started to seize up, her neck to tighten. What was happening now? But she could also feel her body responding, welcoming his big hands as they were winding from her shoulders down her sides to her thighs. Her body knew those hands, trusted those hands. The suspense made her squeeze against his hands, pressing them in as he knelt and licked the wet slickness of her secret, intimate place. His tongue plundered those pink folds until she lost her breath and her ability to do anything except blindly push up and back with her entire backside. She found herself thrusting back helplessly, then in repeated semi-circles, moans rippling out from her throat.

"That's right Jennifer, let me hear you."

She froze, horrified. *Jennifer*. Yet her body kept responding, and didn't care. This was the craziest thrilling thing she'd ever done, and *god* it felt good. Small intense grunts of satisfaction were coming from her mouth.

"I think about those sounds you make way too much for my own good," he murmured to her. The words warmed her inside, until it felt like a blazing sun was under her skin. She gasped and was suddenly coming, coming, coming, the delicious licks not stopping, stroking her onward and forward.

Turning her head she noticed them in the room's mirror. He caught her looking and turned them slightly so she could see better. "Know you like that," he said.

Again her innards fluttered. She did like it, it was amazing, it was all out, and every time she rocked against his mouth with no restraint the flutter happened all over again. He pulled back and played with her with his fingers, his lower face wet, his eyes looking at hers in the mirror. She noticed how serious his face was—his eyes deep under his brows, almost lost in shadow, on the verge of frown.

It was a stare of concentration, and again she noticed those short, sharp lines under his eyes. He placed his head back between her thighs down low. His tongue was magic, she had to stretch forward on her arms and close her eyes—but she wasn't going to forget those shadows. They weren't there at the beginning of summer—she would have gone on the witness stand and testified to that.

His wet cheeks lifted away for a second. "Talkative tonight, aren't you?" Before she could grunt in agreement, he was down low once more, pushing her thighs apart with his raspy cheeks. She gave a gasp of breath, as his mouth sucked her. She was dripping, and her gasps came faster, but not from shock, more as a code. *Don't stop. Don't. Stop.*

His agile tongue knew her, knew her well, its confident probing and teasing groan lower, louder, until she was down on her elbows, her forehead hidden in the covers as she came, helplessly crying out at her tangled unbearable pleasure.

The first rippling pulls inside her died away even as he pulled her off the bed, standing behind her as she looked in the mirror.

Jennifer wouldn't be satisfied by the quick orgasms, nor intimidated when he took one large hand and drew her around until she standing, no, kneeling before him, the broad head of his cock proffered to her lips. Comfortable on his feet, a wet glistening beard across his lower face, his erection pushed past her lips, all silky and rounded. *I've got a fat cock in my mouth* she thought, and sucked harder, whimpering with the pleasure of it, her cunt clenching hard, feeling all hollow and achy. She wrapped her fist around his cock. She sucked and moved it deeper into the back of her mouth, breathing heavily through her nose.

He was grasping her ponytail to guide her, oh-so gently. She lapped him back and forth, up and down with her tongue. She knew that was how Jennifer would do it, both to play with him and tease him and also so he could watch her in the mirror. Meanwhile her lips were getting him wet, her mouth and cheeks and chin slippery as she sucked him off. It made her cunt cry out, her pelvis tingling in demand that *somebody do something* about this situation immediately.

She began sucking him greedily, until she felt him shaking from the effort of holding back. The power of him shaking was hers. It made her want to feel it even more, so she wrapped her hands around his back and grabbed his ass. The pull of muscles trembling there told her again what an effort it was not to pump off into her mouth at once. She wanted him to, but he had other plans.

He withdrew and once again tossed her towards the mattress, forcing her feet into that wide police stance. This time she wasn't afraid. She even enjoyed the cool rush of air there where she was wettest and arching out her ass. This time excitement licked up and down her legs while he easily slid two thirds of the way inside her with his iron-hard, hot cock. She felt him go the rest of the way and she was surprisingly tight, wonderfully so. She found herself down on her elbows, surprised by how he filled her up as he pushed slowly forward. His cock made sucking noises pulling back while she tightened against him and resisted. He plunged forward hard again 'til she was forced to release her grip and ride along with him.

"You like that," he said. It wasn't a question. Soon he was fucking her hard, holding her hips so there was no way she could move them, nowhere to hide from having to take the maddening delicious, unrelenting motion of him. She was up on her toes for him, feeling him put a special effort into each hard thrust, as if his body was saying take *that* one and *that* one, and especially *that*. Her pleasure was sharp, starting deep and diffused inside her, building up along her thighs, wiggling over her shoulders and down her breasts at the same time. Like a harness of pleasure she could feel it taking form and building a tight web all over her body.

He knew her slightest gesture, knew how she came. As her head came up and back towards him, she could feel his belly just brushing her ass, and then he abruptly began giving her faster, shorter jabs that made her grunts go higher and louder.

She was calling out his name urgently with the devastating pleasure he was drilling into her wet, tight pussy. Soon she was undone, pairing his thrusts with the grinding motion of her hips. Her back arched hard, no wonder... Yesterday. She couldn't stand the joy of the jerking thrusts any longer.

She realized he was talking under his breath. What was he saying?

"Have you got a boyfriend? No. Someone else you like better than me? No, somehow I don't think so..." It was almost muttered, but she couldn't reply, not with the deep spring in her body winding up tightly again.

As he kept going it began to implode. First she was a million exploding bits of a thousand stars exploding into nothing. He moved in closer. Now his knees were on either side of hers, his chin brushing her ponytail. His torso hovered inches above her own.

She took pleasure in his biceps, how they were round and strong, how they bracketed her shoulders and flexed with his thrusts. She sank her head lower and pushed herself against him until she felt the sweat seal their skin together. The contact set off the fusion of his orgasm within hers.

That first hollow explosion she felt was replaced by a supernova going off behind her eyes as her pelvis shattered into song, a song of liquid pleasure. Her knees collapsed and Turner followed, falling on top of her. The bed frame dug into her shins, his chin buried into the hollow of her neck and his cock giving a few mindless pulses while his breathing charged along, a whistle in her ears.

Wolverines. He was the world's expert on wolverines.

"Jennifer," he said. He kissed her neck.

"Wolverines," she said. She turned her head. His next kiss owned her. She wanted her lips dominated by his lips. She wanted his hands doing what they wanted to do, which was come up and cup her breasts. She wanted her own hands to know what to do as well, and surprisingly, that was to find his length, let it throb wet and still hard in her own hand, while her lips tasted the salty skin along his infinitely desirable shoulder.

Jennifer didn't talk. She didn't need to. Jennifer didn't worry after sex, and everything was okay.

He roused himself, lifted himself up. Withdrew. No condom, she realized. So that was the smell. She'd always, always used condoms with boyfriends and she didn't realize how it smelled differently without. Less like the faint smell of ammonia mixed with latex, more like she's been marked with his scent. She'd been walking around for weeks marked with his musk and not even known it.

He went into the bathroom, came back with a condom on. *That horse has already left the stable, buddy.*

Wait, no.

She froze for a split second. She knew what he planned to do next. Her first thought was *the jig is up. No way, no way, no way.* She was going to have to say something. But he was already grabbing her, and her body melted and accepted the way he handled her.

His body was already sliding against her backside, and the sliding felt so good. She was deeply conflicted but she was also melting. His chest was rubbing against her back, his stomach and those rock hard thighs, so long, so deeply muscled, they were in between her own thighs. She was so turned on her pelvis was no longer talking, now it was the round circle, the slit of her pussy that wanted this. He was plunging in again, but only to get wet and lubricated it seemed, for after about four deep thrusts he was out and pressing the head of his cock to that inviolate tender button of her ass.

She was so confused, so aroused. She felt the stubble of his shaved pubic hairs against her damp, tender lips. She was very slick there. He rubbed himself against her and she felt herself

112

widen. Then the tip of his penis was in her and she waited. As she waited there was no pain, no discomfort, just that he was wide and deep inside. She writhed with embarrassment that she was actually doing this. And with him. And, and...He went further and concentric circles of pleasure spread from the rim of her ass. He moved another inch deeper, then two. It was intense, so intense, but that wasn't hurting exactly and he pulled out again so fast she didn't have time to even figure out if the intensity was pleasant or unpleasant.

Then he was in again, slower this time, and it didn't hurt at all. He thrust, slowly, going deeper but slower still. That felt good. Oh so good. His hands on her hips, those large hands, they made her breath tremble, they made her belly slide to the sheets. *Oh my god.* He spread her legs more, which arched her ass up more, and her belly was full of dancing shrimp, because it's like nothing—

He started moving, slowly, but she was so damn wet. The thick concentric circle of stimulation went from the outer ring of her ass and spread. It spread and diminished a little with each move, until he was firmly a few inches in. Then it was more intense, and then... he's waiting again. While he waited the deep inner thrill at doing this dirty girl thing took over her. She lifted her shoulders and stretched out like a cat, which excited him. He moved faster. Soon they were rocking together but they didn't stay pressed together for long.

"What's it going to take Jennifer?" Stab, stab. "What's it going to take," stab, "for you," stab, "to talk to me?" Now it was something, something tight and hard but not enough.

Then his finger slid under her, which brought him close against her again, and that closeness made her skin sing. And while his fingers stroked her clit, it was the enveloping warmth of his skin covering her that fed her frenzy. She rocked her hips as he stroked her.

"Harder! Oh fuck me harder!" She submitted to all those licks of pleasure until she couldn't bear to stop, she couldn't speak, or

113

think... Even if she wanted to.

Now now now now. He was taking over, rapid thrusts, then waiting with those strong hands holding her so she could feel him inside pulsing, then his finger on her clit wouldn't stop. She couldn't tell if she was driving them harder or if he was, but they were both slick and wet with sweat and her juices. His six pack was slapping her ass and her feet were arched, her neck fully extended, mouth open as she gave in to his relentless finger on her clit and the slick fullness in her tight ass and started coming her brains out. They both took a big final breath and strained together at the same time. Finally she lay back, and he withdrew and collapsed on top of her. Done.

Okay, she thought, through the thick feeling of orgasm, *that's how it's done. Stranger hook-up complete. Yeah. Wow.*

He was laying there, half on top of her, silent, but not so out of it. He was looking at her. She half-lidded her eyes to be able to bear looking at him. She should get up and go. Get those clothes on and get out. She didn't think she could do that right this second. Whew. Not sure she could even hold herself upright—

"Something's different," he said, his eyes shrewd. Her heart took off like a jackrabbit. He took her chin, looked her face up and down.

"You're...awake."

"What gave me away?"

"You let me kiss you. Jennifer doesn't kiss like that."

Of course not. She didn't kiss well—was that what he was saying? She looked at him, frustrated and puzzled.

"You waited for me to come with you. You didn't try to pull off the condom. You...cuddled."

He thought about it some more. "And then when I was done on top of you, you kind of stroked yourself back against me. Jennifer never does that."

"Yeah, I'm just an amazingly thoughtful lover."

He grabbed her shoulder and pulled her half up looking closer

114

at her.

"What's all over your face?"

She realized he was looking closely at the dots. "So you knew," she said. "You knew I was asleep."

"Not at first,"

"No, you did. I heard you both talking. You knew I was asleep."

He frowned and then his gaze shifted away. "I saw you hanging out with that sleep researcher. I started thinking about it at dinner, and then did some googling. Put two and two together."

He shifted around, put his head on that bicep. She wanted to bite the soft smooth skin there. She stroked it instead, but he tucked it away from her and she pulled her hand back.

"Was that the first time...you know, while you were awake?" he asked.

"The first time I had my ass penetrated. Without anyone asking first."

"Hate to tell you, but that wasn't the first time."

This was starting to feel uncomfortable. She wanted to pull up the bedclothes but he was lying on them. She started picking up her clothes and found herself putting them on. Was there a bell tolling midnight somewhere? Couldn't she just drop a glass slipper instead of getting the third degree?

He was getting dressed too. Having his eyes anywhere but boring into hers gave her time to think.

They were entering the realm of doom, the place where they were supposed to talk. The more they didn't say anything, the more compressed his mouth got, and the more she started wondering how long he knew she was asleep.

Why did she have to take his word for it that he'd just sorta maybe figured it out tonight? On the other hand, why the hell should she? She didn't know this guy. He was a smooth dude. She was a pathetic idiot.

She held up his hairbrush, apparently never used before.

"May I?"

"Sure," he said, but what was he thinking. Those eyes etched into her until she was blushing so hard she thought her face would explode.

Thank God it wasn't Bonifellow, she thought, brushing. Thank God it wasn't Rick, or the psych guy.

Chapter 5

The sudden rapping on the door in the middle of the night scared the hell out of both of them.

"Harrison, shut the f—" Turner said, opening the door. But it was Nadia.

Nadia obviously couldn't take it anymore and had sprung at the door thinking she was being raped.

"He knows Nadia," Jenny said.

"He knows!" Nadia said, not looking at Jenny, keeping her eyes on Turner.

"Where do you get off?" was her first comment.

Turner looked shocked.

"It's like sleeping with an unconscious woman. It's—"

Turner interrupted her. "She's not asleep this time."

"The point is not tonight," Nadia, said, undaunted. "The point is all the other nights. Like yesterday when I found her half undressed and reeking of sex in the morning. A hickey the size of New Jersey on her neck."

It looked bad when Nadia put it that way. But feeling loose, and in fact almost floppy, from great sex, Jenny felt the acute misery of a few hours before grow distant in her mind.

Now Harrison was up, his door open. Great. Just great.

"You could have told me," Jenny said, turning on him. "When you knew. You would have saved me so much torment. You don't get it."

"I didn't hurt you," Turner said.

"No, she was just coming back bruised and marked up," Nadia

said, her tone scathing.

Nadia, Jenny thought, *you're a true friend*, though she found herself wishing Nadia could be full of peace like her at this moment—Or maybe if this wasn't peace, still, chock full of goodwill.

"He's had bruises too," Harrison said, sticking his oar in. "Not to mention some…wicked…rug burns." His cheeks burning pink, Harrison decided to wisely shut up.

Jenny turned to Turner. "It's not about that. I was doing things in front of my colleagues on my way here."

Turner gave her a blank look. He seemed so calm, so relaxed. She kind of started to hate him a little again.

She could feel the agitation cranking up inside her slowly. "It's not like 6th grade sleep away camp where we go home and never see each other again. These are professional colleagues. If you'd *told me* when you *knew*—"

"I don't even know when I knew. It was probably too late by then. It took me time to figure it out. I mean, I'm only one step ahead of you. I didn't really truly get it until you were so different tonight."

Turning to Nadia he said, "She's been like two different people."

And you only want the one I'm not, Jenny thought. *The one that's confident, easy come, easy go.*

He said those things, she reminded herself. But he never said he liked you better, her wicked side prompted. Jennifer was the name on his lips. Not Jenny.

Suddenly she had a bone-deep conviction Jennifer was her enemy. Not just her less repressed subconscious but the *It*, the thing inside her against her will.

The peace of Turner's unrestrained lovemaking ebbed swiftly, replaced by a claustrophobic panic. Meanwhile, his arms crossed, Turner was clearly on the defensive.

"I don't know what your game is," he said, making Jenny blink with surprise at the change in his tone. "But you came here to me.

You know I've been trying to chase you down for two weeks—two weeks to straighten out what the fuck was going on. I've met border collies that have better communication skills than you. If you just stopped whimpering and running away, and tried having an adult conversation—"

She gasped.

"Then maybe you wouldn't be in this muddle. I'm sorry but the nasty hot sex we've been having may not go with your gosh golly church girl image—" Another blow. "—But it's just sex. Your colleagues will get over it. As for them," he said, pointing to Harrison and Nadia. "I'm not comfortable with where this conversation is going. I forced no one," he said.

Turning to her he stabbed out his finger. "*You*—or your alter ego as the case may be—came after me, and did so rather aggressively."

Harrison was giving little nods to the speech his friend made.

"*They,*" pointing again to Nadia and Harrison, "may not have witnessed it," Turner's voice dropped with emotion, "but *you* know and *I* know you liked it. You. Loved. It. Asleep or awake you fucking came your brains out, and I made damn sure you left satisfied every time."

He paused. Struck by the force of this speech Jenny filled up with intense bitter longing, knowing that in some way this— the most honest moment they'd had so far, a moment that she completely agreed with in her heart of hearts—this was the moment she'd lost him.

He gave her a jaded look, "Unless for some twisted reason you were faking everything."

"No," she said, "No, don't say that."

Harrison pointed out Nadia's monitor and said, "Check the machine. The machine don't lie—"

Turner bent his stare upon her again. "Why are you so willing to give yourself all this slack but not give me any?"

"Because she was asleep," Nadia said. "She didn't know, she wasn't awake."

118

But I am now. Except she was also tired, the brunt of exhaustion slamming into her chest.

Nadia was looking at her, but her mind grew thick with the unhappy feelings all around her and she had nothing to say. She'd lost Nadia. The woman was walking into the hall, plainly disgusted.

"I'm out of here. You're giving him too much slack as it is." She fussed with her bag and walked out.

Harrison was quick to follow, "Hey, Nadia—" he said, following the scientist down the hall.

"Do you hate me?" Turner asked.

So many feelings and uncertainties jostled in her mind, she wished she could pick one and stick with it. Do you hate *me*? Jenny wished she could say.

He already seemed colder in the pause of her uncertainty.

"Nadia would say I should," she admitted.

"But do you?" He was so vulnerable, the sex was so good. Even if he was delivering an award winning performance, she couldn't dislike him. But could she trust him?

"No."

"If you didn't run away, could we just talk a minute?"

She sat on the bed. He sat down too. "I didn't like her."

"...Jennifer?"

He took her hand. "Jennifer. I like you."

But I'm Jenny. How much did one nit-pick at a time like this?

"But you had sex with *her*." At least he also thought *It* was apart from who she was.

"Okay, I was initially attracted to you, and then she – I mean, you, asleep – but not seeming asleep at all—though maybe a little stoned—you came and attacked me. And I'm sorry, but I'm a guy. I might have been surprised, but I wasn't going to say no."

She looked at him, feeling more tired, and more drawn to him. He was doing a good job of being a little tortured over it all.

"But you *know*, unlike Nadia," he said, "you *know* I've been trying to connect with you. In the daytime. When you were definitely awake. And I had no idea what the hell was going on."

"So. What do you want, Turner?"

"To get to know you. I mean, *you* you, not—"

"Me. Jenny. You like me. Not Jennifer."

His smile lit up her heart. "Not Jennifer. Jennifer scares me a little."

She gave a small smile. "Me too."

"So maybe the summer isn't a total loss."

There was something so flattering, so moving about the way he looked at her. Like he was very concerned. He'd won her over. Partly for overlooking what a blithering idiot she was, partly for their mind-blowing chemistry, and partly because he seemed like he was a good guy. She was falling for him, no doubt.

"Maybe Jennifer can bring us together?"

Harrison burst into the bedroom again, obviously having no luck with Nadia. He did however, have a bright pink hand imprint on his face. "So now that we know what's what, can I have my video recorder back?"

Jenny stood up from the bed.

"What?"

"Can I have my video recorder back?" Harrison enunciated each word.

She backed off like a trap had sprung. Turner sat on the bed looking utterly confounded. Harrison saw his face and was instantly on the alert.

"Unless you wanted to do another sex tape…"

Jenny swiftly followed him, and Turner was behind her. Something in his expression was making Harrison swiftly back into his room. She could feel Turner's malevolent will like heavy gunpowder igniting behind her.

"'Cause if you do decide to make another tape," Harrison said, his voice going up to the edge of a break, "feel free to keep the camcorder long as you like…" His door slammed shut, and she heard the lock sound.

She'd just escaped. She would have bought the farm, she would have done whatever he wanted, bought all his explanations. *Don't look at him*, she thought. *Run.*

She ran.

She dodged her way through the lounge seeing his body erupt from the dark hall. *His voice, don't listen to him, it's all charm, he sounds reasonable, he'll make up some excuse but you don't know him. Stranger, he's a stranger. Move! Go!* She ran to the glass door at her end of the bridge—which for some reason that night was propped open by a small rubber wedge. She got to the door, popped the wedge out with her bare foot, and pushed the slow spring on the door shut, flipping the lock just as Turner's body slammed against it.

The econ men came out of their rooms, drawn by the noise of his voice and the slamming of his fists on the shatterproof glass, the rattling frame of the door, his voice muffled on the other side as he shouted her name.

Shame put tears in the corner of her eyes as she walked by the same greasy looks that had been crawling over her skin for weeks.

"Who's the guy?" Rick asked. Bonifellow stood in the doorway of his room, looking devilishly tousled, his lower face blue black. He was in a loose navy blue T-shirt and sweats and nodded at Jenny, chin up, those wolfish white teeth slashing through his half-Italian, half-Indian face.

"S'up Jennifer." He stood back, opened the door of his room wider in a silent invitation. "What's the matter? Having a hard time getting to sleep?"

She felt a surge of saliva in her mouth and ran, ran, ran for her room, got into it, locked the door, and made it to the toilet just in time.

Chapter 6

She left the institute within hours. She spent much of that time on the phone with Nadia trying to come to terms with what was going on.

"How can this happen Nadia? Awake and asleep at the same time—what is that? How is that possible?"

"I don't know why, it just is," Nadia said. "We still don't even exactly know why we sleep or dream, we just know we'll go insane if we don't."

Nadia wanted to keep tabs on her—for research—but she said it was also because she considered herself Jenny's friend. A friend. But she thought science would do the trick, so Jenny visited the Stanford sleep center.

In the end, she'd fled not just from Turner and her econ peers, but even from her research and her career, quitting her job at the university by the end of the summer. In less than a month she'd moved across the country to San Francisco.

Meanwhile, one didn't just quit a tenure track job and get another college teaching position, not in as desirable a location as SF, so she accepted a position as a middle school math instructor at a private girl's school.

The real upside to the crisis was that she fell in love with her job. It was a school specifically devoted to shy girls and girls suffering from social anxiety disorder. She taught small classes of sixth, seventh, and eighth grade math. Teaching at the school was her sanctuary.

But the rest of her life was hell. It was as if Jennifer knew she'd been outed and decided to flaunt it. That fall Jenny never woke up at home wondering what happened the night before. Soon, on two or three mornings a week Jenny woke up in strange places, not knowing how she got there and not knowing who was next to her. Each encounter—sometimes there was more than one sexual partner there—and not just men—left her staggering home in the early hours feeling used, exhausted, and terrified. She felt like a whore.

She visited the sleep clinic at Stanford every two months. Now they were moving her up the ladder again. A new doctor was scribbling on her chart, checking his notes again and checking her most recent intake. In between all that he was looking her over, then scribbling some more. He had a salt and pepper beard, acne-scarred skin, a middle-aged barrel chest and a deep voice with an overdone posh accent. What she really didn't like was that he also was very much a man, hairy with a beard, and there was something heavy about him, a rumbling sensuality, a strong magnetism. Given her problems she would have preferred an asexual geeky science type. No such luck.

Finally he looked up. "How are we doing then?" he said.

"I've been having some new issues," she reported.

He went back over the file. "You've stopped taking the Clonazepam."

She was shaking her head. "That was months ago. It didn't do a thing." Except make her a zombie during the day. She'd been worried about losing her teaching job and was teetering on the brink.

"My colleague tried prescribing…ah, let's see here. Trazodone. That seemed to work for a time," he said.

"Um, it's hard to say," she said.

Because she couldn't say. At the time she reported it was working she would go a week or more without waking up some-place new. She was ready to whoop and holler for a while. But her gut said Jennifer wasn't done yet, she was just hiding.

Only it turned out that Jennifer had latched onto one guy, Brett. He was an international model.

So it turned out to be a coincidence that she'd started taking the drug and she'd had fewer symptoms. Brett was traveling for work and Jennifer was waiting for him to come back. One time his shoot was cancelled so he showed up at her place. She opened the door and discovered the drugs weren't working at all. Jenny felt a dip in her spirit remembering. It was all a little hopeless.

"But you stopped reporting as many episodes…for the past

two months. There's nothing new in the way of sex partners is there?" he said, checking the paperwork.

"No, you see...these are new symptoms."

"All right. Tell me what's happening now." His voice hit just the right compassionate note and she found the knots inside her relaxing.

"When I went on the other drug, I was also trying to find a way—a safe way—to restrain my ability to go out at night. I think that the drug wasn't effective, I just finally got a lock for my door that I can't get out of in my sleep."

"What about your symptoms now?"

She told him—part of it. "It's like I'm trying to read in my sleep."

"People can't read in their sleep."

There you go. Doctors loved to state what you could and couldn't do, even if you were doing it and you knew you were. She struggled to tamp down her frustration. "I know. I know you're not supposed to be able to. But I wake up knowing I'm struggling to read something."

"Are you? Are you holding a book in your hand?"

No. She woke up sitting at her desk, or holding her phone.

"I'm not reading pages and pages. It's not like a book. Sometimes I can make out only one a word, or a short phrase—not much. My eyes feel strained, and I feel like I've been concentrating for hours."

"You can actually remember this?"

"Yeah, I'll be aware that I'm asleep, but I finally can read one word—a small word. Then another. But there's a sense that I need string of them together."

Are you okay?

You sure?

I want to see you.

Those little bits she remembered...there were more, but they were lost by the time she was awake.

She couldn't tell the doctor Jennifer was plotting something. She couldn't say, I've locked myself up at night because I'm worried

I'm going to kill someone—or myself.

He switched focus again. "The Clonazepam—did you experience side effects?"

"Yes. And isn't it...addictive?"

"It can be, but if it didn't work before, no need to try it again." He scratched on his sheet. "You're not drinking alcohol, are you?"

"Never."

"How's it going with managing your stress levels?"

"I try. I changed teaching jobs. I like the school where I'm at now."

"Good." He looked at her over his reading glasses. "What grade?"

"Middle school."

"Good god!"

She could tell he was joking with her and started to like him a little bit.

"And that's not stressful?" he asked.

"Not too bad. I love my students and I just had the entire summer off."

"But now you're back in school?"

"We started back in August. I'm trying bubble baths before bed, scented candles. Meditating. Any relaxing device, you name it, I've got it."

"What about sex? Are you sexually active right now when you're awake?" he waited, not looking her in the eye, his pen ready to record what she said.

She swallowed.

"Jenny?" He lifted his head, kindly, but firm.

She couldn't talk about her sex life with him. She couldn't. He wore his sexuality right on the surface, like a lot of charismatic successful men did. The nightmare of waking up with one of her doctors hadn't happened yet. *Yet*.

Once she had a thought it seemed like Jennifer had access to the thought. She didn't actually know for sure if it worked that way. It was all a guessing game.

She wasn't attracted to the doctor but Jennifer would be, and she was at the point where she didn't want to think about things Jennifer might like. Jennifer was pissed off right now. Jennifer wanted to punish her.

But this doctor was far too hands on for her taste. He pressed her again for more details about her recent sexual history and asked about her preferences.

She didn't think she could possibly feel the deep scorching burns of her blushes ever again, but he proved her wrong.

"Well," he said finally. "Let's move on. Perhaps you could update the form for my resident Sandra."

Sandra she could handle. Sandra she could talk to. When Sandra had wanted to know about the sexual partners she'd had in the last year, Jenny said, "Let me write you a list. I've kept a diary." She'd copied out the list, a question mark next to at least five of the encounters.

She'd handed the list over to Sandra, whose eyes widened. By now, Jenny knew that *wow* look of shock when she saw it.

The doctor held up the same list.

"Let's assume for the moment that by day you're celibate." That horrible furious blush again. She couldn't even go there with him. The world she'd been in for the last year had been drowning her in all kinds of filthy sex. She couldn't even dip a little toe into the waters with him, not even to help herself.

"The human animal is fundamentally sexual in nature. We know that. Of course, society represses this. Homosexuals for example, can still struggle against the sense that they're fundamentally doing something wrong. Young women are still repressed. They often pay a heavy price for indulging in a strong libido."

She looked at him with suspicion. Where was he going with this?

"We were indeed able to establish an underlying conscious or subconscious sexual intent in several of our patients with sexsomnia."

126

"What are you saying?" she asked.

He gave the example of a young man who was sleeping in a bed between a man and a woman, when he turned and started trying to have sex with the man in his sleep.

"Apparently he was gay. He came from a conservative background and when he was awake, he quashed his sexual preferences. But when he went camping, got drunk, and went to sleep, it all came out unconsciously."

He rumbled around in his chest a little, giving her time to comment. She didn't.

"Maybe if you let yourself go a little when you're awake, these urges will be satisfied. The pressure, the psychic crank of repression, will be released a few notches."

Again, she couldn't respond. At least he didn't let the pause sit there killing them both. "The body wants sex. Most bodies do. Let yourself out of the box a little. At the very least you might try masturbating, and maybe your symptoms will stop.

Her face was going to go up in flame. She felt like even her eyeballs were blushing.

"In these more extreme cases we can't attribute the problem to sleep itself. Often it's a case of stress affecting sleep."

"Yes, I've been trying to reduce stress."

"A colleague of mine, a Doctor Anderson, theorizes that sleepwalkers will often do simple things that make some kind of sense. For instance, they'll eat if they've gone to bed hungry. The people we work with have complicated lives, but the basic issue here is that if you're depriving yourself of something very important like food, the body is in a state of stress. You see what I'm aiming at? What you're experiencing at night is a confused awake state because your body is seeking something it needs or wants that will relieve the stress. In sexsomniacs, the body is seeking sex."

She nodded in agreement. Inside she was shaking her head no. *No, no.* She could see what the doctor wanted her to do. *No way, no how.*

Masturbating made her think about Turner. She couldn't get off if she didn't summon his face up. Even if she did, then she would lie there in agony for hours unable to sleep from the humiliation of everything she went through. What if the video he made was on the internet somewhere? Most of all she thought of what he'd done to her when they were together. That caused all kinds of other reactions in her.

"One can only try," the doctor was saying. He crossed an ankle and placed it on his knee. "I may have shocked you, but the histories we have of young people like yourself indicates that it's necessary to work with your desires to find a healthy outlet for them, or your own subconscious starts working against you."

She sat twitching her foot, legs crossed, arms crossed, face red, not responding.

"Would you rather risk getting AIDS or Hep C because you're running around at night having unprotected sex with strangers?" He paused. She held her mouth open a little bit so the whoosh of air in and out could pass silently.

"Are you crying? Look, I'm sorry to sound so harsh. It's just this is really the only thing I can recommend as your doctor to help treat your condition. Drugs aren't working, and we'd like to see an alleviation of your symptoms soon. We need to try all the options. I'd hate for you to be harmed by a stranger because we couldn't help you soon enough." He reached forward towards her with a box of Kleenex.

Then, like almost all doctors who made their patients cry but were profoundly uncomfortable with tears, he got up and fussed around, while she made a big effort to control herself.

Dabbing at her eyes, she balled up the tissues and then desperately tried to lighten up. "Haha. It's so funny you should bring up my subconscious working against me." She was very careful. She jokingly brought up the possession angle, telling the story of her mother, the maid in Morocco, and the exorcist who spat some chewed up leaves in her face.

She didn't go one bit further than that, because he was looking at her in a new and funny way. His eyes looked through her almost, and with a poker face, his pen poised, he asked, "Do you think you're possessed?"

This wasn't going to help. This was only going to get her into more trouble instead. Soon they'd be mentioning terms like involuntary incarceration and schizoid beliefs.

She shook her head as if she was promising not to be bad again. "No."

He seemed visibly relieved.

Yes. I know I am possessed. I call her Jennifer.

"Sleep research is new science," he said. "We don't have all the answers yet," he tapped her knee with her thick file that he held closed in his hands, "but we will one day." He stood. "I assure you, there will be *scientific* explanations."

And she was dismissed with that last pat on the head.

Sandra came back to see her in the waiting room and she was taken off into an empty examination room.

"The doctor just wanted me to wrap up some of the details in his notes. So, your sleepwalking incidents almost stopped from February to June last year."

"Yes."

"That was the Brett phase. He was your boyfriend?"

"Not exactly. He was…accommodating about my condition." Now he was dead.

"And then…that relationship stopped?"

"He's deceased."

"I'm sorry." Sandra shuffled some papers to let that moment pass by. "And lately?" She asked.

Shaking her head, Jenny said, "Nothing, really. I was able to finally create this special lock. I can't get it open when I'm asleep."

"Oh, where did you get it?" Sandra asked, crossing her legs. Did Sandra ever think about having sex with the doctor?

Jenny thought about having sex with anyone and everyone.

When you didn't know who you might wake up next to, you tended to size people up in a whole new way. For instance, she'd prefer Sandra over the doctor. The bagel guy with the big Adam's apple over the barista with bad skin where she bought coffee.

"I made it. You have to solve little puzzles before it opens."

"Really?" Sandra perked up. "Little puzzles? Like what?"

"Simple memory games, or you had to learn something easy in order to press the right button that releases the magnetic door lock."

"That's just fascinating. Can I just—I'd like the doctor to hear this."

The doctor came in again and Jenny explained the device to them both. The computer gave you a memory challenge, or an easy little learning challenge. If you could solve the challenge, the door opened. It picked the challenges at random. You couldn't learn to press the same combo of buttons by rote.

"I see. And you created this device?" the doctor said, chuckling, "How clever."

She wished that creating the device allowed her to triumph. To shout *I won, Jennifer, I won*. But given how bad she felt—tired, sleep deprived, ready to shatter—she knew not to underestimate her enemy. Jennifer could make her pay for thinking she'd gotten the last word.

Don't think it, don't imagine it. Plenty of bad things could still happen. *Let's hope Jennifer has a strong survival instinct*.

They talked about the device some more and Jenny offered to email pictures to Sandra so they could share the idea with others in need. The doctor played golf with a patent attorney, and he volunteered to get the man's card and give it to her.

This seemed to get the doctor to take an interest in her again. He remembered that she'd recently been an academic.

As she left, she thought that he was indeed a good doctor. He did all the right things. He took his time with her, he read through the notes most carefully, and gave his best advice.

It was just that he didn't see how traumatized she was. She couldn't date. Well, only if you put a gun to her head. She shook her head. Just walking into a bar…Jennifer would spot the biggest, sexiest asshole in the room and then the next morning…Jenny shuddered.

At home she set the door lock. *What a clever young woman you are,* the doctor's voice echoed in her brain. Clever maybe, but she didn't feel young. Not anymore.

She called Nadia. She could tell Nadia the truth—because Nadia already thought she was crazy. Like bat shit bonkers.

"Let me have it then," Nadia said with a sigh. Nadia didn't believe in the possession thing, but Jenny had worn her down so that at least she wouldn't voice her skepticism and was willing to listen.

The problem was, she confessed to Nadia, she was starting to see some patterns.

"What patterns." Nadia didn't care, but this was their pact for Jenny being a part of her research.

She could never tell the doctor, but when Jennifer slept with someone multiple times… "I think I know what she's doing," Jenny said.

"What is she doing now," Nadia sighed.

"She's killing them."

She explained to Nadia about Brett.

First there was Johannes. Then Turner. But once in SF three times a week, or sometimes four, Jenny woke up in a strange place, next to a strange man. Or strange men. Or strange couple. Yet after a few months there was just the one guy–Brett.

"They all looked a little similar," Jenny told Nadia. "I think she has a type. I think it took her a while to find him when I moved."

The night Brett came to see her she'd told him while rolling her eyes that she was busy. Maybe she'd see him later. He'd accepted that with a nod, and the next morning she'd woken up next to him in his bed. He'd told her where she'd parked the car and then threw an arm across his face, but before he did she'd seen the same raw pink stains around his eyes, the beginning of long blue-purple shadows.

That was when something had clicked. She knew this would be a regular thing. She didn't bother trying to explain it to Brett because, as she explained to Nadia, he was shallow and didn't seem overly concerned with explanations. Like why she had to be told where she parked her car the night before, or why she had to ask him what neighborhood they were in.

"Wait," Nadia said. "You're driving? In your sleep?" Jenny could hear the mad scramble on the other end of the phone line and the tapping of the iPad.

Jenny explained that she'd gotten rid of her car, but then sometimes Jennifer drove someone else's car, so rather than get arrested for auto theft, she bought another one.

"So what happened with Brett?"

She told him he should stop seeing her.

He asked why.

"I'm bad for your health," she said. He ignored her advice. The last time she saw him, she told Nadia, she woke up in a hospital bed. It was the middle of the night. He told her to leave before nurses came through on their rounds.

"He was a sick, sick man," she told Nadia. He wasn't able to look her in the face.

A few hours later she got a call from his parents. It was a Sunday morning. He'd told them that he wanted to see her one last time. They clearly hated her, the mother's tone was dripping icicles, but they called because their son was dying and they would do anything he wanted.

She turned up with flowers. It wasn't even visiting hours, but he was so sick they let her in. They all stood around Bret's bed. She and Bret had nothing to say to each other. Bret fretted about his looks. She leaned over and ruffled her hand over his hair. She lied and said he looked like one of those soap actors in a hospital scene. You know, totally attractive, ready to seduce someone.

"Was that true?" Nadia asked.

"Not true at all. He looked hideous, like someone sucked the life out of him, and left nothing but scraps." Scraps of ego and rage. Perhaps because he was dying young.

"What happened?" Nadia asked.

"I read in the paper that he died in August." She hadn't been invited to the funeral.

But it had seriously motivated her. She didn't know why, she didn't know how, but she became convinced Jennifer had fucked Brett to death. And at that point she also decided it wasn't just about her. It was about protecting others. Innocent others. Brett might have been dumb like a box of rocks, but he hadn't deserved to die.

"But I'm thinking back on things and I have no idea what happened to Johannes, but I think Turner would have gotten sick too if we'd kept going."

She worked like crazy on perfecting the computer lock mechanism. Now she had a system. The computer lock on the front door kept the beast inside.

But for how long? And what happened if there was a break in? The lock did nothing to keep people outside. Others in SF worried about robbery – she worried about fire—more specifically Jennifer setting the apartment on fire to get out. *Don't think about it, don't think about it, don't picture it.* Jennifer had already caused some damage in her frustration...

Nadia asked about the doctor. What did he have to say? Jenny told her that he'd asked if she was enjoying SF.

"And?"

"I told him I was," she said. It was true. She loved the city. Also her classroom, and her students. They loved her back. In fact, the work she did with them was intense, bittersweet, and poignant. If she hadn't been so shy, she would have taken a friend with her to Thailand, wouldn't have been so lonely, and wouldn't be in this mess.

She saw so much of herself in her students. Some were even worse than her—shy to the point of selective mutism. They talked to their parents when alone and to no one else.

Finally she said she had to get off the phone. "Things could always be worse," Nadia reminded her.

"Oh yeah? How?"

"You're not bed wetting. You're not having seizures. You could have narcolepsy. They can't drive." Nadia said. "And there's no cure."

Was there a cure for possession? Perhaps should she fly to Morocco? The idea was starting to sound better every day.

Meanwhile, Jennifer was restless. There were some sexy photos that showed up on her phone last night. Jennifer had taken them of herself—in a bra and undies, thank god, but very provocative. This was new. The last few weeks when she woke up in the morning she could tell Jennifer was itching to get out – her fingernails were often broken down to the quick. There were gouge marks on window sills and on the computer lock—thank goodness the windows were all painted shut.

"She wants out," Jenny told Nadia. Dents started appearing in the floor, and there were complaints from neighbors about stereo noise at night. (She gave away her speaker system—and set the volume level of her iPod at a permanent safe setting. She didn't want Jennifer to blow out her eardrums in revenge.)

Jenny made sure not to live in an apartment above the second floor. Even if Jennifer broke the glass and jumped, she probably wouldn't die. *But you could be maimed. Don't think about being mangled for life, don't imagine it...*

"Look on the bright side," Nadia said. "It's been fun catching up, but I still think you're crazy," Nadia said. "Show me some evidence—"

"I told you about Brett."

"Some underfed model dying is not evidence. You hooked up with him—big deal."

"When Jennifer learns the violin, I'll give you a call," Jenny said and hung up.

She sat on the couch, picking at the furry cover. She hadn't told Nadia that Sandra had ended the interview at the clinic with a brief talk about the doctor's recommendation.

"Just try it," Sandra had said. "It's cheaper than drugs and there aren't any bad side effects," she added with a little laugh.

Except soreness, Jenny thought. Jennifer, locked up in the house with no one to fuck, was masturbating up a storm each night. Jenny was the one who got to walk around the next day with a tender clit.

***

The red rays of the sun struggled to burn through the fog, succeeding just before the light began to fail. The warmth of the day started to fall, like the leaves from the trees. She decided to just *be* the pathetic lonely spinster and changed into her jammies and got out a microwave dinner. It was from a health food store, but still. Cooking was not her forte. She spent a little fb time with her students as it grew dark. The school took their pound of flesh for the decent pay by expecting her to give a lot of extra TLC to the students during non-school hours over social media. It was massive time suckage but being the pathetic lonely spinster dork type, she didn't mind. She needed some extra TLC too.

When her meal was ready she'd eat it and all she had planned for the rest of the night was bed and some needed sleep. She lay there on the couch, lit only by her computer screen, waiting for the timer to go off.

She missed her cat, but worried Jennifer would harm him and had given him away before she'd moved. She was sick of watching TV. As for movies…she could die. Reading was okay, sure. But

135

she itched to read research papers again.

However, searching out current issues of her old favorite economics journals made her twitch. She saw the faces of those men on that strange, sweaty, compulsive night. The flashback always ended with Bonifellow like the last card in a shuffled deck. Blerg!

To distract herself, she remembered that orthodox Jewish couple she'd woken up with. How calm they were as they rushed her out of their bed and downstairs. The mother making breakfast, still in her nightgown, and the father getting out his keys to drive her home. He'd said he was sorry to rush her with an apologetic smile, but the children had Sunday school and they'd overslept. The mother was calling them downstairs even as the husband had ushered her out the door and towards his Mercedes.

Jenny shook her head, and began braiding her hair. She'd modeled her behavior after the Jewish couple from that point on. The hurry to leave, the smile, the matter of fact calm. You were in control of a situation simply by acting like you were. So far it had worked, and no one had locked her up, or killed her.

She took a deep relaxing breath. Could she masturbate and remember Brett? He had an excellent body. Now that dratted doctor's voice was buried in her head. What did her body want?

If she was honest her body wanted Turner.

Put aside Jennifer for now. What does your heart want?

With a grimace she realized her heart wanted Turner too. Not the has-sex-with-unconscious-women Turner, not the makes-video-tapes-of-you-and-doesn't-tell-you guy, but the guy she thought he really was when he sat down with her to 'be honest'. That guy. She wanted him. *Well, you can't have him*, she told herself. She wanted to hear his voice. It was a heavy silk glove laid over rough bark. Deep and soothing, but not too smooth. She had a sudden memory of how it felt to be skin to skin with Turner. To touch him exactly the way she wanted to, with…with confidence.

Okay… She stretched out across the couch and dug one hand down into her pjs.

The front room was painted a deep, dark graphite blue. The couch had a striped grey faux chinchilla blanket that covered most of it. It was the kind of room you could cuddle up and take a nap in. Like a womb. No sharp edges anywhere. Her fingers found her slightly tender clit and began a gentle exploration. Dry.

One time back in the summer before Brett died, before he started looking really bad, she'd woken up and wanted Turner badly. Distraught and unbearably lonely, she'd just wanted to be held by Turner one more time. Hating herself, she'd nudged Brett and asked if he would hold her. He had, without any snarky asides, for which she was grateful.

The momentary sympathy between them had turned into something intimate, and then something sexual. They'd ended up fucking and she'd held on to him during that mini-nova explosion inside her. He'd slid out of bed as soon as they were done and she'd showered a little longer than usual that morning, lingering. She'd heard Bret walking up and down the different levels of his home. He'd been talking to someone on his phone.

"I don't know," she'd heard him say. "Yeah, some pity fuck. Yeah, she's still here…" He'd wandered away again, and she'd been out the door in two minutes.

Her fingers stilled, then came out to rest on her chest. She wasn't in the mood at all now. She got up, began pacing the apartment.

Jennifer was caged…but for how much longer? She was raging. Who was she talking with? Sending pictures to? How? Was it someone she would try to bring into the apartment—someone in SF?

Jenny was used to waking up next to tattooed bikers with a sore neck, next to middle-aged metrosexuals with a sore ass. She found her way around the city by remembering that this was the neighborhood with the guy who had the two pit bulls and told her to 'stay sweet'. Something was going to happen, she could feel it. She just didn't know exactly what and she didn't know exactly when. Soon. Her finger traced the screwdriver marks that scarred the computer lock on the door.

Finally the microwave timer went off. The main door to the apartment buzzed down below. She shuffled into the micro-kitchen and got her plate, bringing it back into the living room and turning on one light.

Someone wanted the neighbors. Or more likely, since it was a Friday night, a delivery man was bringing the people below a more tasty and fattening version of the dinner she was apatheti-cally swishing around on her plate.

They knocked on her door. Happened all the time. She put her food on the floor and wandered over to the peephole, again wishing it wasn't so dark in the hallway. Sure they saved on electric bills, but—

"Jenny?"

She froze in place, though it felt like her guts splattered all over the floor.

The voice spoke again. "It's me, Turner."

Chapter 7

Words failed her. Talk about the devil. She swallowed once. Twice.

"How did you find me?" Her voice sounded guttural and harsh. Her whole body broke out into a sweat.

"You've been sending me photos."

Photos? On her phone. Oh shit.

"I think…I think I'm going to call the police."

"Don't do that. Please."

His voice. It enfolded her, all warm and aching.

She hated the silly naïve part of her that already wanted to forgive and forget the past, fling open the door and let him have whatever he wanted. As long as what he wanted was her.

But the hard lessons she'd learned over the last year made her a little tougher.

"You're stalking me." Her words were quiet, diffident, factual. It was an accusation. He was silent, yet she could feel the force of his presence behind the steel barrier. "I think I should call the police," she repeated.

"Please don't, Jenny." His voice was split open, a vulnerable throb resting in the center. She simply couldn't resist that voice. "I really don't mean to scare you. Honestly."

She hesitated, her hand hovering over the mini screen asking her for the answer to a simple puzzle before the door would open. She answered it.

The computer asked her if she wanted to open the door. Her finger hovered over 'yes'.

"How did you find me?" she asked. "What do you want?"

"I want to make sure you're okay."

Shit. Now it was her turn to be silent. She bit her fingertip.

"I've been worried about you." His voice dropped. "So here I am."

"What photo did I send you?" *Please don't let it be a photo of someone having sex with me. Please, please.*

"Of you. Her. Jennifer."

The magic words. She let him in. He had a backpack with him, and a waterproof winter jacket. He looked straight out of the frozen tundra, a little scruffy beard going on. It was only with great self-restraint that she stepped back to let him in instead of wrapping her entire body around his. She ushered his big, reassuring presence through her door, pinching the coat at the back, where he couldn't tell, since she couldn't hug him.

He took his jacket off but held it in his hand, as if he wasn't sure if she was going to let him stay awhile.

"Sit down."

She walked over to the sofa, and he came and sat down at the other end, facing her, eyebrows knit with worry.

"Where's your phone, let me show you," he said. He put his

backpack down in the center of the floor.

Obligingly she got her phone, handing it over to him. He passed the photo from his phone to hers. "Look, I'm deleting mine," he said.

She plunked down on the couch and studied the photo.

"It's a selfie," she said. Jennifer, in her best panties, was leaning topless out the window, giving him a half lidded stare. *You know you want some* was the best way to describe the look in her eye. Her hair was slicked down and over to the side. She wore heavy eye make-up smeared across her lids. It looked like something from the ever-popular "How to put on make-up drunk" YouTube video her students loved. More arresting still was the composition of the shot. She was out the window from her knees up, not holding onto anything. Jenny automatically twisted around and looked behind her. Turner followed her gaze. He was up off the couch.

"Is that the window?" he asked.

"It's painted shut," she said, even as he raised the window sash smoothly upward. Agitated, she went and leaned out with him. The second floor looked a long way down on the sloped street outside.

"That's how I found you," he said, nodding. She looked across at the lights from the local public library. Looking down in her hand she saw the familiar neighborhood landmark building in the background of the photo.

The sneering yet stoned look on Jennifer's face made her skin crawl.

"We don't have to get involved again," he said. "We don't have to do one single thing you don't want to. I just wanted to make sure you're all right. You could really hurt yourself if Jennifer is hanging out windows like this. I'm just worried about you is all."

Her heart was beating loudly, so loudly in her ears. She had one hand on the phone, and her voice was cut off, choking inside.

"If you need someone to talk to, I'm here."

She put her face up against his faded red thermal underwear top. She stayed there, while he was frozen, and let her forehead rest against his amazing pecs. A tingling sensation came up from the bottom of her ribs and spread to her nipples.

"Just talk," she said, snuggling up into his chest. "Keep talking."

"Nice place," he said, looking around. His fingers barely touched her shoulders, like she was going to shatter. "Kinda dark though."

"Thanks. It's a sublet." She talked like she wasn't standing there so desperate to be held by him.

"I came out here thinking I could stay with my college buddy and his wife, but I hadn't been in touch with them for a while. And I forgot it's Halloween. They've got twelve kids at their place running around screaming, so I was kind of uninvited to spend the night."

"Oh," she said, not caring, savoring the bliss of human body contact.

"You want to stay here." She said it factually.

"On the couch? Sure," he said. He didn't seem sure. His hands fluttered around behind her back.

"Swear there will be no touching, no pressure, no videos—" she demanded.

"That was not my idea," he said.

"No, nothing. Swear it."

His hands lifted up, uncertain. "Though we are touching, you know."

She probably seemed so crazy to him. "You know what I mean," she said, her face smooshed against his pecs. They were great pecs.

She hesitated. What about when she went to sleep? She looked up at him. No raw pink. No shadows. He looked well rested compared to the end of their time together. That frowny look was gone from his face. She had actually kind of gotten off on the frowny look, but still... He seemed to read her mind, or at least the dubious look in her eyes.

"Even if you're sleepwalking...or whatever. Nothing. Not with Jennifer—not with you. Promise. Hope to die. I swear."

She thought about it. She gave him a pass on sleeping with

141

her. Everyone else did it, she thought, and didn't seem to think sleeping with someone who couldn't talk very coherently was a big deal. Why not him? Videotaping her...that was a horse of a different color. Now he had come all this way because he was worried she was hanging out a window. It made her want to cry.

"I reserve the right to change my mind at any time." *And kick your ass out.* By a huge force of will, she pulled herself off him. "Coffee?"

"Coffee is good. Great. I can always sleep at the bus station if it gets down to it."

Ten minutes later he was pulling the cup away from him and frowning at it.

"This is horrible coffee."

"You're just a snob," she said.

"There's a reason I accepted a job in Seattle—well, near Seattle." But he took another polite sip.

He was sitting on the couch. He looked good sitting on the end of her couch. She realized how tired she was suddenly. With his arrival all complex thoughts were just beyond her reach.

"I can't stand this," he said and got up. She thought he meant he was leaving and leapt up as well. Instead he strode into the kitchen, him and his fine ass, and poured the coffee out into the sink.

"You got anything else to drink? Beer?"

Her body was cooking. Her stomach was making funny noises. He was ignoring them, he must be. She felt fevered. "No. I'm not supposed to drink at all."

"At all?" He asked.

"Well, it can exacerbate the sleepwalking."

"Oh. I see."

Chapter 8

"Are you worried?" he asked.

142

"About you being here?"

"About what's been going on." He motioned to his phone. "You don't have any copies of that photo on there, do you?"

"Of that picture? No!" He got out his phone. "Here." He tossed it to her. "Do what you like with whatever you find in there."

"Okay, okay, don't sound so outraged, Mr. Sex tape."

"I didn't save any pictures of you."

"Thank you."

"Is this thing…are you isolating yourself a lot?" He looked over at the computer lock.

She followed his gaze, wanting to laugh her head off. "I'm trying to stay safe. I'm trying to lock her in."

"But you need to get out and see people, don't you?"

The fog was building up outside. Living in SF was like living in London sometimes. She took comfort from the billowing clouds that settled on the streets outside. She felt hidden, anonymous.

"What are you *doing* here?" she said.

"You, ah, I mean, Jennifer asked me to come," he repeated.

"How bad was it?" she asked.

He pulled up the text messages and showed her.

"Wow." She studied the messages. *Are you cumming?* "You really think I would spell it that way?"

"Wishful thinking?" he said.

Then catching the look on her face he said "Okay, that was too much. Too soon."

She was shaking her head.

"Did you get my letter?" he asked her.

"What letter?" Her hands—she didn't know what to do with them. This was why people had cats. Though a cat would probably spring out of her hands because they were icy cold.

"I left a letter in your room. That night… well, that morning."

"No, I didn't get it," she said softly. "What was in it?"

The letter was to reassure her that he put the fear of God into Harrison to never breathe a word to anyone about the sex tape.

"I didn't think he would talk," she said. "I thought he— or you— would post this on the internet."

"God no," Turner swore. "Here," he said, digging into a small zipper pocket in his backpack, fishing out a DVD in a blue jewel case. "Here it is, and it's the only copy, I swear."

She knew this was wrong. So wrong. She took the DVD from him.

"Did you edit this on Harrison's computer?"

"No. On mine. It's not edited, it's just saved. And I erased it from my computer."

"There are ways, I've heard, you can recover what was on a camcorder, even if—"

"I didn't give him the camcorder back. I gave him money to buy a new one instead."

"So what did you do with the camcorder?"

"I busted it up. Threw the parts away. He wasn't there when we did anything. When Jennifer and I...he just let me borrow his camera and showed me how to use it. She – you – actually plucked it from his hands that night."

He stood up and walked around the room. Her eyes tracked his body and her stomach was setting up a different kind of yowl, no longer remotely hungry.

"He was just playing around with it, making a video for his friends from college."

"You don't have to plead his case."

"I'm not, I just want you to know what happened. Then— Jennifer walked in, and took it from him. She walked into my room and plunked it on the dresser, setting it up. You...she was pushing all the buttons trying to make it go. I didn't have to be a rocket scientist to figure out what she wanted."

"You didn't tell me, and you didn't give this up until now," she tapped the DVD case. "So why are you trying to act like the good guy here all of a sudden? What changed?"

"I was sitting there with you finally talking about what

happened...I wanted to take things very slowly. I guessed you'd be upset, given what you're like."

"I'd be upset?" She couldn't stop the tone in her voice from escalating. "Given what *I'm like*?" From zero to sixty the anger came flashing out of her.

"Yes. You're a good girl." It almost sounded like an insult.

She frowned. "I'm not Jennifer. And I'm not ashamed of it." Her guts were turning back flips, but she wasn't ashamed.

"I know that," he said. She couldn't look at him. She found herself twisting up the cuff of her pj bottoms and forced herself to stop it. He sat down again on the couch facing her, hands on his knees.

"But I didn't know where you were. And I'm not a stalker. Then I guess Jennifer found me and sent me—that. So I came here to check on you and see if you're holding your own. That relieves my mind. But you've got the DVD, you've seen everything is off my phone and nothing's popped up on the internet. So look, I don't have anywhere else to stay. I'll just go to sleep here on the couch and head out in the morning back to Seattle."

She almost decided to let her bad girl out for once.

"Will you," she began.

"Will I what?" The luminous heat was in his eyes in a flash.

Scared, she backed down.

"Nothing. Let me get you a pillow and a blanket."

"I'm sorry about this mix up," he said as she walked to her bedroom.

Deliberating, she turned back before she had a chance to make up her mind.

"I'm glad you're here. You believe me—that it's not all in my head."

"It's not all in your head. Well, it is your head, it's just there's someone else in there with you."

"Watch over me." She rocked back and forth on her feet holding a blanket. She looked up, down, anywhere but at him.

145

"What?"

"Will you watch over me? While I'm sleeping."

"I...thought you wanted me out here on the couch. You didn't trust me."

"How can I worry about not trusting you, when I know I can't trust myself?"

"What do you want me to do?"

"Don't let me out of the apartment." She couldn't help whispering. "Or let Jennifer set the place on fire." He was going to think she was just *looney*.

"I won't."

"Don't let me do anything I shouldn't."

"You can trust me."

She gave him a hug. He felt so good. Smelled good too. Probably used scented deodorant, but travel had worn that off. What was left behind was something not bitter or pungent to her nose. A smell that was human, and slightly tangy. She controlled herself from burying her face in his armpit and smelling more. "You smell good," she found herself saying. "Like chicken soup." She could tell he was smiling.

"Thank you."

She gave him a soft kiss on the cheek.

He was frozen in place, as if afraid to move.

Then his hands slid away from her body. She could tell he had his hopes up. Or, not that, but that his body was on the alert every bit as much as hers was. She went into the bedroom, and looked back. He was peering after her.

"You want me...out here?"

She nodded. "Leave the light on." Then she lay down in bed.

She put the pillow over her face and groaned. She'd told him he smelled like chicken soup.

"Jenny? Are you okay?" he called out from the other room.

"I'm fine," she called.

The next morning she woke up…and found herself tied up. This was not a new sensation. She turned her head. His face was right on the other side of her arm, asleep. Such a straight nose. He looked a little more determined asleep than he did awake. Not so much Grecian soldier, more Grecian general.

That whole how do you handle an awkward hook up? She was so over that. She gave him a poke with her knee and his eyes opened.

"Good morning," he said.

"Good morning." *Let them say what they want to say, echo it back at them, and then follow right up with ask them to untie you. People are expecting you at Sunday school, and you're already late.*

"Let me explain," he said, though he was blinking like someone trying to start their brain when it was stalling.

She tried to aim for a neutral tone, a matter of fact, yet friendly command.

"Where did these come from?" she asked calmly wiggling her fingers. They were cushioned restraining straps—and not bad. Natural leather on the outside, pink terrycloth on the inside. The pink was a nice reassuring touch.

"I brought them."

Don't think about what else he brought in the large duffle bag. She was naked except for her undies. She swallowed.

"Must have been fun going through the airport." The thing was, her calm confident act only lasted so long. Right now she was burning to the end of her limits. She was going to start screaming in *ten, nine, eight…*

"Oh, it was."

"So. Can you…untie me?" She didn't say please, it'd just reinforce her subordinate position—which for some folks signaled that she was ready for round two.

Seven, six… He sat up on the bed, still dressed in jeans and the waffle shirt, and rubbed his eyes.

The trick is that you're not really asking, she reminded herself. She didn't care really, just another walk in the park and now that was over, she had things to do.

He started to untie her left hand.

"So you had a busy night," he said. *Three, two...*

"Thanks," she sat up, pulling her wrist free. "I can get the rest myself."

"Oh. Okay." He got up from the bed. That hair. It was mashed into a standing position on the left side of his head. Like a cartoon character hit with a shovel.

"I'm getting the sense that this is not your first time at the rodeo," he said.

"True." She started untying her feet. Three straps, and her fingers weren't totally steady. "Sometimes they don't want to let me go, but saying I teach Sunday school usually does the trick. It gets them laughing as they remember the night before."

His smile was a total apology.

"What's up with the tattoo?" he pointed. She pulled her arm across her chest, trying to see what he was talking about. Across her left arm was a red heart with a skull in it, a dagger through the skull. It said Brett in cursive across the bottom. *Her first kill.*

"That's Jennifer's idea of a joke," she told him and went back to the straps.

"No...seriously?"

He ran his thumb across it. His fingers felt warm, sensuous, causing a prickle in her breasts that was noticeable. She moved suddenly away from him on the bed. She twisted over to work on the other foot. It was easier to talk if she wasn't looking at him. She used the same busy, practical tone as her fingers fumbled about.

"So you did Jennifer last night. Hope you had fun." *Hope you die.*

"No! I told you, you can trust me."

"Look it's okay." It was not okay. It was *so* not okay. "Can you get me a robe out of the closet? And you don't have to lie." Unless he was such a habitual liar he couldn't help it.

"I didn't," he insisted, throwing the robe on the bed. "And she was..." His eyes opened wider at the memory. "Not happy about it."

148

She believed him. It felt like she could take a full breath for the first time in forever. He was looking at her, frowning, trying by sheer force of will to get her to believe him and now that she was looking at him full on, he still had the faint pink imprint of a hand on the left side of his face.

"Come here," she said. He bent down to her. She stroked his cheek with her hand. He needed to shave. "Sorry."

His face close to hers, she thought about how that rough, prickly beard would take the skin right off a girl's chin... if they were making out like mad.

"Not your fault."

She pulled the robe up over herself and let him finish undoing her feet.

"Thank you."

He was rubbing her ankles. It felt good.

"My pleasure." His thumbs—those were talented thumbs. She refrained from rubbing her legs together.

She hopped off the bed and tied the robe tightly. Moving away, she headed to the kitchen. "So what did happen then?"

"Not much," he said, following her. "Jennifer got up, Jennifer got naked, and when I wouldn't go along with it, Jennifer got pissed. Then she wanted out, and started climbing out the window. We tussled."

She looked around the living room. The lamp was still on, but the shade was dented and the rest of the room was trashed.

"Sorry about the mess in the living room by the way," he said behind her shoulder. They started straightening things up together.

"And then we went another few rounds, while I managed to keep my dick out of her—you, I mean, and finally put her down for the night." He gestured with his arms to the bedroom. She saw the flash of some wicked nail marks through a tear in his shirt on his right arm.

"Oooh," she said, peering through the hole to look at them. The cuts were going to scar.

149

"Yeah, she doesn't fight fair."

"Poor guy." She had to let go of his arm, had to step away, walk away. She just wanted to rub herself all over him. *Did the mean nasty Jennifer hurt you? Come here, let me kiss it and make it better.*

"So who lets us out?" he said.

She showed him the system. There was a new puzzle card in the door. She showed him how to solve the puzzle so you got a three number code.

"Memorize it," she said.

"Easy." The code went away.

"It's supposed to be easy." A minute later the computer screen asked for the code. He plugged in the correct three numbers and they heard the magnetic lock released with an audible click. The door opened.

"And Jennifer doesn't know the code?" he asked.

She explained the code was always different.

Knowing Jennifer could read and type was alarming. But she was still safe. The puzzles required just a little more. Not much more, but a little learning and some memory stopped her partially sleeping brain in its tracks.

"Nice," he said. "But you should really nail the windows shut too. I'll do that for you today, if you've got a hammer and some nails."

Who was this guy?

"I'm taking you out to brunch right?" he asked.

"Sure. Let me get dressed."

When they left the apartment he took her hand. The smallest gesture, but it set off a wave of feeling up and down her entire body.

"What if there's an emergency and you need to leave the apartment quickly?"

"I thought about that. I could rig the computer system to the fire alarm so if the alarm went off the door would open automatically."

"Sounds like a good plan. Why haven't you done it yet?"

"Because I think Jennifer would set the place on fire to get out." He stopped, holding her hand tightly. Then they kept walking.

Her face was flushing. He got it, he really got it.

Over brunch she proposed they just spend the day together and not talk about Jennifer at all. He agreed without the slightest hesitation, and the day seemed to pass in a blink. She showed him her school, her classroom, the photos of the girls on a trip to Seal Beach.

"I never thought middle school could look so peaceful," he said, staring at the photos.

"They're happy," she said, stroking the pictures of the girls with big grins, skinny arms tight around each other's necks.

They brought a pizza back to the apartment. She wasn't hungry, but Turner was huge, so she needed to feed him something.

"I have to explain something," he said. He stood up and was pacing back and forth in front of the couch. "Sometimes a guy's brain...okay, it's a lot like what you said. About waking up next to someone and thinking 'I can't believe this guy got with Jennifer'. And he looks as surprised as you are. I mean, it's like when you stumble onto porn on the internet. Okay, suddenly you're looking at porn. You didn't set out to, but now that it's happening you're going with it. That's how it was with me and Jennifer. I didn't set out to, but it happened and I got lost in the woods."

She tried to say something but he put his arm out. "Wait, wait just a sec. So that video... The honest truth is, it's so hot, I couldn't let it go. Even though another part of my brain was kicking me, but—"

"Don't explain, it's fine," she said, wrapping her arms around her knees.

"No, I need to. It was just sex with Jennifer—but not with you. If you watched the video you'd know that what I had with Jennifer, and when I'm with you–you'd see that they're two completely different things."

"It's fine," she said. "I've seen Jennifer on video."

"You have?" he said, then remembered. "Oh, that sleep researcher."

151

"Nadia."

"Nadia, she had a camera too, didn't she?"

She nodded.

He thought she knew what she was doing. Reading these cases of sexsomnia she knew that even husbands and wives who knew their spouses were often fooled during episodes and assumed the other person was awake.

He listened to her, he believed her, he wasn't trying anything. He had the claw marks to prove it.

He narrowed his eyes. "I'd still like you to watch the video."

Her heart lumped up in her chest. "Why? Because you want to enlighten me, Turner, or because you want to seduce me?"

He looked over her hair, her face, and his hands slid up her arms. "Because I want to seduce you."

She brought over her desk chair and set up her computer on it. Then she slid the DVD in and sat back on the couch. With him. She felt like her joints would crackle with each move.

"Porn," she said. "Oh goodie." She wondered if it was appropriate to offer him popcorn, but she was so nervous she thought she would yak at the smell. He was wearing a long sleeved T shirt and darker jeans today. He looked good. She didn't look as good. She wasn't wearing make-up. She wasn't ready for this.

"I don't know, Turner."

"Don't think of it as porn. Think of it as, um, you. I mean, her."

"I don't want to see this."

"Only a few minutes. It's the only copy. I'm leaving it with you. You can rip it out of the computer and smash it to bits."

"That would be lovely."

She settled back closer to him. He was at the corner of the couch, facing her, an arm—Jesus he had long arms—stretched out along the back. She was about six inches away, arms crossed tightly, legs crossed tightly, vibrating as much with nerves as from her proximity to him.

The recording was suddenly there, and she on all fours turned away from the camera with her ass in the air. Jenny felt her attention stretch out like salt water taffy. There was her body, in the dim glare of his fluorescent desk lamp. The bluish glow fell over her face, but at the moment she was just flexing her back, her face turned away to look at whatever he was doing.

Jenny was observing her body, observing how it felt to watch her body naked in a video, observing what it felt like to have a guy watching you watch yourself naked in a video.

Her ass was biggest because it was close to the camera but it was like a firm peach, round and not too big and not too small. She gave her ass an A+.

She peeked out of the corner of her eye. Turner was not watching her ass, Turner was watching her. But then on screen Turner walked back into the frame and she was observing him as well, kind of peeking at his naked body between her fingers. She'd been behind him when they'd...now she could see he was... wow. Now *that* was an erection. An unfocussed excitement began worming its way through her body.

Part of it was that she was crawling with self-consciousness that the real Turner was there, not even six inches away from her. He wasn't watching the video. He was completely focused on her. The distracting heat of his eyes taking in her slightest reaction was creating a painfully sensitive feeling down there. It was all she could do not to visibly squirm. Her mind was kind of squished, and all analytic thought went out the window.

On camera her ass was still the focus, slowing waving back and forth as he came forward.

"Ready for this?" he said. Jennifer nodded and tossed her slutty pony tail. His back to the camera, the large hand came out and left a hot pink imprint. *Slap*.

"Kind of like your face this morning," she said.

Then she ruined it, as a wave of hot blood forced through her cheeks and beat against her skin.

"More, Jennifer?" Turner on camera asked. She waggled her

head up and down.

"I look slightly drunk."

He shot her a look. "True. But...*Jennifer* seemed to clearly know what she wanted."

On screen he was thinking about it. She saw harsh angle of his jaw and tilt of his head.

"What were you thinking?"

"I was thinking, I wouldn't have picked this as my thing, but if she wants it, I'm going to give it to her," he said, turning to look at the computer for the first time.

That caused a complicated reaction in her chest. Her blood was rushing through her veins and the odd tickling sensation in her pelvis was growing. It was like her cunt was shouting at her. She crossed arms over her chest, squeezing hard.

Now Turner on screen was focusing most of his attention on her tender thighs, while her ass was pink all over. She imagined how her body would feel bent over her own bed and how it would feel with her backside naked like that. To give him that power over her. The tingling became stronger and stronger. Meanwhile, on-screen Turner, who was not nearly as friendly as he was with her now, was giving it hard to those thighs, his face stern.

"This is turning you on," he realized.

"Fuck off, Turner."

"It is."

On-screen Turner spread Jennifer's legs and did something with his fingers between those legs that made Jennifer's head snap back with a jerk.

She forced herself to look away. Unfortunately she met Turner's eyes and could read his mind: *Spanking excites her. Noted.*

She stood up abruptly. "I'm not going to watch this." She was pacing, hoping it was hiding the twitching going on all over her body as her fingers were already imagining him standing up, already imagining the feel of his skin beneath his shirt, the heat. A new kind of hunger, raw and naked, grew inside her. This wanting him so badly sucked.

He stood up. She backed away.

"There's nothing wrong with getting turned on. We made the video, we're watching it."

"It's porn," she said instead.

He looked at it. She could see him decide he wasn't going to go there.

"What if what turns Jennifer on turns you on?"

She could hear the spanking on the screen resuming even if she couldn't see the screen. Jennifer's pleasured grunts squealed out into the air between them. He turned back to her.

"I promise you, only three minutes more."

The tight hot clench in her sex throbbed out its own measured beat between her legs, a reminder that she was missing the spanking.

"I'll fast forward to the part I mean," he said and fiddled with video.

"Okay, that. Watch that." He sat back and she perched tentatively on the edge of the couch next to him, ankles crossed, fists clenched in her lap.

"What am I watching?"

"Just look."

They were having sex from behind. They'd turned or they'd repositioned the camera so Jenny was facing it this time and Turner was kneeling behind her. Both their faces were clearly visible. As he was finishing, he grabbed her hips and was going at it hard, face determined, jaw thrust out. Then it was over. He was caressing her slowly. Up her sweaty thighs, across her back. Lovingly. A shadow passed across Jennifer's face as she ducked away from his touch. He was bent over her, behind her, and yet he noticed she didn't like it. He paused and leaned over her.

"Are you okay?"

She flicked her head in the other direction and began thrusting again.

"Hey Jennifer, what is it?" He tried to withdraw, but she pulled him back with one hand. He was confused. She picked up her thrusts.

He tried caressing her cheek, and she twisted her face away again. His expression changed to uncertainty. She thrust harder. He steadied himself with one hand against her hip. "I wish you'd talk to me." He put a hand out on her neck, stroking her throat, then her shoulder blade. Again she twisted her back like a horse trying to swish off a fly. This time he clearly go the message and stopped.

His face had a *what's your problem* kind of look, but his eyes closed briefly, and then he was obviously hard again. They carried on. There was something there, the expression on her face, that so deliberately turned to the camera.

"I don't usually look like that do I?" She asked.

His gaze flicked towards her. "Evil? No. You don't usually look like that."

His expression grew intent. "That's Jennifer. That's her face. That's why I wanted to show you this."

A flood of relief coursed through her like adrenaline, radiating out of her arms.

"I mean, it *is* like porn," he said his voice tight. Clearly Jennifer had gotten to him too. "She wants minimal contact," Jennifer at this point started bucking her hips, her head going up and down. "It's not about intimacy. It's pure, unadulterated fucking. If I wasn't fucking her, then I was kind of disgusting. It didn't make me feel particularly good about myself. Hey," he nudged her. "I'm not boring you, am I?"

"No."

He leaned over and began to fast forward the rest of it.

"What—what are we missing?"

"The part of the night where I try to hold a conversation with Jennifer. Not scintillating stuff."

The video showed him trying to get her dressed. He even tied the pink tie on her black and white cow print pj bottoms. The jerk he gave on the tie, the pissed off look he gave down into her face, it sent a stab straight to Jenny's cunt. So. Hot.

She flicked a look back up at his face. On screen was a reminder of the shadows beneath his eyes. The ever slightly raw looking skin looked more light brown on screen than pinkish. There was nothing like that across his eyes now. Just a mere pencil tip of light grey.

It was over. He cleared his throat. An arm came out and pulled her over to him. She let herself be reeled in resting against his side.

"So what do you like to do?" She asked, her finger picking at his navy shirt and feeling the muscles underneath.

"I'm game for pretty much anything as long as there's a connection," he says.

"Typical guy answer."

"I'm a typical guy," he said. His voice dropped about two notches, his lips coming right up against her forehead. "Why? What do you like?"

His words were a shot right to her core. She felt cold, she felt wiggly and liquid. It took total concentration to formulate words. She was surprised by how horribly hot watching the video made her. Her eyes were riveted to her fingers, her fingers had nothing to do except pinch the fabric of his long sleeved tee.

"Ow." He said, and caught her hand in his larger one.

"Watching that made you hot."

"Yes," she said in a suffocated voice.

"Have you ever done that before? Spanking?"

"Not that I'm aware of. How'd you feel the next day?" she asked, curious, and yes, stalling. "After...all that?"

"I don't know. I've actually never had a girl just fuck me and want absolutely nothing else. I mean, not that there aren't girls... it's just I didn't know how to handle it. So I tried to get you to talk to me during the day. To form, I don't know what—a friendship?—with me. But you kept ducking me."

157

He was looking at her again. She couldn't handle the intensity in those eyes and bent her head down.

"And you were really cold," he added.

"I am. I guess I was very insecure around you."

"Games you play because you're insecure are still games."

She completely disagreed.

"I was getting nowhere with you, but she," he said pointing at the screen, "kept coming by at night."

She turned and draped herself across his chest. He pulled his other leg up onto the couch and adjusted her so she was lying fully on top of him. She put her head slowly down on his chest.

"I'll admit," he said. "I liked that world for a bit. I felt powerful, until it seemed really lonely. I…I haven't been with anyone since then."

He was playing this whole indifferent to sex guy. She wasn't buying it. She could feel the rather wide and obvious bulge under the jeans. She rocked her pelvis against it.

"How'd you avoid being with someone? A cute guy like you," she mocked.

Looking away, he rolled his eyes. "It wasn't easy."

"And?" She rocked again. The bulge seemed to like this. It was bigger and harder. "I lied. I said I had a girlfriend. I meant *you*, in case you didn't get that," he said, lifting his head up.

She rocked again and his head dropped. She felt all woozy about that and her throat closed up.

"It wasn't true, but I wanted it to be."

She sat back up, straddling him. "Here are the ground rules. You use protection, no drugs, no permanent marks, don't scare me, and please go slow."

He began to kiss her, caressing her breasts, unzipping the oh-so-*not*-sexy oversized hoodie she was wearing and tossing it aside. The way he caressed her nipples brought feelings right down between her legs. She squeezed her thighs together, feeling his hand there.

"Can I tie you up?" he asked quietly.

"Yeah. I'd like that," she responded.

He was kissing down her neck, her bra straps going down, her breasts pushing up until the nipples were out and he was caressing them, making them tighter, harder, then sucking them, licking them. She found herself straddling him on the couch, naked on top, jeans unbuttoned, his hands sliding around her hips and over her ass, squeezing it.

He drew her into the bedroom where, conveniently, the restraints hadn't been removed from the night before.

"Do you want to be on your back or on your stomach?"

Even those few paces made her tense up with self-consciousness. She looked up at the ceiling and said, "Both, please."

His eyes were hazed with a film of lust. In the bedroom he shucked her out of her open jeans and he tied her up. Once she was in the restraints she thought she'd relax, but this was a different kind of nervous, a different kind of pent up shame feeling that flooded her entire body.

She was in his hands.

He kissed her for a long time, until his roving hands had sensitized every part of her frame and she was aware of a warm overriding feeling of pleasure as he sucked her breasts. Then his lips moved down to her hips, where his fingers soon followed. As he pushed her thighs apart, pulling up her bound feet, he placed his head firmly between her legs. Her thighs tightened involuntarily as his tongue delved into her core and swiped along the ridge that led to her still delicately sore clit. He worked it gently, sucking her, and her clit sang with pleasure.

She pulled against the ties, arching hard as his hands grabbed her ass and held her up. He began seriously eating her pussy, the feeling of his harsh beard gently scraping against her tender skin making her undulate and bite back a groan.

Her face turned into the soft skin inside her forearm as she began whimpering when he started sucking her clit harder, licking little horse shoe shapes around the top. His beard stimulated the tender folds, his chin rode up and down as he was fucking her pussy with his tongue, sucking her clit. She was thrusting herself up to him, and he made her wait, staring at her, while he used his fingers on her until suddenly he rose up and was covering her.

He entered her hard and fast. She was so wet, she used her muscles to pull him in, but he jerked out and back in again, hard, over and over. He was in control. That look was on his face, stern. No mercy for her, he gave it to her hard until with almost a painful crest she felt her orgasm coming, sweeping over her, and his mouth covered hers. Every muscle in his arms stood out as he held firm, letting her buck against him as she shattered and fell, shook and thrust her hips up, greedy for every bit of him.

It was over and she realized that they had forgotten about condoms entirely. Then all her feelings of worry and agony were wiped clean from her mind as she felt every molecule fill with happiness. She let that feeling permeate her, interlacing her fingers with his. She was on the pill, and they could have the talk in a moment. He began unstrapping her and rolled her over onto her other side.

He remembered the condom, got up from the bed and after a moment of rustling in the living room came back with one on.

"I—" she hesitated. "You know last time was the first time I'd done that."

"Good," he said.

There didn't seem to be the need to say anything after that, did there? He did it right then and he did it right again this time too. No pain, and he went slow enough to make her feel squirmy about herself and her reactions to the sex they were having. Who was this person she'd turned into? The one chanting *fuck me, fuck me. Harder.* Then it was bliss, bliss, bliss. How many times did she come? *Let me count the ways.* He was lying on her and his weight felt enormously reassuring, like he was pressing her back into her body, owning it, ruling it from the inside once again. He started to shift.

"Don't move. Don't take this away from me," she muttered and he stayed there on top of her while she drank in the feel of him all over her skin.

Later when they got up from the bed she saw new shadows under his eyes. What if she was killing him? Only the expression on his face was entirely different from before. It hurt to look at him, so she went into the shower.

God, she was cold.

It was sex with Jennifer that killed them. He was just tired because he hadn't gotten any sleep last night.

But what did she know for sure?

He slipped into the shower with her and she wrapped her arms around the tanned skin of his neck while he held her.

"I want to be with someone like you," he said. The look was still there. He was happy. She'd made someone happy. Her hands were covering his sternum, and he was holding her close, arms across the wet hair streaming down her back.

"What would it take for you be with just me?" he said low and quietly in her ear.

"I don't know. You've got heartbreaker written all over you." she replied, with a slow smile, a little shy, a little afraid.

"I don't want to break your heart. Just take a little piece of it. Just a tiny little piece." He began using the soap, rubbing it between his hands and then caressing her shoulders, her sides. "You could come visit me in Seattle next weekend."

She nodded, happy through and through.

Chapter 9

On Monday morning she had to go off to school while he went to the hardware store to buy nails. He had to go back to Seattle Monday night so he could teach his Tuesday morning class. They got to do all the pleasantly clingy couple stuff at the airport, and

161

she sent him off, telling him to say hello to the varmints.

He texted her Tuesday morning.

How'd you sleep?

She smiled at the text, typing back.

Well. All's quiet. Then she turned back to her busy day. She was behind on class prep and stayed late so she'd be enough ahead that she could fly out to Seattle on Friday evening and stay without needing to do any work except grading. Her mind wandered into a pleasant fog for most of the afternoon.

By the time she returned home from work it was dusk. She hurried a little up the front steps, her bag in one hand, a small pizza box in the other, knowing what the villagers much have felt like way back when. That sense of impending doom grew upon her as it got darker and she yawned with fatigue from the weekend and the long day.

Her phone rang as she got in the door.

"I couldn't wait any longer," he said.

She smiled into the phone.

"It's good to hear your voice," she said.

They chatted for a while, and she said her appetite was coming back, she even got pizza for herself. He talked while she chewed a slice. She happened to look at the mini-computer screen on the magnetic door lock. It was smashed, a crack running across it, like a witch's pointing finger. She went over and tried it. It still worked.

She listened to him in strained silence a little longer, but her appetite was gone and she shoved the pizza box in the fridge. Then, plucking up her nerve she said, "Turner, I'm nervous." She told him about the cracked computer screen.

"Just three nights before you're here. Hang on and then I can watch over you. At least for a few days."

"I'm looking forward to it. I don't want to be all needy and freak you out, but..."

"No, you're not. Jesus. I don't know how you get to sleep with this kind of thing hanging over you."

"I thought about checking myself into a mental asylum."

"Frankly, I don't think that would stop her. Anyway, I'm here. It's so much better when you let me know what's going on."

"But I'm going to run out of minutes on my phone."

In the end they Skyped on the computer. She set up her laptop on her bed and let him watch her fall asleep. They did the same thing each night and, holding her breath, she got on the plane Friday night. She was walking through JELL-O, the deep exhaustion settling all around her as she walked slowly through the airport, but he was there at the gate to meet her with a bouquet of Black-eyed Susan's and Queen Anne's Lace. She ran into his arms.

"You made it," he said.

"It can't be this easy," she said.

He had a giant reddish-black mutt in the back of his car.

"That's Rusty," he said. She didn't mind Rusty hanging over her shoulder, his gentle drool spooling onto her thigh every now and then while they drove out to Bellingham. She petted Rusty, who was half Newfie half mutt. With each mile the trouble she felt brewing and building at home backed off. By the time they were rolling into the bay, she could even look around her, eager to see things in daylight the next day.

They didn't even try to have sex after she tripped into his shabby log A frame house. She dropped her things in the living room decorated with cast off dorm furniture, and went into his dark bedroom. Stripping off her clothes she threw one of his t-shirts on, jumping into the middle of his big bed.

"Come here," she called to him. "I want to collapse in your arms."

He stripped down to his boxers, launched himself towards the bed, and soon enough they were snuggled together under the somewhat clammy covers.

"These sheets could be washed," she said, her voice muffled a little against his naked chest. Long waves of relaxation began to overtake her. She felt her body draining stress and found her eyelids wouldn't open.

"Beggars can't be choosers," he said, shoving aside some of her long blonde hair and kissing the side of her neck.

He talked about his week and classes, the chatter so comforting that Jenny felt as if Jennifer and all her problems were far, far away. All her woe drained away, and sleep stole upon her.

"You hid the car keys?" she mumbled.

"I did. Don't worry, we're on a ground floor, and I'm a light sleeper."

"I'm such a bother," she said, feeling a stab of shame through the waves of sleep overwhelming her.

"You're not a bother," he said kissing her head. "I love you."

And then she was out.

When she woke it was still dark. Turner was not in the bed. She got up and padded out into the rather cold open living room and kitchen space. He was kneeling at the woodstove in a flannel shirt and jeans, barefoot, stuffing the stove full of wood. Then he got up and went back to cooking.

"Hey," she croaked rubbing her eyes, and went up to hug him from behind. He felt good, but he kept cooking, and her radar went off. Something was wrong.

"What time is it?" she looked around for a clock. It was over the sink and said four thirty.

"Couldn't sleep?" she asked. Trepidation was eating away her mental fogginess. Something was clearly wrong. She looked around for Rusty. He was there lying on the floor near the sliding glass door like a tame black bear, his pink tongue leaving a small pond on the slate floor. She went and knelt next to him and then melted down against him to hug his mane and bury both her hands in his fur. Then, despite the cold slate flooring, she turned to lean up against him like he was the back of a couch.

"How'd you sleep?" she asked, thumping the dog's side with her hand. She wanted to be timid, but was trying to be brave.

He glanced at her and there was a look in his eye. A look that said *don't ask.*

"What happened? What's wrong?"

He finished putting the eggs on two plates at the counter. They steamed on the plates full of red peppers and other yummy bits. She shuffled over and slid onto one of the barstools.

"That bad?" she said, not able to look him in the eye.

"After breakfast," he said.

Smashed mirror? Obscene message written on the wall? Maybe Jennifer erased everything on his laptop. Jenny felt her shoulders creeping up to her neck.

"Was it Jennifer?" she asked. Of course it was. He chewed his food, concentrating, and she joined him. Her eyes filled up with tears, every bite tasteless.

How was he going to be able to sleep with her at night if he had to be on the alert every moment to make sure she didn't harm his things, or him, or Rusty? She suddenly realized the impossibility of carrying on this way. She'd have to be tied up every night. And who would want to give up their normal life to live like that?

He finished his eggs and shoved his plate away. She put her hand out on his big wrist.

"I love you," she said, wanting to melt towards him. He had such a grim look on his face, it was hard to choke out the words. "You can tell me whatever it is. It's okay."

"It's not okay, and I videotaped it...on my phone."

"You *what*?" Her accusatory tone shot out at him like an arrow.

"Not to share it! Jesus, I wanted you to *see* it. I didn't think you'd believe it if I just told you."

He brought her the phone and she stood back against his chest, leaning into him as they watched it together.

The screen wobbled and went to Jennifer's torso, then steadied on her face. She was tied up.

"Tell me what you want Jennifer."

The lizard eyes looked at him while the body shifted below,

restless. He began stroking her face, her jaw line, and then a little lower. "Come on, I know you can talk," he said, his voice enticing and flirtatious.

Her eyes didn't track well, and her face screwed up three or four times as various expressions morphed and faded before finally a twisted come hither expression settled on her features. "Play with meeee," she mumbled.

"Yeah? How?"

"Put your hands around my neck," she told him. The screen shifted. He was now straddling her body, torso naked, but Jenny noticed he was in his jeans. She looked over to the bedroom, seeing the cuff open on the floor. He must have uncuffed her later.

From within the shelter of Turner's arms, she watched the video screen as one hand came up and around her neck. "Like that? And then?" She rolled her head around as if it felt good.

"Squeeze," she said, her body writhing "Oh—like that—and fuck me."

"You want me to fuck you?"

"Yeah." His pelvis made a back and forth movement and that set her body writhing.

"Then what?" he asked. He was moving his pelvis more, humping her through his jeans.

"Harder, harder," she pouted, commanding.

The movement of his pelvis stopped. His hand came away.

"But if I do it harder, I might hurt you," he said.

She was nodding. Then she blinked hard and started shaking her head. "Noooo. Won't kill meeee." The implication was clear. It would kill Jenny, not Jennifer.

He got off her body entirely and leaned down getting a clearer shot of her face, but his own outline shadowed the glaring lights.

She pouted and her fingers curled closed like she wanted to grasp him, but she was all tied up.

"Is that what you want?" he asked. She smiled, stretched, gave him a sideways glance, but didn't answer.

166

"You're hot," she said finally.

"Jennifer, do you want me to kill Jenny?"

"Mmm-hmm."

"What did she say?" Jenny asked, looking up at him and putting her hair over one shoulder.

"Yes."

She looked at the screen again, riveted. Her arms wrapped around his as he braced himself with one hand on the counter and the other held the phone low so they could both see it.

"Then we can't have sex anymore. You'd miss that."

"No I won't. I'll go inside someone else."

"How would you do that Jennifer?" She didn't answer. "How?"

"You'd help me." By this point, Jenny could tell the conversation was getting to him. The picture was bobbing up and down more as if it was harder for him to hold it still.

The lizard eyes came back though her voice still had that whiney little girl quality. "Anyway, you'll do it, or you'll be gone too." Jenny felt herself turn icy cold with horror hearing those words come out of her own mouth. She leaned forward.

"What do you mean I'll be gone?"

"You just will." The evil face smiled sloppily. "Jenny knows..." The evil face was smiling. "Hee hee."

"Why?"

She could hear the tension in his voice. He wanted to fight the thing but he couldn't, and she could see his other hand clenching and opening, clenching and opening.

"Why would I kill Jenny for you?"

The cold horror filled her, made her want to struggle and thrash and kick to get away from him. Jennifer on screen was starting to struggle as well, and her limbs strained, tendons popping as she struggled with the bindings.

"There's a price to pay," the voice coming from inside Jenny said. It was deepening, getting harsh. He stopped the video.

"This is where she went all exorcist on me," he warned Jenny.

They were standing apart now. He started it up again.

" W h a t   p r i c e ? "

"A blood price. For this." The demon wiggled her hips at him, smiling.

"She means for sex," Jenny said, looking at Turner for confirmation. He nodded.

"I'm not going to kill Jenny," Turner said. The finality of his decision was like the closing of a heavy lid on a truck that would be forever locked.

Jenny's eyebrows went up and on screen she watched her body go berserk. The thing went total demon, the bellowing voice no longer sounding female, or human. The limbs popped against the restraints in grotesque ways.

"Stay with her and die," the voice, octaves deep and harsh, said.

Then the demon's smile came out again. "You won't be the first," it said.

She stood there wiping her eyes. He looked pissed off.

"It's true," she cried. "I should have told you. She killed that other guy. She killed Brett." She found her arms were around his neck. He was holding her off the ground in a fierce hug.

"Oh my god," she said sobbing into his flannel shoulder, "I didn't know. Not for sure. You were getting tired…it was starting with you too. You should leave me."

"Nobody's leaving anybody," he said.

He was stroking her, calming her, setting her on the ground but not letting go. She hiccupped and turned her head to lean it against his right shoulder this time, feeling her hot eyes and the freezing tracks of her tears as they dripped down her face. Her feet were so cold they were numb, but she didn't care. She was not leaving the warm circle of his arms. Not until he pried her out of them. But even as she squeezed her eyes tight with the thought, she felt the knife go deeper into her soul. She would have to leave him. She didn't want him to die, did she?

"What's that?" he asked. He was looking at something, but with

168

her head down, she couldn't see what it was. His thumb stroked over the back of her neck.

"What?" she asked.

"Oh, nothing," he said. "I didn't realize you had gotten a tattoo. It's cool."

"Where?" She looked, craning her neck around trying to see the skin under the stretched out neck of his green t-shirt.

"Right there," He put his finger smack dab on the back of her neck.

"I don't have a tattoo," she said.

"Course you do. Like a Chinese coin."

Like hundreds of butterflies beating their wings all at once against her skin, she felt her body tingle all over then go numb suddenly. "I need a mirror," she said.

Chapter 10

In the end she needed two mirrors to see the back of her neck, which he didn't have, so he took a picture of it on his phone and showed it to her.

"You don't remember getting it?" he asked.

She gave him a look.

"Okay, well, we know how that happened then." He paced. "But wasn't there a bandage or something? You'd notice that, wouldn't you?"

She shook her head. "No. Sometimes I came home and my neck was sore but—" She hesitated. "There was never a bandage."

"But what?"

"But we know how that can happen. With Jennifer, I mean." She didn't say any more. She watched as he looked at her intently and then the mental picture formed before his eyes. His face became suddenly grim, and she knew if Jennifer were here in another body, he'd be throttling her. A violent speculation, but one that made her feel all warm and fuzzy inside—and a little bloodthirsty. A little horny on top of it all, too.

She looked down at the back of her neck on the phone.

"Look, there's this notch in it, through here," her finger traced it. "Straight up at twelve o'clock. And see there's this kind of maze etched inside the rest of it."

"We need to see it better. Let's blow it up on my computer."

He hauled out some glasses and sat in front of the screen.

"You wear glasses," she said.

"Yup. Okay, well, it looks old."

"I don't think you look old at all." She ruffled his hair and sat on his knee.

"The *coin*. I think it's old."

"I've seen this before." She bit her lips. Thailand. Shit.

"If it's an image of a real coin, then chances are someone who knows coins might know what it is. You want to tell me how you found it?"

"I didn't find it, someone was wearing it."

His pencil was tapping on the table. "If you're possessed—and we think of possession as similar to a kind of infection, then when were you infected? Who infected you? By what means did it occur?"

"Johannes. He was the one wearing the coin." She gave him a brief sketch about her encounter in Thailand.

"I really don't want to hear about your adventures with other men, okay?"

She looked at eyebrows raised.

"Sorry, I'm jealous as hell, is all."

So sensitive.

Then just like that all the tension went out of his shoulders.

"Okay, sorry. Tell me."

Turner lived in the moment, she realized. When he was bothered, he said so. She played with his hair. Then the clouds blew away and his usual can-do attitude took over.

"We were travelling around Bangkok together, and Johannes wore this coin around his neck on a string. Like a necklace."

"It looked like this."

"Exactly."

He drew her back to his chest and pushing her hair aside, kissed her throat.

"Don't."

"I'm kissing your neck, not the tattoo."

"Whatever."

"So he was wearing this symbol. He wore it when he had sex with you."

She remembered the pinkish exhaustion bruising around his eyes. She scanned Turner's face. The skin around his eyes was clear, completely unsmudged by fatigue. "Then he tried to give it to you. Did you wear it?"

"Just until he left. Not even an hour."

"Did—do you think you had sex with him in your sleep? Do you think Jennifer got into you somehow when you had sex?"

She shook her head. "I don't know. I didn't sleep well after that, but I thought it was jetlag." She played with his hair some more. He needed a haircut, but seeing him with groomed hair at this point was going to seem rather strange.

"But if just having sex with someone wearing the symbol—" a symbol now permanently tattooed on her neck, "is enough to infect someone…" She looked at Turner, her heart squeezed tight with concern.

"Think the tattoo might be part of it?"

"It's definitely a part of it," she said. Poor Brett. She didn't want to think about him.

"Look," he said, as Rusty waddled over to them wanting to share the love, "we're smart people. Academics are useless for a lot of things, but we know how to do research." He put his finger down on the phone as she petted Rusty. "If anyone knows anything about this coin, we'll find them."

"How?"

"By playing six degrees of separation."

The rest of the day was spent playing phone tag with fellow academics and hopping on and off internet databases.

She marveled at Turner's connections. He knew biologists all over the world, and they knew other academics. She admired the way he could reach out and connect with total strangers, getting them on the phone even though it was Saturday night. Meanwhile, she didn't even like to call the local pizza place and talk with them long enough to place an order.

He got academic friends going on Facebook by making it a competition, by offering beer for everyone at the next biology conference. He was obviously very popular.

By Saturday afternoon Turner's connections had narrowed down the likelihood that the image was not of a coin, and was not Chinese.

Turner knew someone who knew an art historian who claimed to know something about the design. He was at Heidelberg University. Professor Frey spoke English and specialized in mediaeval monastery artifacts—and he was willing to answer a few questions over Skype.

With a *schwoooop!* noise, Skype loaded up onto Turner's big screen monitor.

While they waited for the German professor to come onscreen, they talked about the future.

"Clearly we need to stay with each other until this gets resolved," Turner said.

"I've been holding my own."

"Jenny, she wants to kill you. She's got access to your phone. What if she gets some guy to come over and strangle you?"

Jenny didn't know what to say to that.

"Can you take time off from the school?"

"No."

"Well, I'll take time off then."

"Leave in the middle of the semester?"

"Yeah."

"You can't do that."

"I'm not going to leave you alone with her at night. It's not safe."

The emotion gave an edge to the soothing rumble of his voice. It got her going, and she turned to straddle him, pulling his shirt up, her hands exploring the firm pale muscles of his ripped torso.

"Your farmer's tan is sexy to me," she said, gasping. He wasn't slow to respond. Her shirt was already up, his hands flaring out over her bra cups, making her nipples stiffen and harden, making her sit up suddenly and hold on to him when she immediately wanted to melt again. She pushed herself more insistently into his hands, rubbing against them while his mouth captured hers, his lips soft, tongue sensuous but demanding. She was undoing his pants while responding to his kiss with her own naughty tongue and feeling the shape of him under his boxers, teasing him with her fingertips. He undid her jeans and pushed them down her hips so they were lower on her ass and cupped her two suddenly naked cheeks with his big hands, making her feel a spurt of wetness down below. She was torn, arching her back, aiming her ass further into his hands, and stretching to get breasts up towards his mouth, cups down so that her pert nipples could feel him sucking on her, gently biting her suddenly hot skin.

Just then the Skype noise signaled the professor's incoming call. Startled, Jenny moved off Turner's lap and scooted out of range of the computer screen. Turner merely pulled his shirt down.

"Professor Frey! Thank you for your time. Anthony said you knew what our little design is."

"Yes," said the man on the screen. Jenny adjusted herself and edged over a foot to see a bobble headed bald man with a prissy little mustache in a coat and tie purse his lips on the screen. "It's a map," the art expert explained. "A map of hell."

Chapter 11

"Perhaps you've heard of Alphonso de Spina?" Professor Frey

173

continued.

They shook their heads.

"Alphonso de Spina finished his greatest creation in 1467: an illuminated grimoire of all the demons in hell," Professor Frey prompted.

"Sorry. I haven't heard of him," Turner said.

"He was exceptionally capricious in his writings." Turner shot a look at Jenny. *Capricious, eh?*

"It's apparent that he stole from everybody," Professor Frey continued. "And not very well, but there are indications he stole an exceptional amount from someone he notes in his writings as the monk from Aquitaine."

"Very mysterious," Jenny piped up. Turner introduced her and the professor gave her a tiny nod in return, his lips crimping up again.

"It may not actually be that mysterious. It's possible that by the time he sat down to write of his meeting with the monk he simply forgot the man's name."

Professor Frey gave a small cough into his fist.

"This monk from Aquitaine created a grimoire of all the demons in hell about fifteen years before Alphonso de Spina. It was later lost, so all we have are de Spina's writings and notes concerning what the manuscript looked like.

"De Spina says the grimoire was rather vague but that, in a letter, the monk claimed he had actually visited hell and had escaped in a hurry. He apologized for his recollection being so hazy.

"He said at first he did not believe the monk, but that the monk gave a detailed description of everything he saw and had such a sincere and honest way of relating his story, soon all the monks were convinced, with de Spina remaining the only skeptic among them."

"So what does this have to do with our coin?" Turner interrupted.

"Professor said it's not a coin," Jenny reminded him.

"Suck up," he whispered.

174

Professor Frey cleared his throat. "De Spina said the monk described entering through a cleft and going down a long vestibule into an underground maze, the center of which was a large square where Satan held court."

"Oh."

"As demons were leaving hell, de Spina relates, they apparently walked the long vestibule, loudly boasting of the wicked deeds they would do upon their return to earth before disappearing in a noxious vapor."

"Vestibule?" Turner asked.

"Yes."

"You mean a foyer or something?"

"It's a long hall between the entrance of a grand building and its interior." Professor Frey was exacting, Jenny thought, but clearly Turner was wearing down his patience.

"So it's not a coin from Diyu," Turner muttered.

"What's Diyu?" Jenny asked.

"It's the Chinese concept of hell. Which is an underground maze."

"You said it wasn't Chinese." Jenny looked uncertainly between Professor Frey and Turner.

"It's not," Professor Frey said. "There are also writings in Sanskrit, backed up by Sumerian cuneiform tablets that mention the entryway to hell in the form of a cleft with the rest of it being an underground maze."

"So...the Chinese picked up the same concept and ran with it?" Turner asked.

"Exactly. However, they never minted representations of Diyu in any coin form that I am aware of. Yet de Spina later claimed the monk from Aquitaine carried with him a token of his visit to hell—he showed de Spina the token. It was small and round. It is a representation of the maze, and a cleft."

"Sound familiar?" Jenny suspected the professor had a very dry sense of humor underneath his uptight European manner.

"So what happened to this token?" Turner challenged.

"De Spina asked the monk if he could have it but the monk said no, it was a parting gift from a demon. De Spina is recorded by another monk as saying that it was an actual portal to hell, and if the gateway were ever opened, the owner would suffer visitations from demons."

"Suffer how?" she asked.

"I'm afraid de Spina did not record an answer to that question."

"Why if it was such a dangerous token would someone keep it?" Jenny asked.

"My dear child, I haven't a clue."

"Perhaps as a constant reminder that hell awaited sinners?" Turner offered.

"Perhaps. Apparently de Spina stole the token from the monk or the monk changed his mind and in the end gave it to him. It was found amongst his things after he died."

"Thank you so much Professor." Jenny said. "I think we've solved our mystery."

"If you have such a token, I suggest you look into verifying its provenance. It could be quite valuable."

"You've been such an amazing help," Jenny said again.

"My pleasure. If that is all, I will leave now for my Schubert symphony which is starting in less than an hour."

"Certainly," Turner said. "We owe you one." Then he signed off.

"You miss it?" he asked Jenny.

"Miss what?"

"Playing in the big leagues? Doing research like this?" She pursed her lips, "No."

"That was so entirely convincing the way you said it."

"I enjoy how cozy the school is where I teach. I've got my own little classroom, I know all my students." She thought of the way the morning sun hit the windows of her room, her big solid desk, all the photos of the girls on the wall. "I care about them. I think the work I'm doing with them is meaningful."

"So you don't miss this."

"Well, I miss research." Looking at the old books Turner had hauled out from his book shelves that were open on the table before them. "Definitely."

"You know, Bellingham is hiring in the econ department."

"I don't know if I could get a teaching job with the way I left. And my evaluations were lousy."

"Never say never. There's always spousal hire."

"Great. We'll get married and I can ask Jennifer to be my bridesmaid. I can't see myself committing to a long term relationship. Not now. Not like this." She peeked at him to see how he took the news.

"Okay. So back to work."

"After Brett I can't. Don't you see? If we can't defeat her, I couldn't allow us to be together. Not if she's still in me. Not if you might get hurt."

"Until then...should we be pumping you full of caffeine? It's getting late, you know."

Jenny shook her head. "Now that we know what the design is, sort of—now what?"

Turner thought, his fist up to his cheek. Jenny paced.

"Something about this symbol helps Jennifer," she insisted.

"Having sex with someone wearing the symbol allows for a sort of infection to occur." He looked out the window. "The infection being Jennifer. You were infected by Johannes. Brett was infected by you."

"And you?"

He shrugged. "I'm fine. But I haven't had sex with Jennifer while the symbol was present."

She cocked her head. "How would you know?"

"Well, you—she was always wearing that ponytail up high." He mimed a water spout coming out of the top of his head. "I spent a lot of time looking at the back of your neck. And I know you weren't wearing a necklace. Anywhere."

She felt very self-aware, but not self-conscious. She promised him things with the smile she gave.

"Okay, so if we do something so the symbol's not present on me or with me, then she can't infect anybody else."

"I'd bet the farm that if she can't infect anybody else, she'd go away."

"Really?"

"Yeah. Because where's the fun in that? I am *starving*."

They decided to go out to eat and got shoes, keys, wallets.

Back in his beat up Volvo, she smelled the pines and caught glimpses of the gorgeous bay. Behind them a snow capped mountain presided benevolently over the smaller pine covered hills.

"Look, it's not just a map of hell, it's a portal to and from hell," Turner said, driving with one finger, his hands resting on his thighs. "That's where she goes back to when you're awake. That's where she's coming from every night when you got to sleep. She's using the tattoo to come through the vestibule thingy of hell and into you."

She imagined Jennifer pimp walking through a line of demons in the vestibule, boasting of the decadent things she'd do with Jenny's body that night, high fiving the other demons and then diving through the noxious fumes.

He stopped in front of a café. "Well?"

"Cute." She took in the little bakery attached to the café on one end, and the bar on the other. "Very cute."

"Thought you'd like it. And I need a beer."

Of course the waitress was young, gorgeous and a former student of his. Jenny tried not to be too happy when he couldn't remember her name even as the woman beamed at him like a puppy eager to please.

"The national park is just over to the east a little, if you like hiking," he said.

"Turner, you don't need to audition. If we get this thing resolved with Jennifer, you can plan our future together to your heart's content."

His face lit up for a moment, then clouded over. They drank in silence.

"I need to get the symbol off me," she said, "Just cut it off."

"That's one possibility," he said. "Though a lot of nerves run through your neck. You'd want to be careful. But just destroying the symbol might not work. What you really need to do is...you need to close the gates of hell."

"Yeah, right. That's impossible," she said.

He looked up at her.

"What?"

"No it's not." He gripped her hands and pulling her across the table, gave her a full kiss on the mouth. "It's not, Jenny. Look—" He held her face, his own turning red with excitement.

"We change the tattoo."

Chapter 12

In the end they drove an hour and a half south along the Puget Sound to Seattle. Jenny fed Turner fries from their abandoned dinner along the way. He said he knew of a place the students recommended highly and eventually they pulled into the parking lot for Scully Tattoos. Getting out of the car, their forms were dyed deep blue by the neon sign that was as long as the shop itself and even more brightly lit. Soon they were in the back, and Jenny was invited to stretch out on the retro red leather and chrome chair while Scully himself finished up with another client.

"I like your chair," she said, stroking the red leather arms.

"Old barber's chair," Scully said. He had a worn, pale Irish face with a love patch below his lip and an expression that said he'd seen a lot of freaky things in his time.

Soon she was straddling the tilted chair and leaning over to rest on her arms as Scully took a dentist's lamp and placed it so the light illuminated the back of her neck clearly.

179

"Across that wedge there, that's what you want?" He asked. He started putting on rubber gloves, and digging through a deep tray for his grip, the ink cup holder, and the needles.

Four minutes later, he said "You're done." His bifocals were put away, and he was wiping at the back of her neck with a sterile pad, tossing the bloodied pad in a bio canister.

"Don't I get a lollipop now or something," she said. "That hurt a lot more than I was led to expect."

"Sensitive skin," Scully said, putting his tools of the trade back on the tray and turning to face her again. "You can pay at the front desk."

"Thanks, Mr. Scully," she said

"Pleasure." He ducked his head and left the room, leaving them alone.

"You were very brave," Turner smiled, holding her hand between his own.

"What's it look like?" she asked. He took a photo, and she was slightly disappointed to see that there was just a short, thick blue-back bar across the notch in the round shape.

"Is that all?" she said. "It felt like it hurt a lot more than that.

"How does it feel?"

"Hot. Like it's burning."

He looked at the back of her neck. "It's uh, smoking," he said.

Scully came back in. "Still here, hun?"

"It hurts," she said, twisting a little in the seat. "Stings."

Scully looked at it. "Her tattoo is fading," he said.

"What?" Turner said, whipping around to bend her neck down and examine the image.

"See, originally the bar I made between this point and that one matched. Now it's darker than everything else."

They both stood there bent over, staring at her neck. Jenny didn't notice Scully, she only had eyes for Turner. When he was seriously thinking hard, the Grecian general's face came out. She wanted to kiss that face.

180

"I'll be damned," Turner said.

Scully shrugged. He wanted to see it again, and rubbed it. "It's permanent. I don't understand what would cause it. We're not in any special light or anything."

Jenny listened to the two men talk over skin acids and other peculiarities Scully had encountered after thirty years in the biz. The back of her neck felt like someone had poured a drop of acid upon it. It burned and the itchy agony she endured was fierce.

"Little lady, feel free to stay in here until you're feeling okay," Scully said.

"Thanks." She smiled.

"Not at all. You want some ice?"

She shook her head. "No thanks."

"Well, we got business, Saturday night and all." With that Scully went off.

"I like this chair," she said again once he was gone. She stretched out on her side.

Turner nodded, frowning.

"I don't think you understood me. I *like* this chair," she said, running her hand along the red leather.

Turner's head came up. He got up, locked the door, and came back.

"It's a nice chair," he agreed.

She sat upright, her legs on either side of the chair and bounced a little, testing. It was bolted solid into the floor, with only some faint creaking protest.

"You're...sure you're not Jennifer?" he said as she got up and pushed him back in the chair. "Because...she could be pretty aggressive sometimes."

"Is this aggressive?" she asked, unbuttoning his jeans.

"In the nicest possible way," he said, his hands coming down to her neck.

"Are you okay?" he asked.

"It burns," she said, holding his dick and sucking on it, then

181

letting it slide out of her mouth, wet and dark pink. "And I need a major distraction."

"I'm here for you," he said. She stood up, shucked her jeans and got back on him.

"I noticed that," she said, starting to stroke the wet, slick core of her sex over his cock.

"Prove you're not Jennifer," he said. She impaled herself on him and began to rock. "Prove it," he repeated between grunts.

"How?" she asked, rolling up her shirt and placing his hands where she wanted them. He scooped them into her bra and she closed her eyes with a shiver.

"Tell me how you feel about me."

She didn't know what to say. She was feeling lots, but the words suddenly got stuck somewhere between her throat and tongue, her mind wiped clean.

"Cat got your tongue?

She nodded.

"Well, we can work on that," he said. She put her hands on his shoulders and rode him, taking pains to roll forward with a controlled motion of her hips and then up and hard down again. She bent down as he shifted his grip to her naked ass, and she licked her way up his salty chest, her teeth scoring over his nipple. She saw his head arch back, the veins throbbing in his throat, which was turning a pinkish color with his arousal.

"I love you," she said. She said it like it was the answer to the bend of his neck, like it was the flavor of his skin, and somehow they felt different to each other in that instant, their hold on each other more snug, more alive, the heat between their skin going up another notch.

"And?"

"And what?" She began picking up speed, riding him cowgirl style. The buildup of her orgasm caught her by surprise. She pressed her knees down into the leather and her rocking became more urgent.

182

"What else do you say?"

"I don't know. What?" She felt fretful. Her neck no longer burned but she was burning up below, and that patient expression on his face left her wanting...she didn't know what, she was aching, she was...

"You say, what are you making me for breakfast Sunday morning?"

"What are you making me. For. Breakfast." Her words came out in little gasps.

"Whatever you want."

"Shut up," she gasped. "Oh, god, oh my god." Her hand came down and felt his face, her eyes closed. She felt him sucking her fingers and then he was up, taking her with him, sitting on the highest point of the chair. He pulled her down on him, then pulled her up and down again, hard. And again. Harder.

She put her nipple in his mouth and between thrusts said, "I liked it when you tied me up."

"We've already done that."

"Well we could do it again." He thrust her down. She thought she was going to go mad, the feeling was so aching and pleasurable and the two were mixing in her brain.

"Or maybe I could get some special lingerie."

Turner agreed lingerie was nice.

"Why don't you spread me out on this chair?"

He picked her up again and deposited her on the chair, spreading her legs wide.

"Like this?"

"Yes, and then, your tongue," she said, eyes half closed. His body looming over her made her thoughts incoherent. Her fingers slid between her legs, showing him. "Like you did before."

He straddled the chair and his face was between her legs. She knew that she shouldn't scream out, there were other people in the shop, but she had to bite her fist as her hips scooched up and urged him along.

183

"Please, please, please," she said.

"What do you want, Jenny," he crooned, lifting his face up, his chin awash in gleaming juices.

"You know."

"No. You have to tell me. And we don't have much time."

In the end he tied her hands together with her twisted underpants and put her face down across the hump of the chair and fucked her hard that way. She felt a kind of controlled brutality to his movements and wondered if there was a way to explain that she loved this about him as much as she loved the rest of him. I love you squared, she thought, and then the pinwheel rockets went off in her head, and she was utterly limp, her breath harsh, the thump of his heart pounding against her back.

There was a tentative knock on the door.

"We're just leaving," Turner called.

A low male voice said, "No worries."

"Hey, it's gone," Turner said, lifting off her. He took another snapshot with the phone. There was a pinkish scar left behind that had raised ridges here and there but it looked clean and healthy with just the little black bar at the top that Scully had inked.

But by the time they left the blue neon was turned off and the parking lot was wet, rainy, and dark. Jenny found herself with her feet up above her head in the back seat, pressing into the roof. They couldn't get enough of each other. The car rocked and it rained harder. It was so wet outside, and so deliciously wet inside. She was smirking, because she reeked of sex. They made it to his doorway back at his house and then he was pushing her up against the frame, wrapping her legs around his waist. The nice thing was that out in the woods she could grunt and growl and shout out his name. She might be shy, but when it came to sex she didn't want to be quiet.

"You sure you're still Jenny?

"Yeah."

"There's a price to pay for all this."

"What?"

"You already gave me your pussy."

She nodded, ready to fall asleep as he held her in his arms. That deep resin smell of the forest mingled with the rain and a strong nip in the air, but she didn't feel the cold.

"And I've had your ass, which is magnificent," he said.

"Hmmmm," she agreed, swaying in his arms.

"The price is that I've fallen for you."

"That's not such a bad thing."

"Maybe for you. I feel like I'm going to curl up and die. I hurt when I'm around you Jenny, I love you so much."

She was silent. Suddenly her chest hurt too, if only out of sympathy.

"Even without the thing cursing me?"

"I want you to give me your heart. I lied before. I want all of it. And you've got mine."

"I know that. You don't even have to say it."

"I do have to say it."

Smiling into his eyes, there was a kind of strangled feeling in her throat, but that was okay.

"I love you," she said again, and he ignored the tremble in her voice that almost broke the words apart. She'd have to practice. "I love you."

Divine

By

Elizabeth Shore

"Bolt cutters."

Faith Luna held her hand out like a surgeon as her videographer, Cam Rosario, slapped the requested item into her open palm. She closed her fingers around the rubber-gripped handles and glanced around, triple checking that they'd not been spotted. Weed-choked grass stirred in the light breeze. A rusty soda can rolled and clinked along a cracked cement pathway behind them. Apart from that, silence.

"Everyone ready to go?"

"Whenever you are."

She lifted the heavy-duty cutters to the lock, releasing a deep breath to steady her nerves. It wasn't every day that she broke into abandoned psychiatric hospitals, and Faith was well aware that this could land her in jail. Not that it would stop her. She'd get her film made no matter what it took, but it'd be a hell of a lot easier without needing to post bail.

The jaws of the bolt cutter clamped down on the lock as she jammed the handles together, but the damned thing stayed intact.

Despite a chill in the late afternoon air, trickles of sweat rolled between her breasts.

"Crap," she muttered, gritting her teeth. "You dirty, no-good, son-of-a —"

Pop! The lock snapped. They were in.

Faith handed the bolt cutters over to the film crew's runner, Kelly Stahl, and then she hauled the thick chain off the fence. Shoving the gate open, she grabbed her bag of gear and led the way, her film crew right behind her.

Racing as quickly as possible while carrying pounds of camera and lighting equipment, they covered the area between the fence and the abandoned hospital in seconds. Faith rounded a corner to one of the side doors. A source she'd interviewed for the film had told her about this specific entrance, saying that once you got through the chain link fence on the hospital's perimeter it was easy enough to get inside the building. The hospital had been abandoned for nearly twenty years and intrepid trespassers had broken several locks long ago. Some of them had been replaced, but not all.

She cast another look around. Still no cops. Approaching the side entrance, she grasped the rusty door handle and turned. It groaned in protest, hinges squealing, as Faith bumped a hip against it and shoved once, twice. Reluctantly, the door swung open.

Her crew was assembled behind her, already setting up for outdoor shots. They had to be as quick as possible, knowing the area was regularly patrolled. Their late afternoon arrival was purposefully orchestrated to give them enough light for filming but not so much that they'd be easily spotted. Still, time was tight. Faith cocked her head toward Dana Stewart, her lighting assistant.

"Ready?"

"Yep. We've got everything."

Alongside the building, Tyler and Cam had their camera hooked up to the battery packs and were ready to start shooting.

"Hey guys, gather 'round. We need a quick huddle before we

get started." Faith crooked an arm to call them toward her, like a shepherd gathering her flock. They stepped forward into a semi-circle around her as she faced them on the steps before the door.

"I know we've gone over this but bear with me. I just have to be sure." She took a look at her faithful crew, all but one of them with her since her first project ten years ago. They'd worked in some hell-hole conditions with bare-bones equipment and zero money. More than one dinner had consisted of packets of ramen noodles. At times even less than that. But they stuck with her because they were as passionate about the causes Faith documented as she was.

She pulled a folded blueprint of the hospital's interior from her back pocket. Faded with age, there were parts of the map that were impossible to make out, but it was better than nothing. Harlem Valley Psychiatric Hospital was spread out over 800 acres and included 80 buildings. They risked getting lost without some kind of map.

"Okay, so we're here," Faith said, pointing to a spot in the middle of the crinkled paper. "Cam, you and the crew take as much exterior as you can get but focus on the main building first. If there's time, then spread out."

"Got it," Cam assured her.

Faith glanced over at the youngest member of her crew, twenty-three year old Kelly Stahl, a recent grad from the New York Academy of Film and Television. As junior member, he was their runner, acting as pack mule and hauling loads of equipment on location and making sure supplies were in good working order. With bodybuilder biceps he lifted pounds of equipment like they were made of feathers, and with misplaced lust Faith sometimes couldn't help but covertly watch Kelly when he loaded up their van. At ten years her junior she felt like a cougar on the prowl so she made it a point to keep her peeping discreet.

Now, however, as she looked over the scattered piles of gear, she couldn't help but frown.

"I thought there were two more battery packs." She directed

the question at Kelly but it was Cam who responded.

"They're both dead."

"Dead?!" *Shit*. This she didn't need. "What happened?"

Cam shrugged. "They're old, Faith. Packs only last so long." He was quick to reassure her. "Don't worry, we've got enough for this shoot. We'll recharge later and be good to go for tomorrow, too."

She gave the crew a smile, despite the coil of anxiety unraveling in her gut. Where in the hell was she going to come up with money to replace those packs? Damn, what she wouldn't give for just one percent of a Hollywood big movie budget. They'd struggled for so long on nothing, fixing busted equipment with duct tape and crossed fingers, praying things would hold out just long enough for them to finally catch a break.

"Okay, let's get to it. Dana and I will shoot as much interior as we can while the light holds. You guys do the same out here." She glanced at the thick clouds forming in the sky. "I'm hoping the storms they forecast will hold off for at least a couple of hours, but do your best. And don't forget the most important thing."

"Don't worry about the cops." Tyler Kannon cast a grin at her. "We can't tell them what we don't know, right?"

The chances of them getting arrested for trespassing were higher than she'd like, but Faith knew her crew was as committed to taking their chances as she was. If Cam, Tyler, Travis, and Kelly were spotted by the cops and arrested, it was agreed beforehand they'd go without protest and not reveal that Faith and Dana were inside.

It would've been a lot easier if they'd just been given permission to film, but the city had repeatedly rejected their requests. Faith was determined to expose abuses in the mental health industry, and capturing its ugly history was integral to the film. Her eyes traveled over the stark red brick administration building and a cold finger of fear tracked down her spine. Her grandmother had died in a place just like this, locked up in an asylum hell-hole for "psychotic episodes," which nowadays would have been diagnosed as severe bipolar disorder. But without proper treatment

189

Nana had suffered, and an orderly found her one dreary winter morning, hanging from an exposed pipe in her room, bed sheet tied around her neck.

She pushed away the swell of sorrow that always bubbled up from thoughts of Nana. Faith had been only fifteen when the suicide happened, and over the years she'd cried buckets of bitter tears from the pain of her loss. She used that pain now, as an adult, to spur her on toward making this film and honoring the memory of the grandmother who'd left this world far too early.

"Ready, Dana?"

"Whenever you are."

"All right, let's go." She turned once more to Cam. "We'll text you when we're wrapping up and all of us meet back here at this door. Then Kelly will bring the van around and we'll load up." She hoisted a duffel bag filled with equipment onto her shoulder. "See you in a few."

"Later." Travis waved a hand and then turned away to help the other guys with the exterior shots. Faith and Dana walked through the metal door and stepped inside.

Maybe in its own way it had once been an attractive building, but the abandoned hospital was now little more than a shell of its former self. Chunks of old plaster, scattered papers, and frayed wires littered the floor. A spiderweb of cracks stretched across the ceiling. Peeling paint hung like dead layers of sunburned skin. Insects scattered as they walked: spiders, cockroaches, silverfish, racing toward corners of the room to hide in waiting until it was safe to come out and crawl. A shudder of revulsion slithered down Faith's spine.

Despite it still being daytime the interior of the building was dim. Its small barred windows didn't allow for much light, even on the sunniest days, and of course the electricity had been shut off years ago. Dana flicked on the flashlight, revealing a concrete archway through which they could see the expansive admittance area, stark and severe like the hospital itself.

"Let's start here," Faith said, stepping around the stiff carcass of a long-dead rat as she carefully lowered her pack to the filthy floor. Her nostrils flared from the thick, musty odor permeating the room; the haunting smell of abandonment and death. Despite her stalwart nature, she shivered.

She guessed her trepidation was reflected on her face, because Dana grimaced as she looked around. "I've been in plenty of abandoned buildings, but this place is creeping me out."

"It's not that bad." Faith forced a lightness in her voice she didn't feel. Countless patients had suffered and ultimately died in the hands of those who'd worked here, using cruel treatment methods like electroconvulsive therapy and prefrontal lobotomies. The cobwebs and dark shadows seemed like remnants of those long ago tortured souls.

Dana set up portable lights around the main reception area as Faith assembled her camera. Minutes later she began recording footage, going wide at first before narrowing in for detail. She captured the dozens of cracked and broken windows, abandoned sticks of furniture, filth and litter scattered across the floor. Plant tendrils pushed through the crumbling walls, like gnarled fingers of nature creeping in to reclaim its territory. And everywhere — rats. They skulked in the corners, beady eyes glinting in the light, whiskers twitching. Their long claws scratched against the floor as they raced around and screeched.

"Crap, I didn't expect so many damn rodents," Dana grumbled. "Gross."

"I know." Faith looked around. "We can only hope it's not like this everywhere."

"I'm not optimistic. This place has been abandoned for so long. It's not like anyone's around laying traps."

"Just try to ignore them," Faith urged. "The sooner we get our footage the sooner we can get outta here."

They fell silent and kept walking, scouting for sights to film. Aside from the quiet squeaks from the rats and the light scuff of their shoes against the squalid concrete floor, an eerie silence pervaded the room. Anything louder than their breathing seemed obnoxious. Faith tried ignoring her jumpy nerves, but she couldn't quiet the machine-gun thumps of her heart. She wiped her shaking hands against her jeans and set her jaw, focusing every ounce of energy on the job at hand.

Dana walked ahead of Faith and entered an adjacent room. Seconds later, she peered around the corner and crooked her finger in a "come here" motion.

"Check it out." She kept her voice low, as if they were in a library. Speaking any louder than that seemed wrong, like laughing at a funeral. Faith made her way over to where her lighting assistant pointed.

"Looks like they used to keep medicine in this room," Dana said. "I see a lot of small shelves where pill bottles might have been stored."

"Perfect." Faith glanced around. "I definitely want footage in here."

She passed Dana and walked through a set of double doors covered with peeling and crackled green paint. Aiming her camera toward the storage shelves, she could see as she approached that each compartment on the shelves had been precisely labeled, indicating the drug stored there. She zoomed in on the names: prolixin, serentil, thorazine, vistaril. The names were familiar to her, having learned about them through research prior to filming. Powerful drugs used to treat psychosis, sometimes with dangerous side effects.

Once finished in that room they made their way down various hallways, capturing footage of abandoned patient rooms, dining areas, and large spaces where equipment had been stored. They saw gurneys still folded and neatly stored although covered with thick layers of dust. There was an odd proliferation of broken fans scattered about, their long frayed cords reminding Faith of rat tails.

They decided to head down toward the old boiler room. It

appeared from the map that a tunnel down there connecting the main building to some of the others would allow them easy access to move about. Suddenly, in mid-step, Dana froze.

"Did you hear that?" Her wide eyes reflected fear.

Faith stood still, ears craning for sound. She shook her head.

"I didn't hear a thing. I think you're imag — " Then she heard it. The noise was low, soft, at first indistinct, but then...

"It sounds like a...like a moan."

"Yeah," Dana whispered. "That's what I thought, too."

Faith's heartbeat tripled in speed, quick staccato beats like a snare drum in her chest.

"Well, what the hell," she said, trying to keep the tremor out of her voice. "Are there kids in here?"

Another moan floated through the air, louder this time. Dana clutched her arm.

"That doesn't sound like kids to me."

It didn't to Faith, either, and despite her shaking hands she was trying to put on a brave face for Dana. Her mind raced for a logical explanation, bound and determined not to succumb to temptation and admit what the noise really sounded like, which was an other-worldly — No. She wasn't going there.

"I'm sure it's nothing," she said, striving for confidence. "But just in case, I'll see if I can record it." She flicked the camera back on and pointed the lens in the direction of where they thought the sound was coming. Before long they heard it again, this time from behind them.

"What the fuck!" Dana spun around, her head whipping back and forth trying to spot whoever was making the noise. Just then, accompanying the moans were deep, lust-filled sighs. Faith's nerves eased, replaced by a thread of anger. Whoever was making the noises was hampering her project. They had a very short window of time in which to film and she wasn't about to let some sex-starved teens screw things up.

"This isn't funny!" she called out. "Whoever you are, you better show yourselves. We've got a camera and we're filming. You're not supposed to be in here and you're about to get busted."

Not that she and her crew had permission, either, but that was beside the point.

Apart from the distant rumble of thunder, all around them was silence.

"Think we scared them off?"

Faith shrugged. "Maybe for the moment. Although if those teens are anything like I was at their age, they're not going to give up on a good fuck space quite that easily."

Dana raised an eyebrow. "Really? I didn't realize you were such a wild child, Ms. Luna. Do tell."

Faith grinned. "What happens in college dorm rooms stays in college dorm rooms. My lips are sealed."

"Fine," Dana huffed as they started back down the stairs. "I'll get vodka when we're done and *then* you'll tell me."

They chuckled as they headed toward where the boiler room should be. As they walked they could see that the floor in the basement area was covered with patches of moss that had pushed up from the ground, like in a forest. They spotted the boiler room. As they made their way toward it, a pack of startled rats raced in circles around them, their sharp squeals as they ran causing both women to jump.

"Cripes!" Dana clutched her heart. "I'm twitchy as those damn rats."

Faith expelled a long sigh. "Me, too. The noises from those screwing teens put us on edge." She lifted the camera back up to her shoulder and prepared to shoot footage of the room. Her camera light started to dim.

"Damnit. I don't know how long this thing's going to last." She looked around the room. "And it's getting darker from those storm clouds."

"I'll head over to the room ahead," Dana suggested, "and set up more lights. According to the map it's an equipment area so there might be some interesting things to film."

"All right. Get set up and I'll be there in a few."

Dana grabbed her lights and exited through the door in the back. Faith stayed behind, poking around the massive boiler room to see if she could find the entrance to that tunnel. She'd just decided to head toward where Dana had gone when she heard it again — a long, low moan. This time there was no mistaking the distinctive groans of someone in the grip of a powerful orgasm.

"Ahhhh!!!"

"Dana?" Faith whispered. She'd wanted to shout, but her voice wouldn't cooperate. Those teens had to be close by; their sex sounds echoed all around her. Despite her annoyance about her project being compromised, she couldn't help her body's response to the teens' noises. Being so focused on this project hadn't left much time for her love life, even just a casual partner. The deficit was making itself known now, as every groan caused her pussy to clench with growing arousal and her nipples to harden to stiff peaks beneath her blouse.

She raised a hand, for a split second tempted to slip it down her dampening panties and give herself relief. But with a curse, she resisted the powerful impulse. What the hell was she thinking? *Focus on the project, Faith.* Forcing herself to move and find where Dana had gone, she shook off the odd temptation to masturbate and pulled her thoughts back to the business at hand, which was finding Dana.

Maybe her lighting assistant had found the teens, which was why she wasn't answering Faith's calls. Rushing toward the back door, she pushed it open and entered the adjoining room. Her foot kicked something and sent it spinning across the floor. Beams of light shone on the ground where the object lay. Faith stepped toward it and a shiver of fear raced down her spine. It was Dana's flashlight.

"Dana?" This time her voice obeyed and she loudly out called her lighting assistant's name. No response.

Propped up against a crumbing wall was Dana's lighting equipment. Faith set her camera down next to it. She retrieved the flashlight from the ground and waved the beam of light around. The room was massive, the size of a gymnasium. She wondered if that was what it had been but didn't feel like wasting time consulting the map. Right now she had to find Dana.

She continued calling out her name, her nerves getting more frayed as seconds ticked by without a word from her friend. She tried telling herself to be logical. Dana couldn't have just disappeared. *But what about those teens?* her worried inner voice whispered. *Maybe they weren't just a couple of lusty co-eds. Maybe they were strung out meth addicts. Or criminals. Murderers.*

Faith cursed under her breath. What the hell. She had to stop freaking herself out and focus. Find Dana.

But half an hour later, her friend was still missing.

Denying her fear had become pointless and Faith knew she needed help. She pulled her phone from her back pocket, tapping on Cam's number from her favorites. No signal.

"Fuck!" Faith screamed her frustration as she turned back in the direction she'd come to head upstairs. She raced through the door but didn't see the stairs. She must not be where she thought. Then she remembered that she needed to go back through the boiler room and keep moving straight. Heart pounding, blood roaring in her ears, she ran through the boiler room, the light beam from her flashlight guiding the way. More thunder, louder this time. She wondered if it was raining yet but couldn't tell since there were no windows in that area of the basement.

She pushed through the door, searching frantically for the stairs. Not there, either. The cold grip of panic clutched her throat, cutting off air. She opened her mouth, gasping like a fish out of water as she strained to breathe. Loss of control danced on the edge of her sanity. Time to do something, fast. Resting her hands on her knees and lowering her head, she fought off the panic. Techniques from yoga flitted through her mind. Her eyes fluttered closed as deep breathing took over, long, slow breaths that eased her pounding heart and kept her fear at bay, at least for the moment.

With deliberate slowness she lifted her head and shined the flashlight beam around the room. There. The stairs were straight ahead.

She raced up, two at a time, back to where she and Dana had started their journey what seemed like hours ago. Again she tapped at her phone, sure she'd have a signal, but the result was the same. Nothing.

Damn it! Why hadn't they thought to check for signals before they even started? Too late now. The only thing Faith could do was to get out of there, grab the guys and head back inside to find Dana. Pulling the map out of her pocket, she traced her finger along the route they'd taken to begin with, determined not to lose any more precious seconds by wandering aimlessly through the hospital.

She sped down the hallways through rooms that were now familiar. Minutes later she found the door. Her hands slammed down on the release but the door didn't budge. Frowning, she pushed harder but still it wouldn't give. She stood on her tip-toes and peered out the small narrow window. The storm clouds and waning light combined to make it look like nighttime outside. She saw no sign of her crew. Her heart stopped as she realized what must have happened. The cops had discovered the guys filming out there, rounded them up, and relocked the door. And, as agreed beforehand, her crew assured the cops that no one was inside.

Faith lifted her fingers to the sides of her head, her temples throbbing. How could a day deteriorate so quickly from bad to hell? Her crew was in jail, her assistant missing, and her phone dead. Fitting irony that she was locked inside a looney bin, because she felt like she was going to lose it at any second.

Her lips curled from the dark humor. She took a deep breath, considering her options. Since they were locked inside, Dana *had* to be here. She couldn't have escaped any more than Faith could.

Even if Dana had found another busted door she wouldn't just leave Faith behind.

She pulled the map out of her pocket, wondering if there were any rooms she'd missed or not noticed, maybe small ones where Dana could have gone to explore. She herself might be lost, and Faith was the one with the map.

But what about the flashlight?

Yeah, that was a problem. Even if Dana had set down her equipment to go exploring, she wouldn't have discarded the flashlight. Faith bit her lip, thinking. It wasn't worth trying to figure out the answer. Her sole focus now was finding her friend.

More thunder, this time followed by streaks of lightening. She aimed her flashlight beam toward some windows. They were all covered with crisscrossing iron bars allowing no chance to crawl through them and run for help. Fat raindrops began pelting the glass. Faith opened her mouth, breathing deeply, doggedly fighting her growing sense of panic.

She turned back toward the direction where she and Dana had gone. Her plan was to retrace her steps, go over every inch of ground they'd covered until she found her. She wasn't leaving this place without Dana.

Her steps were slow, deliberate, determined not to skip any place they'd been. When she entered one room her flashlight reflected the beady eyes of a rat as it plucked at the carcass of a dead pigeon. Fighting off a surge of nausea, she turned away and continued.

Heading back toward the stairs that led to the boiler room, she heard what sounded curiously like the caw of an exotic parrot. She stopped walking, feet glued to the ground. Her flashlight revealed nothing but seconds later she heard the sound again, this time followed by the menacing growl of a lion.

The hairs on her arm shot straight up and she screamed, whirling around, searching frantically for the source of the noises. The room was empty.

"Hold it together, Faith. Hold it together." She uttered the words aloud, over and over, an incantation to keep herself calm. Unknowingly her steps had been reduced to tiny shuffles as a river of fear coursed through her blood. Her body was drawn tight as a wire as her eyes flitted around like a lab mouse in a maze, searching for signs of her friend.

A breathy whisper tickled her ear.

She jumped back, gasping, craning her neck to see who stood next to her, but there was no one in sight. Her trembling fingers aimed the flashlight around an empty room.

Faaaaiiiittttthhhhhh . . . . .

What the hell? How did they know her name? Suddenly an icy finger, cold as death, brushed along her cheek. She screamed once more and spun, frantic, her arms pinwheeling as she stumbled backward and away from whomever was tormenting her. The flashlight flew from her fingers and clattered to the ground. She glimpsed it spinning across the floor right before it went out, probably broken. Near darkness consumed her, with the curious exception of a light ahead. Its source was unknown but it seemed she had no choice except to move in that direction. It was too dark to walk anywhere else.

She advanced slowly, heart ricocheting in her chest, but threads of annoyance also wove their way in. Who the fuck was screwing with her project? And why wouldn't the bastards show themselves?

"Who's out there?" No response. A slow burn of anger simmered her blood. "C'mon, you people, game's up. I have work to do and no time for your bullshit."

She thought at first that she'd get another round of silence, but then,

Ooooooooh yeeeeaaaaahhhhh!!!

Seriously? They were at it again? Who was having sex for that long? Or was this round two? The moans and whispers increased in volume as she moved toward the light and Faith was certain that this time she'd discover the identities of the sex-starved teens. They'd probably found some old mattress, plopped it on the floor, and were going at it with the vigor of youth and raging hormones. Probably gave them a creepy thrill to be doing it in an abandoned psychiatric hospital, too, like having sex in a graveyard.

The light grew stronger as she walked. The sighs and moans continued, becoming more frequent. And, just as before, Faith's body responded. Low pulses throbbed between her legs, moisture soaking her panties. Her breasts grew heavy, aching for touch. Without being aware of what she was doing, her hand drifted over to her breast and began teasing a hardened nipple through her blouse and bra. She crept forward, now able to see a dim corner of the room. Nothing was there beyond a single metal chair and chunks of fallen plaster. An empty cabinet hung crookedly against a wall, its shelves devoid of whatever it had once held.

Faith approached the threshold, her shallow breaths echoing in her ears as she peered around the corner, expecting to see naked students in the middle of action. Judging by the noises there was more than one couple, a veritable orgy of college kids in the midst of sexual awakening. A crazy, illogical thought about whether they'd welcome some company flashed through her head, but then her mind went numb and all thoughts vanished as she stepped into the room.

Directly in front of her was the ghostly, eerily erotic image of a couple making love. Their features were indistinct, no more substantial than cobwebs. They floated through the air, curled around one another like wisps of smoke, their sinuous bodies writhing in ecstasy as they mated.

A spear of terror pinned Faith's feet to the ground and froze her in place. Her mouth fell open as she gasped, at once horrified yet unable to look away. The sighs and moans she'd been hearing clearly came from the ghostly couple before her, the loud noises strangely at odds with their delicate images.

She was unaware of how long she stood there, transfixed by the sight, until she once more heard the whisper of her name.

Faaaaiiiittttthhhhhh . . . . .

The sound broke the spell and she looked around, desperate to identify its source.

"Dana?" She knew it wasn't Dana calling out, but maybe her friend was here somewhere, trapped by whatever entity haunted the hospital. She looked back to where she'd seen the couple but now they were gone and the room stood as empty as if they'd never been. The light remained, however, yet Faith was unable to identity its source. It was almost as if its origin was the room itself.

She inched forward, casting her gaze everywhere as she looked for Dana. Her earlier arousal from seeing the couple had been replaced once more with fear. She wanted nothing more than to find Dana and get the hell out of there. She'd figure out some other hospital where they could film. No project, even one that was as important and personal to her as this one, was worth her or her friend's life.

She walked through the door on the opposite end of the room from where she'd entered, still following the trail of light. It almost seemed to pulse within the hospital, the weird, unidentifiable glow not fading but remaining steady as she made her way through what appeared to be a tunnel connecting this building to the next. Goaded with purpose she picked up her pace, stepping swiftly through the tunnel to reach the next building.

There were more windows there than in the building she'd just left, and the rumbles and crashes of the storm were more prominent. The rain had picked up, sounding like huge shovels full of gravel pummeling the glass. Water poured in where some of the windows were cracked or broken, accompanied by the high-pitched howl of the wind, like the screams of a tortured soul.

A flash of lightning lit the room, drawing Faith's attention to another ghostly image. This time it was a man and two women. Again, as before, they were transparent, but the muted glow allowed her to see what they were doing. In this scenario the man lay on his back while both females straddled him. The first had her thighs on either side of his hips as she rode him like a bull, pounding

201

his cock with her hungry pussy. Her female companion faced her while straddling the man's head, perfectly positioned for his tongue to lick and tease her clit. As the women took their pleasure from the man, they stroked and fondled each other's breasts, their deep whispered sighs floating through the air.

Suddenly the women broke apart, as if sensing they were no longer alone. Then, like a movie in slow motion, one of them turned her head and stared straight at Faith.

Her mouth went dry, terror racing through her blood as she gasped, stepping backward, wanting to get away. The spirit rose from the man and began floating toward Faith, her arms reaching out as if to grasp hold of her. She cried out and spun around, not knowing where to go but desperate to run. A long corridor loomed ahead to her left and like a panicked animal she took off, feet flying over the littered ground. The muted light remained, enough for her to see, but as she ran deeper through the corridor the light began to fade and soon she was barely able to make out where she was going. Her foot kicked something, hard enough for her to cry out but still she fled, frenzied panic gripping her.

"Dana!" The scream ripped from her throat as she ran. She didn't chance a move back, wasn't even sure if the ghostly spirit was still in pursuit, but all logical thought had vanished. All she knew was that she had to get away. She made out another hallway, this time to her right. She rounded the corner, hoping for a place to hide or even better to get the hell out. There had to be an exit somewhere, an old door that kids had busted through and cops hadn't yet discovered. Faith just had to find it.

She called Dana's name once more, hoping against hope that her friend would hear, but there was no response. Just then she thought she saw a door. It was difficult to know for sure, but she'd head in that direction. Her ragged breaths echoed in the hallway, blood roared in her ears. She was just about there and yes, it was a door, she was sure of it. All she had to do was —

"Ah!" She ran straight in to something hard and low. Maybe a table. She flew through the air and landed with a thud, her head smacking the ground. All breath left her body and she lay sprawled where she fell, resigned to her fate. She groaned and lifted a hand to her head, feeling for blood. Her fingers came away sticky.

Dying in this hell-hole asylum was not an option. She'd figure a way out of here. Her natural resilience would not allow her to fall into hopelessness and accept that this was the end of Faith Luna.

"I certainly hope it's not the end of Faith Luna."

A man's voice, seductively soft, floated across the room to her left. Faith groaned and turned her head. As she did so the light returned, allowing her to see the source of the voice.

In an enormous ornamented chair, almost like a throne, sat the most beautiful man she'd ever seen. He wore robes similar to those of ancient Romans, draped casually to partially hide his naked body. His muscled calves were exposed, and Faith's eyes roamed over them and then down to his sandaled feet. He sat languidly upon his throne, like a bored king, eating bits of fruit. With long, beautiful fingers he slid spears of apple between his lips, slowly sucking in the fruit as a devilish smile played about his mouth. It was as though he could tell, in spite of everything — her missing friend, her fear, her injured head — that Faith was aroused by him.

He was right, of course, for in spite of her throbbing head she couldn't look away. The sight of this man — if that's even what he was — mesmerized her like she'd been placed under a spell. Even when he rose and stepped down from the dais upon which the throne was placed, Faith was helpless to try getting away. Her head felt stuffed with cotton, she was dizzy and bewildered and her feet refused to move. She was as trapped as an insect in amber.

He walked to her, so lightly he seemed to float, which was astonishing considering his size. Built like a Viking, his chest and shoulders were enormous and his height looked well over six and a half feet. Yet he retained a surprising fluidity, his taut body moving with the coiled sleekness of a panther's. When he reached her he crouched down and tenderly placed a hand against her forehead. From his deep, mellifluous voice came sounds like an ancient chant. She caught a glimpse of dark, chocolate brown eyes just before they fluttered closed as he continued chanting, infusing the air with hypnotic verse.

Faith's body went limp, freed from every ounce of tension and pain. Pleasurable warmth spread like molasses from where the man touched her to all the joints, muscles, and bones in her body. She turned her head, cautiously, bracing for the throbbing ache, but it had vanished into nothingness. With baited breath she lifted her hand to touch the bloody spot on her scalp, but like the pain, the blood was no more.

The final notes of his chant hung in the air, wavered, then at last dissolved. The room went quiet. Faith's mystery man or whatever he was opened his eyes and looked down on her. Despite her dire situation, her breath caught in her throat. Now that the haze of pain had lifted, her vision was clear and she could fully appreciate the man's ethereal beauty. His features were nothing short of perfection. From his eyes, to his lips, to his chiseled jaw, every detail was flawless. Her gaze drifted downward. His robe had slipped from his shoulder, unveiling ripples of taut, sculpted muscle like a gladiator. He radiated power.

"Your pain is gone?"

He posed it as a question but it was clear from his smile that he knew the answer. Faith licked dry lips and nodded.

"Yes."

"Then rise."

Hypnotized by the silky sound of his words, she moved to obey, but before she could lift a finger she was standing upright and he, inexplicably, was seated back on his throne.

"How—" The words died on her tongue. She and the man were surrounded.

Faith gasped and whipped her head around, ready to flee, but escape was impossible. Seemingly out of thin air dozens of people had appeared and linked hands to form a circle around the dais, effectively trapping her and the mysterious man. They were dressed similarly to him, in loose, flowing robes, although unlike their apparent leader, their feet were bare. The women had flowers and ribbons adorning their hair, like mythical forest nymphs.

Suddenly, as if they'd all understood some silent cue, they began moving forward, closing the circle like a noose tightening around its victim. Their steps were slow, deliberate, bare feet whispering across the floor. Faith's heart leaped in her throat. Her mouth went bone dry. She tried to scream but could only muster a cry no louder than a kitten's mew. Her panic seemed to strike her captors as funny and they began to laugh, at first softly but then louder and more boisterous the closer they came. To her ears the noise was tinged with evil, like mean kids taunting a hapless victim in the schoolyard. But these people looked like they'd do more than tease Faith with childish pranks, especially when she looked into their coal black eyes.

She finally found her voice and pierced the air with her terrified plea.

"Get away from me!" She held both hands before her, shielding her body as she whirled around, not wanting to be attacked from behind. Her gesture only made then laugh harder, revealing perfect rows of gleaming teeth. She imagined them biting into her, ripping away strips of skin from her body, sinking those evil teeth deep into her flesh. As the horrified image flashed through her mind she screamed again, a primal animal screech of sheer terror.

"That's enough!" The sharp command was issued by their leader who remained casually lounging in his throne on the raised dais, as if bored with the events happening before him.

"But we want her. To touch her. Feel her." One of the women turned adoring eyes toward him. "She's the one."

"That's for me to decide." His voice was laced with a touch of irritation as he rose from his throne. "As you well know."

As far as Faith was concerned, whatever they were talking about was for *her* to decide, and she already knew which way she'd go.

Way the hell out of there.

Right now, however, she had to keep her wits about her and figure out how to escape. She'd find an exit, get help, and then come back for Dana. She'd bring the cops, she'd bring attack dogs, she'd —

"Now, is all of that really necessary?" Crazy ancient Roman man stood beside her once more, waving his finger back and forth like a parent scolding a child.

"After all," he continued while slowly licking what looked like honey from his fingertips, "I haven't done anything to you." He placed his index finger beneath her chin and tilted her head up to look into his blazing eyes. "Yet."

The touch of his finger sent shockwaves through her body, currents of fire that roared through her blood. Astounded by her reaction from just that slight touch, Faith gasped and stepped backward. At once the swarm of people moved in but their progress was halted by the barest of nods from their leader.

He stepped toward Faith once more and she had no choice but to remain bolted in place. His devoted posse wasn't about to let her go.

"Yes," he murmured, almost to himself. "It's just as I thought. I sensed it with the healing touch, but now I know for certain."

"What are you talking about?" Faith hissed. "And who the hell are you?"

"Ah." He smiled, perfect lips curling upward, and despite the fantastical situation in which she found herself, Faith couldn't ignore the swirl of desire in her belly as she watched those beautiful lips.

"Of course you would want to know that. Come." He held out his hand. "Sit. Have something to eat. You must be famished."

It wasn't until that moment that Faith realized she actually was hungry. Starving, more like it. She hadn't eaten in over twelve hours, not since she'd gulped down a dry muffin for breakfast. But she'd rather be starving than poisoned. She shook her head.

"Just let me go. I need to find my friend."

"She's fine." Despite her resistance he took her hand and led her to the dais. As if by magic, the single throne was replaced with two. Faith allowed herself to be drawn forward, the man's vise-like grip leaving her no choice.

She sat, pulse racing, her mind whirling with questions. Dana's fine? His answer could mean only one thing: he was the one who'd taken her. But if so, where was she? And was she really all right? Damn it. She released a ragged sigh. What the hell was happening?

The loud caw of a bird shook away her thoughts. Faith glanced up, looking around to see where the noise came from. At once the hairs on her arms shot straight up. Her mouth fell open as she gasped.

All around them were animals, as if Noah's ark had pulled up and dumped its load in the asylum. At their feet were cats and dogs. Rabbits hopped up and down the stairs of the dais. Birds circled the air above them. In the distance were larger animals — tigers, zebras, lions, crocodiles, gazelles, ostriches, bears, snakes. Many more, *hundreds* more. But they weren't just hanging out in the abandoned hallways of a psychiatric hospital, because the room they were in had been transformed. Concrete floors were now covered with thick, soft moss. Walls disappeared, replaced with enormous trees: soaring oaks and long-needled pines. Instead of being in a hospital, Faith found herself in a lush, dense forest.

"Do you like it?"

The man beside her chuckled and as Faith swung her gaze toward him she saw sparkles of humor reflected in his eyes.

"I...I...."

"Never mind." He waved his hand to dismiss her. "I realize this is all overwhelming for you now. I shall explain. But first," he nodded toward platters of food all around them, "you will eat."

Enticing aromas drifted through the air, and suddenly Faith felt she understood how the biblical Adam was tempted with forbidden fruit. *And look how that turned out.* She decided to pass on the offering but her captor shook his head.

"There is no choice in this matter," he said, his silky voice smooth but tainted with a hard edge. "Eat."

The one-word command spoke volumes. Accepting her fate, Faith selected a handful of grapes and popped one in her mouth, chewing slowly. It was delicious, succulent and sweet, unlike any grapes she'd ever had. The fruit teased her, reminding her of how hungry she really was. She took more and noticed that it seemed to please her captor, who sat back in his chair and watched her while she ate. All around her the animals played. Her captor's posse, who'd seemed so threatening only minutes before, now lounged on the grass like friends at a picnic.

"My name is Alexandru," the man beside her suddenly said, without preamble. "And you are Faith."

Her gaze snapped over to him, brows furrowed. "How do you know that?"

"There's a good deal I know about you, Mistress Luna. Much more than you realize."

The smooth words unsettled her, and her stomach twisted. She set aside her bread and cheese.

"Fine," she said, mustering courage. "And since you seem to be able to read my mind, you know how much I want to leave this place. So let me go."

He pinned her with a stare. "I'm not going to do that."

Cold fear coated her tongue. She sat back, putting every possible inch of distance between herself and this crazy beautiful man. Her fingers gripped the edge of the chair.

"Why not?" she whispered.

Alexandru leaned forward, his powerful frame filling the space she'd just created. "Because you are my queen."

A strange, mystical shimmer radiated from him as he spoke. It was as if he were surrounded in a sparkling cloud of gold dust. Faith nervously licked her lips and glanced around. The area was infused with Alexandru's aura. The oak trees, the meadow, the babbling brook in the distance, even the animals and people around them all suddenly seemed to shimmer in gold. A whispered chant arose from the followers, like the low hum of insects, becoming steadily louder. Faith sensed that they were scared.

You've angered him, you've angered him, you've angered him.

"I—" She was about to protest her innocence. She'd done nothing, after all, except sit and listen to Alexandru talk. But even before she could speak she realized they were right. His lips were twisted in an angry grimace, brows furrowed, hands balled into fists. He shook with emotion, making the colors all around them deeper and more vibrant. Yet suddenly Faith realized they were wrong, all of them, because it wasn't anger that was fueling Alexandru. It was desire.

She could smell his arousal, flowing from his body toward hers like the heady musk from an animal in heat. The force of his lust consumed him, the passion so strong it was mistaken for anger. He held himself from her but she sensed, she *knew*, that he was on the brink of losing control and allowing his powerful emotion to take over and consume them both.

She made her voice soft, to soothe the wild beast. "What do you mean, I'm your queen? Talk to me. Help understand."

His words were coated with lust. "I have searched for you, Faith Luna. For thousands of years. And at last, I have found you."

"Yes," she agreed, not knowing what he meant but understanding that she needed to keep him talking. Bit by bit, the intense colors surrounding him started to fade.

"I am the ancient one. Alexandru. And you belong to me."

At this the followers released a collective sigh, as if the dangerous grip of his fevered emotion had begun to loosen, allowing them to breathe. Faith turned back to face Alexandru, irritation zinging through her blood.

"I belong to *no one*," she snapped. "And what you say makes no sense. How could you have been searching for me for thousands of years? I'm mortal. I've only been around a short time."

He chuckled, a deep baritone rumbling in his chest, devoid of humor. Cold fear traced a finger down her spine. Had she inadvertently angered him?

"That is why my journey was long," he said quietly, almost wistfully. "I searched for something that did not yet exist." He leaned forward and grasped Faith's hands in his while piercing her with his stare. "But now you do," he said. "At last."

His eyes blazed like the sun as his gaze burned into hers. She wanted to recoil from it, to turn away from the intensity, but found she could not. Once more he'd hypnotized her, although this time it wasn't only through the beauty of his intent look but the spell of his touch. His skin was as soft and beautifully smooth as a dove's breast. The fingers which grasped hers were long and straight, his hands perfectly formed. As she looked at him, caught in the web of his gaze, a million thoughts swirled in her mind. Who was this mystical god? Why did he claim to have been searching for her? And why, oh why, was she suddenly no longer afraid but intensely, dizzyingly aroused?

Alexandru's eyes began to change color, shifting from the vivid deep brown she'd seen at first to a vibrant blue, then purple, before returning back to brown. With the tip of his tongue he licked his lips, moistening them, and Faith had a crazy thought that he meant to kiss her. Then another, even crazier thought: she wanted him to.

A touch of amusement caught the corner of one of his perfect lips. He raised an eyebrow toward her.

"I know you want this as much as I do," he murmured. He released one of her hands and slid his palm along her arm, caressing her. His breath shuddered. "To think how long I have searched for you. At last you are mine."

With that statement he broke the spell and Faith's sanity returned. She pulled back, welcoming the infusion of anger heating her blood.

"I'm not *yours*," she said, crossing her arms over her chest.

Her statement did not please him. His lips pulled back and he snarled. Once more the air seemed to swirl with debris sparked by Alexandru's emotion. This time, however, the particles were black instead of gold, and they filled the room like a cloud of locusts. Out of the corner of her eye Faith saw Alexandru's followers gasp and clutch one another, shielding themselves from his wrath. In seconds she understood why. He lifted himself from his chair, rising higher and higher until he hovered over Faith like a vulture just before it swoops in for the kill.

"Yes you are!" he growled, baring gleaming teeth. Despite wanting to be strong, Faith cowered in her chair, terror like a vice around her throat. Screaming was impossible. Not that anyone who cared would even hear it.

She watched him as he stood there, trying to anticipate what he might do next. Despite the seeming impossibility of her situation, she refused to go down without a fight. If this crazed god or whatever the hell he was wanted to harm her or worse, he was going to have to work to do it.

Swallowing her fear, she shoved her hands against the arm rests of the chair and pushed herself up so she stood right before him. He towered above her, his height like a mountain casting her in his shadow. She tilted her head back and looked up, meeting him eye-to-eye. Her heartbeat slammed in her chest as her eardrums roared with the rush of her blood. She wiped slick palms against her jeans and balled her hands into fists, giving her strength.

"Now you listen to me," she hissed, giving him a taste of his own medicine. "I want out of here — *now!* And let Dana go, too. I know you've done something with her." She stepped forward, anger fueling her courage. Her body trembled as rage built. She welcomed it. She refused to keep cowering before this asshole, having him act like he owned her. Screw that. He may be beautiful and sexy as hell but no one, no matter how hot, claimed her as his without her say so.

"Did you hear me?!" Scalding hot fury boiled her blood. She lifted her hands, palms up, and shoved against his chest as hard as she could. It felt like driving her fists into a wall. Despite the force of her shove, Alexandru didn't budge, not an inch. It was as though he were cemented to the ground. Faith was incensed, crying out in frustration.

"Damn you!" She shoved again, over and over, but it was like trying to move a mountain. Around and behind her she could hear his disciples gasp. They probably knew something she didn't, but Faith didn't care. She was so enraged she could no longer see straight. Rational thought was a thing of the past. All she operated on right now was pure emotion — raw anger more powerful than the most lethal narcotic. She screamed in outrage, the sounds echoing through the abandoned hospital like the cries of patients from long ago.

"Stop!" Alexandru bellowed, but still she went on.

"Fuck you!" She'd stopped shoving and now simply pummeled, balling her hands into fists and pounding at his chest. "Tell me where Dana is! I want my friend and I want to leave. I'm not your queen, I'm not anybody's queen, I'm just—"

The crash of his lips against hers silenced her screams. His powerful arms, like iron bars around her body, stilled her fists. His kiss matched her fury as he ground his mouth on hers and plunged his tongue into the moist depths. She initially tried pulling away, furious at his arrogance, but seconds later desire roared to life as an atomic explosion of need surged through her veins. Her breasts ached and her nipples tightened and strained against her blouse, begging for his touch. She was engulfed in a wall of fire, heat as scorching as the sun enflaming her senses as her pussy throbbed and grew damp. She rocked her hips forward and teased the huge bulge of his cock, easily felt through his robe. He groaned and pulled away from her lips to feast on her neck.

She let her head fall back, exposing her throat to him as he kissed and licked her skin. He had relaxed his unyielding grip and now slipped a hand beneath her blouse and bra to caress her breasts. She sighed, arching her back to fill his hand. In the distance she became aware of other noises around her, moans and sighs that were identical to those she'd heard earlier when she and Dana were filming. Those college kids, the ones from before. Her eyes snapped open and she looked behind her to where Alexandru's followers had been lounging on the grass. They were all still there, except now they were naked.

Scattered across the lawn were piles of discarded robes, tossed away with the impatience of illicit lovers meeting for a secret tryst. The scene before her, however, was far from secretive as couples and trios openly kissed and caressed, their passionate moans drifting lazily through the forest. It was some kind of bizarre spiritual nymph orgy. Faith's mouth fell open and she jerked away from Alexandru.

"What... what *is* this?"

"Enough!" He clapped his hands and the activity stopped at once.

"Shield yourselves," he ordered, and the nymphs scrambled to obey, donning robes in seconds. The reassembled themselves in a circle around their master, eyes shining up at him, faithful disciples eager to please.

Alexandru nodded and smiled, then invited Faith to sit back on her throne.

"In their desire for the mating ritual, my followers have gotten ahead of themselves," he chuckled.

Faith frowned. "The...*what?*"

"This is the reason we were brought together, Faith. To mate." He spoke slowly, like someone speaking a foreign language to another who struggles to understand. Faith pushed herself back in her chair, needing as much distance as possible between herself and the crazed lunatic sitting across from her.

"I'm not mating with you," she said, defiant. Yet even as she spoke the words, the sizzle of heat between them flared anew.

"Oh, but you will," he murmured, faint shimmers of gold arousal swirling about his head. Faith's gaze flicked down and saw the tent

213

beneath the robe where it draped over his thighs. She licked her lips, her breaths becoming shallow. The pull of this crazy god was undeniable. Still, she had to keep her wits about her. Summoning strength, she steered her gaze away from him.

"I know you want me, Faith," he said. "Though you try to pretend differently." He sighed, a low, heavy sigh, like that of a teacher disappointed in his pupil. Sitting back in his throne, he steepled his fingers beneath his chin and locked his gaze directly with Faith's. "Let me tell you a story," he said. "After which, if the story pleases you, the mating ceremony shall begin."

"If the story pleases me?"

"Correct. If it does not, you are free to leave."

"What about Dana?"

"I shall release her as well."

"Unharmed?"

His voice took on a sharp edge. "I already assured you, she is unharmed."

She bit her lip, considering. There had to be a catch. All she had to do was say that the story displeased her and he'd let her go? Why would it be that easy? She chanced a look around. The nymphs sat in rapt attention, their gazes still cast upward, like earth's faithful looking toward heaven. But these nymphs were no earthly beings, and they prayed to a very different God from the one she knew. Still, if she had any hope of escape, there appeared to be little choice but to go along with what he wanted.

"Fine." She shrugged. "I'm game. Tell me your story."

"Very good," Alexandru said softly. "I'm pleased you have agreed."

"Did I have a choice?"

"My mistress has claws," he responded, ignoring her comment. "I like that." He clapped his hands together and in an instant a servant appeared out of nowhere. He was strong and athletic, like an ancient Greek sculpture come to life. His hair was dark, almost black, and his skin deeply tanned. If he were an earthly being, Faith

would have guessed his age to be in the mid-twenties. As it was...
hell, who could say. He could have been a thousand years old for
all she knew. Draped in white robes like the rest of Alexandru's
followers, he held a silver platter in his hands bearing two goblets
filled with dark red liquid.

"Ah, Eryx," Alex took the goblets from the servant, setting them
on a table beside him. "Thank you, my love." Eryx smiled and bent
forward, leaning in to Alexandru. The god looked up, locking gazes
with the younger man before giving him the barest of nods, as
if granting permission. Slowly the servant lifted a hand to touch
his fingertips softly, almost reverently, against Alexandru's face. He
slid his other hand through the god's hair as he closed the gap
between them, bending down to sweep his tongue over the god's
lips before eagerly plunging into his open mouth.

Alexandru circled his arms about Eryx's waist and guided him
forward to sit beside him on the massive throne. Once the servant
was settled, he lifted his hands and slipped them gently, worship-
fully, beneath Alexandru's robe. Seconds later the god broke the
kiss and cried out, a low, husky moan drenched in passion. He
bucked his hips, gyrating against Eryx's ministrations. The servant
dipped his head and ran his tongue along Alexandru's throat,
leaving a trail of moisture in its wake. Then he kissed the god
on the mouth once more, long and deep, as he and Alexandru
groaned in ecstasy.

Faith watched the duo, almost feeling as if she were invading a
private moment but unable to look away, helplessly aroused. Out
of the corner of her eye she spotted some of the nymphs locked
together in their own passionate embrace. She couldn't deny the
hypnotic pull of the erotic scene before her, shifting in her chair
as she watched the two men. Her pussy throbbed, begging for
touch. A sudden, powerful urge to give herself relief flooded her
body but she resisted, telling herself it was all Alexandru's doing.
He'd put her under some kind of spell and she needed to, *had to*,
resist it. She would not be a puppet to this crazy god, allowing

him freedom to do as he wished. With iron will she gripped the sides of her throne, ignoring the pulsating ache between her thighs.

Eryx slipped down the throne to kneel before Alexandru. One hand remained beneath the god's robe but with the other Eryx drew aside the robe from one of Alexandru's legs, exposing a smooth, powerful thigh bulging with muscle. The servant began kissing Alex's leg, starting low, his mouth voyaging over the side of the calf, up over the knee and then along the thigh, all the while his hand continued its work beneath the god's robe.

Alexandru groaned loudly and Faith looked up, straight into his deep brown eyes, although now they were coated black with lust. *He likes me watching him.* Alexandru nodded, a coy smile playing about his lips.

"Yes I do," he whispered in a ragged voice, reading her thoughts. "And as much as I love my dear Eryx, I would prefer you in his place." His breaths were quick, shallow, as the servant continued lavishing attention on him. Alexandru refused to break eye contact with Faith, drawing her into his lust-filled world through the power of his gaze.

"Join me, Faith," he urged, gasping as his arousal grew. She shook her head, barely able to resist him but knowing she must. Despite the enticing scene before her and the hypnotic pull to do as he asked, a small part of her instinctively knew escape would be impossible should she allow herself to be sucked into his world. She bit down on her lip, tasting blood, and allowed the pain to distract her so she could pull away her gaze.

Alexandru's curse vibrated throughout the room. "Away!" he shouted, and as Faith looked back over she saw Eryx rise and scamper off. The god readjusted his robes. His eyes shot sparks at her and his skin was flushed. Despite her determination to stand up to him, she couldn't stop the tremors coursing through her body, as if she'd been shocked by a lightning bolt. Her eyes grew wide as he approached her throne, his great height making her feel like a mouse in a hawk's shadow. But then, to her great

216

surprise, as she braced herself for the onslaught of Alexandru's fury, instead the god's mouth fell open and out came a great bellowing howl of laughter.

All around her the laughter increased, voices joining in and growing louder, like the chorus in a sympathy. It echoed off the trees, rolling across the meadow, and Faith could see the nymphs shriek, holding themselves as they shook with mirth. She had no idea what was so funny but couldn't deny she preferred that over Alexandru's bone-shaking anger.

When at last he brought himself under control, he looked upon her with what could only be described as pure adoration shining in his eyes. "My queen," he said, extending his hand out to her, "I laugh from sheer joy. My happiness at finding you knows no limitations. Come join me for a walk and I shall tell you my story."

Faith shook her head, wary of being led away. "Just tell me the story here," she said, determined to keep her voice from trembling. "I don't want to go anywhere."

"You don't trust me?"

"Why should I?" She frowned, angered by his arrogance. "You've taken my friend, you've turned a hospital into a forest, you claim to be not of this world and you've got an army of nymphs who'll do anything you command. We humans are taught from a young age not to trust strangers so I'll stay right here, thank you very much."

"Rise." Ignoring her, Alexandru held out his arms like a conductor signaling for the music to begin. With slow but deliberate purpose he swept his arms upward and, in spite of every ounce of resistance within her, Faith began to rise. Her body lifted from the chair as if pulled by invisible strings. She felt the ground beneath her feet, yet the strides she took seemed to serve no purpose. Rather than walking toward Alexandru it seemed as if she were being transported, like being on one of those moving walkways in an airport terminal. Whether she took steps or stood still, in the end she was nonetheless brought before the god.

He smiled with satisfaction, reaching out his hand to take hers.

Once more his touch sparked desire and she wondered again if he'd cast her under a spell. The urge to resist him waned, then disappeared. She was a sleepwalker in a trance, unable to pull away. "We shall walk," he said, softly this time, and Faith could do nothing but follow, helpless as a lamb being led to slaughter.

They descended the stairs onto the soft meadow grass. The nymphs parted to allow their passage like the Red Sea before Moses. Alexandru guided her through the trees and toward the crystal stream. Casting his gaze before the sight, he murmured, "How I love water."

"So do I," Faith agreed. "I always have."

"Of course you do."

His cryptic talk unnerved her. "What do you mean? How would you know?"

"The story first," he said, waving a scolding finger. "Then it shall all make sense."

She sighed with impatience, although another side of her was excited, like a child at a party awaiting gifts. Inexplicable as it seemed, Faith felt that she was about to receive answers to things in her life she'd always wondered about.

They reached a fallen log alongside the stream and it was here where Alexandru led her. They sat side by side, shifting positions so they could face one another. The god smiled and snapped his fingers. Eryx appeared once more holding the wine he'd brought earlier. This time he did nothing more than hand each one of them a glass before slipping silently away.

Alexandru tilted his glass toward Faith "*Noroc.* That is what we say in the language of my old country. I believe here you say 'cheers'."

"Cheers," Faith replied, though she refrained from drinking. Could be a glass full of poison for all she knew.

"It's not poison." Alexandru drank deeply, emptying the glass. He signaled for more and the chalice was refilled at once by the ever-attentive Eryx.

Faith frowned. "I don't like you reading my thoughts."

"I can't always, my queen. You are exquisite at shielding them, most of the time. But every so often an unguarded one slips through." He took another drink of the wine. "I think it happens when you are nervous. Your control weakens."

She tucked that bit of information in the back of her mind, silently celebrating the fact that she'd just been given an essential tip for getting out of here. *Stay calm and carry on. Oh, and don't let crazy gods read your mind.*

Her gaze slid sideways to study Alexandru while he drank more wine. His robes did little to mask the sculpted body beneath, his steely muscles bulging defiantly against the draped cloth. Strong fingers lightly grasped his ever-present chalice. As she watched him she noticed a strand of ivy hanging around his neck, curiously reminding her of the titanium rope necklaces often worn by baseball players. It was said to give them energy, she recalled, wondering if ivy did the same thing for Alexandru.

All at once, as she idly sat waiting for the god's story to begin, clarity struck with near violent force as she realized who he was. It had all been right in front of her, the answer there for the taking, but until now she hadn't seen it. Her mouth dropped open in an astonished "o" and she let out a small gasp, pushing her hands against the log as she jumped up and stepped back.

"You're…you're…"

"It took you long enough, my queen."

"I'm not your queen, *Dionysus*," she hissed, jaw clenched tight.

"Or Bacchus," he calmly replied, "depending upon whether you favor the Greeks or the Romans."

The picture rapidly came into view, like a mirror cleared of steam. Suddenly Faith understood everything: the nymphs, the wine, the ecstatic atmosphere surrounding her. She thought back to what she knew of mythology. Dionysus' father was Zeus. He was the last god to be accepted into Mt. Olympus and the only one to have a mortal mother. He was worshipped for being the god of winemaking, harvest, madness. And ecstasy. At that last thought she was scorched by a heat wave, infusing her body with a heady rush of desire. And once more, like a drug, Alexandru's irresistible pull intoxicated her senses.

No, she reminded herself. *Not Alexandru. Dionysus.*

"Why did you lie to me?" she asked, ignoring the ache of her sensitive nipples as they strained against her blouse.

"A small test," he shrugged, waving a hand in the air as if to brush away a fly. "I needed to see if you would figure it out on your own."

"And I did." The heavy pulses between her legs had slowed but still she didn't trust herself to be near him. She remembered her body's reaction when he had first touched her. And then kissed her. Knowing he was the god of ecstasy reminded her to keep her distance.

"Now tell me the story so I can leave."

"If the story displeases you," he reminded her. "But only then." He patted the empty place beside him. "Come back here, Faith. I need you next to me."

She shook her head. "No. I'll stay here."

His dark eyes blazed into hers. "You know I can force you."

A sizzle of anger ripped through her veins. She gritted her teeth. "Why even bother with your story, then? If you can make me do whatever you want, why not just go ahead? Screw your pretense of a story and acting as if I have a choice." Her body shook as her fury grew, like a tornado gathering energy as it roared across the plains. She wanted to lash out at him, to yell and scream and pound him with her fists. But she remembered what happened the last time she'd beat at him. Her mortal strength was no match for a god.

"It doesn't work that way," Alexandru replied evenly. Faith could tell by the twitching muscle at the back of his jaw that she'd angered him, but for the moment he kept his cool. Still, the swirl of black in his eyes teemed with foreboding. She needed to get herself under control if she had any chance of getting out of there alive.

With trepidation she stepped back over to the log and sat down, keeping a safe distance between them.

"Fine," she said. "Tell me the story."

He released a slow breath and then drank deeply from his chalice, emptying the silver cup. He set it down on the ground beside his feet and turned his attention to Faith.

"You know who my father is," he began, "and I assume my mother as well?"

"Semele," Faith confirmed. "You rescued her, did you not?"

"Yes. From Hades. And forevermore my mother presides over my frenzies as we celebrate freedom. Her freedom and the freedom of all who have been imprisoned." He shifted his body, turning to face her more directly. "That is why I am god of madness," he said, his words laced with conviction. "Madness imprisons the mind and denies it the freedom we all desperately desire."

Faith's eyes unexpectedly filled as she thought back to her beloved Nana, locked away for her "madness." She'd lost her physical freedom, but Faith realized that the undiagnosed mental illness had cost her grandmother emotional and psychological freedom as well.

She swallowed against the lump in her throat. "The "frenzies" you mentioned," she said, her voice halting. "Are you talking about the bacchanalia?"

The god smiled. "It is what others have called them. But yes, the bacchanalia I am known for are nothing less than a celebration of freedom, a way to cast off fears and restraints."

"But how does this all apply to me? I still don't understand."

"Soon you shall, my queen. Very soon." His soothing voice drew her back into his web, and without his urging she moved closer, his body heat flowing into her like steam from a sauna.

"Many years ago, when I was young and foolish, I lusted after a beautiful, powerful goddess. She consumed my every thought and my desire was unquenchable. I burned for her." He chuckled at his last sentence, but Faith scarcely noticed. Irrational though it was, she struggled against the great roaring beast of jealousy that howled within her as Alexandru spoke of his lust for someone else. She balled her hands into fists, driving her nails into the soft fleshy part of her palm in an effort to banish the monster. At last, in a tight voice, she said, "I don't understand why this is amusing."

The god reached a hand out toward her and lightly traced a finger along her thigh. Even through her jeans, her skin tingled where he touched, the energy like an electrical current. "Because the goddess I burned for was Vesta."

Despite her jealousy, Faith smiled. Vesta, goddess of the flame. She now understood his humor, that he burned for the goddess of the flame.

"But..." She frowned, remembering something else about mythology. "Wasn't she a virgin?"

"Alas, yes. In spite of my best efforts."

"What happened?"

"I pursued her for years, stealing kisses whenever I could but never more than that. She absolutely forbade it. Finally I grew weary of her denials and turned my attention to others. I thought Vesta would be relieved that I no longer chased her, but I was wrong."

His earlier humor gone, Alexandru frowned at an invisible speck of lint on his robe and with quick flicks of his wrist brushed it away. "*Very* wrong. Vesta still wanted my undivided attention and she was furious when she realized that my interest in her was gone." He expelled a deep breath. "In her fury, she vowed revenge."

"Revenge? How?"

He leaned down for his chalice, expelling a snort of annoyance when he remembered it was empty. He snapped his fingers for Eryx. "Join me," he invited Faith as the servant appeared to fill the cup. "As I told you, it's not poison."

Faith's cup, still full, was at her feet. Leaning down to retrieve it, she decided she may as well. Alexandru had consumed enough wine to down an elephant, yet remained alert and lucid. To be fair, she hadn't exactly been schooled on alcohol tolerance levels for gods. But instinctively she knew he wasn't out to poison her. She lifted her cup and tilted it toward him.

"*Noroc.*"

He smiled. "*Noroc.*"

They drank deeply. It was, without question, the best wine Faith had ever tasted. She nodded toward Eryx to top off her glass.

Once the servant had departed, Alex resumed his story. "Vesta vowed to destroy any lover I take with an arrow of flame." His eyes filled with sorrow. "And Vesta is a goddess who keeps her promises. As I have found out the hard way."

Fear as cold and dark as a python slithered down Faith's spine. "But you want to mate with me," she whispered, her heels digging into the ground to get herself away from him. She wanted to take off, to run screaming through the unreal forest he'd led her into and not stop until somehow she figured a way out of the madness. But she knew she couldn't. He'd pull her right back before she even started.

"That's just it," Alexandru replied, jerking Faith's attention back toward him. "Vesta's revenge cannot reach this world. I've discovered it's the one and only way I can break her curse and the torture she's cast me into. I need to find my mortal queen, hold a ceremonial mating ritual with her, and the spell will be broken. It is why I have searched for you for so long, Faith. The spell won't be broken with just any mortal. It must be the one to whom I am destined. My queen. It's the only way."

Fine hairs on the back of Faith's neck prickled, and a boulder settled in the pit of her stomach. Something told her that wasn't quite all of the story.

"But what happens —" She cleared her parched throat and swallowed a lump of fear. "What happens to your mortal queen?"

"Well…" He glanced away.

"Even though you'd be free, the mortal still dies, just as Vesta vowed. Isn't that right?"

He let out a soft breath. "Yes."

Without a second thought, Faith bolted. Consumed with blind panic, her feet flew across the forest floor, arms pumping as she raced. "Dana!" Her friend's name ripped from her throat, hoping against hope that somehow Dana would hear her cries and they'd find each other and figure out an escape. Branches scratched and clawed her arms, painting them red with angry streaks of blood. Still she ran, amazed that she hadn't reached the end of the forest. Its infinite length taunted her, as if she could run forever and never reach the end.

Her head whipped around, fueled by desperate hope that she'd spot something familiar to guide her way out. A path she thought she'd seen before was her best hope and she raced toward it, her labored breaths wheezing as she struggled to get away. She'd hardly run more than a few frantic steps toward the path when suddenly her feet snagged a thick tree root and she flew forward, crying out as the ground rushed up to meet her. Slamming down hard, the air whooshed from her lungs. Her heart thudded within her chest and she gulped air, yet still she scrambled to push herself up and keep on running. Her eyes darted around, frantically seeking a way out, but in that very second, hope died. Blocking her way like a great concrete pylon stood Alexandru, his face dark as murder.

"Get up, Faith." Not bothering to help her, he merely stepped back to give her room. She stood, the earlier fear gone, likely depleted by her mad run. Ironic, that. She'd tried to get free from the very god who claimed to celebrate freedom.

With a quick glance, she realized she'd somehow ended up back at the very place from which she'd fled. All that running had gotten her nowhere. Alexandru sat, saying nothing for a few moments but nodding at the empty place beside him, indicating he wanted her to take it. Recognizing the futility of arguing, Faith sat.

The look on his face remained dark. He drank wine and breathed deeply, collecting himself. At last, he spoke.

"Do you really think," he began, his voice low, "that I would propose death to someone I have repeatedly referred to as 'my queen'?"

"How the hell should I know?" she snapped, anger taking hold. "If I'm threatened with death, it seems like a good idea to try getting away."

"What I'm proposing wouldn't bring you death, but rather, eternal life."

A collective cheer rose up and Faith whipped her head around. She realized they were once more surrounded by Alexandru's nymphs and that she and he were back on their thrones atop the dais.

"How did we...how did you...?"

"A simple transport." Alex shrugged. "I wanted to be back here, among my people."

In the distance, music began, the whispery tone of a pan flute so light and beautiful it seemed to shimmer in the air.

"Behold my vision for you," he continued, drawing Faith's attention back to him. "Forever more you shall have all the resources you need for your films. Money, people, time, ideas. Nothing will stand in your way. I will provide you with riches beyond your wildest dreams to do with as you wish. Success is within your grasp."

He smiled as he spoke, revealing white, even teeth, and she was reminded of the god's striking masculine beauty. His face was a model of perfection; his body nothing short of miraculous. As she studied him, he shifted in his chair. A section of his robe slipped down his arm revealing a tanned bicep rippling with muscle and lightly covered with golden hair. He lounged on his throne like a lion, relaxed and powerful. As he spoke, golden sunshine filtered through the trees and into the meadow, casting its glow onto Alexandru. He looked in every way an exquisite, immortal god. And she was the one he wanted for his queen.

"All you need do," he finished, "is mate with me and everything you desire shall be yours."

225

Faith emitted a decidedly unqueen-like snort. She couldn't deny the thrill skating through her at the thought of never having to struggle again for funds for her projects. At the same time, she remembered the well-worn phrase: if something seems too good to be true, it probably is. The words, like a ping pong ball, bounced maddeningly in her head.

"You said you'd be free if you mate with a mortal, yet the mortal would die. At the same time you offer eternal life. How can that be?"

He straightened in his chair, facing her straight on as he penetrated her soul with his dark piercing eyes. "Your mortal life would die," he said softly. "As your eternal one begins."

She sat, unmoving, riveted in her chair as if actually bolted in place. Yet her heart raced wildly, thundering in her chest. Eternal life? Like a vampire?

"Not a vampire." He shook his head. "A goddess. *My* goddess."

"But — " She cleared her dry throat. "You said I could make my films. How could that be? If I'm imm...imm..." The word refused to come.

"Immortal?" Alexandru finished for her. "Why, that's the beauty of it all, Faith." He chuckled. "You could walk the earth if you wish. Live among the mortal beings. There's nothing preventing you from doing so."

She frowned. "Is that the same for all, um, gods?"

"It is."

"Then why —"

"Why don't we? Is that what you want to know?" Not waiting for her response, he shrugged one sculpted shoulder, causing the robe to slip off. Faith's breath caught in her throat.

"You'll be the one to decide what you want to do, my queen. But you see, in short order the urge to resume your former life grows weary. Mortal creatures live short lives. They get sick, they die, and then what becomes of you? Sooner or later people notice you're not aging and it forces you to move on, endlessly searching for new places to go and new people to meet, slipping out of their lives when it's no longer feasible to live among them." He breathed deeply, as if the very thought of it exhausted him.

"But if I wanted to do that," Faith pressed, "to live among mortals, in spite of what you say…?"

"You could do so."

His words laid before her a treasure chest of possibilities. Financial problems washed away, more new equipment than the biggest of Hollywood blockbuster budgets. Most of all, time. An endless, insurmountable sea of time, complete with an ending that did not exist. A heady sense of purpose lifted her spirit, making her long to rush out the door and begin new projects at once. Of course, it wasn't that simple. The admission price of immortality was steep. Prickles of apprehension knotted her stomach.

She lifted her eyes to meet Alex's gaze. "Why me?" she whispered. "Why did you choose me?"

"*I* didn't." He slowly shook his head, a wry smile playing about his lips. "The universe did."

"What do you mean?"

He leaned forward in his chair, his gaze burning into hers. "There are no coincidences, don't you know that? We're meant to be together, Faith. Everything in your life tells you so; all you have to do is look."

Behind her, the nymphs giggled, as if they knew the punchline of a joke to which she wasn't privy. She frowned.

"I don't know —"

"Yes you do." Alex's lips hadn't moved, yet she heard his honey smooth voice echoing in her mind as clearly as if he'd spoken aloud his words. "*Think*, Faith. About your life, and everything that's happened in it thus far. Think of your grandmother. Of yourself."

Despite not fully understanding what he meant, she sat back and did her best to follow his instructions. Visions of her child-hood swam before her eyes. Her parents, where she lived, her friends. Yet nothing she recalled from the past brought clarity to the unreal situation she faced right now, sitting before a god, in an abandoned psychiatric facility cum forest, with a promise of immortality weighing on her mind.

Think, Faith. Alexandru's words floated through the air like delicate strands of cottonwood. She let her eyelids drift closed, imagining herself slipping into a fragrant hot bath, the aroma infusing her with calm. Suddenly small remembrances of her past took on deeper significance, and understanding became crystal clear. Her grandmother's mental struggles, Faith's outrage over how Nana had been mistreated. Her determination to show the world. Even her own name factored into the equation. Faith Luna - moon faith. She'd always felt oddly exuberant every month during the full moon. Now, all at once, she understood why, as if a curtain in her mind had at last been drawn back to reveal long buried secrets.

Faith worshipped not just this world, but the larger one beyond. She fought against madness, celebrating freedom with near reckless fervor. Becoming Alexandru's — no, *Dionysus's*— queen. Suddenly it all made perfect sense. Becoming his queen was her destiny.

She looked up at him, seeing the god with new eyes, a strong sense of fate penetrating her soul. Her one-word response to his question was all that was left to say. "Yes."

A collective sigh from the nymphs rose throughout the forest. The air shifted, becoming heavy and sultry, infused with erotic heat. Dionysus pinned her with his stare, his eyes coal black with desire.

"You are certain?"

She nodded, suddenly so aroused that speech became impossible. She could only think, and feel. An overwhelming urge to join with the god and become one seized hold. Desire as she'd never before known surged like a tidal wave in her blood. Her body trembled, her hands shaking where they lay atop the armrests of her throne.

Dionysus rose and walked toward her. A glittery glow radiated from his body and Faith knew it was from the force of his arousal. He held out his hand and she grasped it, desperate for his touch.

She rose and stood before her god.

"My beautiful queen," he murmured, looking at her through heavily lidded eyes turned black with desire. "I worship you."

"And I, you."

"Come." He led her toward the stairs leading down from the dais. "Let us mate."

A rush of moisture flooded her panties. On trembling legs she descended the few stairs. Her tight nipples brushed her blouse; her pulse raced. Looking around, she noticed that the nymphs were similarly affected as she by the sensual atmosphere invading the forest. Couples, trios, even larger groups kissed and touched one another, peeling away clothing, lips and tongues sliding sensuously along naked skin. The air was heavy with sighs and groans. Those nymphs not yet caught up in the sexual feast danced about the meadow, laughing and playing instruments, gorging themselves on food and wine.

A short distance away, in the midst of a clearing yet surrounded by soaring pines, stood an enormous, ceremonial bed. It was enveloped on each side by translucent, gauzy curtains, like the veil of a bride. It was the largest bed Faith had ever seen, looking as if six people lying side by side could be comfortably atop it. Placed at the headrest were dozens of white plush pillows, like a mound of fluffy clouds. As they approached the bed their steps were muffled by millions of soft pine needles cushioning the ground beneath their feet. The bed itself was perched on a raised dais, elevated like a stage so onlookers below would have a clear, unobstructed view. Faith froze in her tracks as she realized what it meant.

"No, wait." Her firm voice stopped Dionysus. He turned lustful eyes upon her.

"I'd rather not."

"But…are we, um, mating *here*? In the middle of this clearing where anyone can see?"

A bemused look crossed his face. "Of course, my queen. Where else?"

"I had in mind someplace more secluded."

"Whatever for?" He chuckled at her seemingly trivial need for privacy. "Important ceremonies are always witnessed, are they not? A wedding, a baptism, the celebration of a notable achievement?"

"Well, sure, but —"

"Why would the crowning of a queen, *my* queen, be any different?" He tugged on her hand, leading her forward once more. "My nymphs have been awaiting this moment for thousands of years. This will be a bacchanalia for the ages. Of *course* there will be witnesses, hundreds of witnesses. No one would miss the lustful initiation of this moment."

Hearing the excitement and sultriness coating his words, Faith's initial resistance began to transform into deep, carnal desire. Slow, steady pulses throbbed low in her pussy. Her breasts swelled, aching for the warm, wet attention of his mouth and tongue. Suddenly she longed to be rid of her clothes, to live in the forest like a mystical fairy as her king and lover Dionysus ravished her. Perhaps she was an exhibitionist after all.

They climbed the few steps to the dais upon which the bed was perched, but instead of climbing atop it, Dionysus turned to face the crowd of nymphs who had gathered around them, like a politician about to make a speech. For a moment the music and all activity fell silent, even the birds and animals made no sound.

"Behold the woman who will be your queen," Dionysus said to the crowd, spurring excited gasps and whispers. The atmosphere tingled with anticipation, like in an enormous arena at the start of a sporting event. Faith saw the nymphs press forward, craning their necks for as close a look as possible at the ceremonial bed. *Where I'm about to transform my life.* She released a breath, trying futilely to calm her racing pulse.

Dionysus turned to her, his eyes sparkling with lust. "I will now disrobe you," he said in a low voice. "You must walked naked in one complete circle around the bed so that everyone will get a good look at their queen."

Unexpected heat warmed her cheeks, but at the same time she tingled with excitement. There was no judgment here; she was not on trial. It was, instead, a celebration of freedom. And of love. Even as the thought filtered through her mind she knew it to be true. It was inexplicable but nonetheless without dispute. She was destined to be with this god, with Dionysus. She was destined to be his queen for time immemorial, and to love him as he would love her. Her gaze sought his and she knew from the burn of desire she saw that he'd read her thoughts. But this time, she was only too happy to have them shared.

"Beautiful, Faith," he murmured, leaning in to breathe deeply of her scent as his fingers worked the tiny buttons down the front of her blouse. Her heart pounded so wildly in her ribcage she was certain he must have felt it. For a moment she closed her eyes, wanting only to experience this moment through his touch, her breath catching in her throat as his fingers brushed her burning skin.

Cool air surrounded her as Dionysus whisked away the cotton fabric. Faith opened her eyes once more. Hundreds of heated gazes were traveling along her bare arms and stomach and nodding with wanton approval. Dionysus reached behind her, for one swift moment sheltering her breasts as he removed her bra. But then, as the clasp was undone, he drew away the garment and stepped to the side so that Faith was unobstructed.

The sultry atmosphere skyrocketed as she stood bare breasted before the admiring crowd. Some of the nymphs had resumed leisurely fondling their partners as they watched Faith's disrobing. It was the most bizarre strip show she could ever have imagined. Instead of being looked upon by creepy losers in a dark smoky club, her audience was a fantastical gathering of otherworldly sprites and fey who awaiting her coupling with a mythical god. Not exactly how she'd envisioned her day when she got out of bed that morning. She smiled at the thought, but then gasped as Dionysus unbuttoned her jeans and pulled down the zipper.

"Step out of your shoes," he instructed, and she easily kicked off her flats. The dais was cool to her feet, but she gave little thought to that as Dionysus' hands brushed her legs as he peeled off her jeans. He held her steady as she stepped out of one pant leg and then the other. All that remained was her panties. Wasting no time, he kneeled before her so that his head was level with her stomach. Leaning forward, he pressed gentle kisses against her skin as he hooked his thumbs around the delicate silk material and slowly slid them off.

Dionysus rose and stepped away, leaving Faith standing naked before the admiring crowd. *Ooooh* she heard them gasp, and she couldn't prevent the smile the touched her lips. They made her feel like a proud, beautiful goddess.

"Walk," Dionysus reminded her, and like a model on a runway Faith made her way around the bed. She took her time, letting the nymphs get a full look at her as she sensed it was exactly what they wanted. Some of them, in fact, bowed low as she passed by, already showing obeisance to their queen.

As she reached the other side where Dionysus awaited, she noticed his dark, lustful gaze as she strode toward him. He was still fully clothed and a surge of longing for him to be as naked as she engulfed her like a wave. She slowed as she approached, swaying her hips to entice him. He reached for her when she neared, but she purposely stayed just beyond his outstretched hand.

"It's your turn, my king," she said softly. "Strip for me."

He drew in a sharp breath at her seductive words, but they served their desired effect. Never breaking eye contact, Dionysus began removing his robes. With one hand he reached to his shoulder and unclasped the jewel-encrusted fastening that held the garment together. Folds of draped material slid down his torso, revealing the most perfect man Faith had ever laid eyes on. She took her gaze on an erotic journey, traveling over wide, powerful shoulders and rock hard pecs before moving down along the ladder of sculpted abdominal muscles. She sucked in a breath.

"Like what you see?"

She shrugged, biting her lip. "Maybe."

"*Maybe?*" His eyes widened. "You don't know?"

"I need to see more. To be certain."

Her words brought a smile to his lips. "Then of course, my queen," he murmured. "Let me honor your most noble request."

He undid the belt at his waist and the rest of the garment dropped to the floor, giving Faith a clear view of everything her god and lover had to offer. It was, she decided, a bounteous feast. He was built like a stallion, rippling with steely muscle. His thighs were cut like marble, as were his calves, looking as if he could bench press a house. But in spite of the glory on display before her, Faith's gaze was riveted to his thick, aroused cock.

"For you," he murmured, noting the path of her vision. He turned toward the bed and with one hand lifted aside the gauze curtain.

"Come," he nodded to Faith. "Let us begin."

It seemed almost off-putting to be so official about the proceedings, but once Faith climbed into bed, Dionysus ensured that her world exploded in a dance of carnal lust.

They knelt on the bed facing each other. Though he towered above her even while kneeling, Dionysus brought his hands to either side of her face, softly caressing her skin as he leaned down to capture her lips. His kiss was at first gentle as rain, a tantalizing sample of the passion that he held, for the moment, in check. With the tip of his tongue he gently swept her lips, painting them with moisture. He probed at the slight gap where they parted, requesting admittance. Faith sighed, opening her mouth wider, and felt the sensual slide of Dionysus' tongue against hers.

His hands slipped down to caress her shoulders and then along her arms. Goosebumps dimpled her skin at his gentle, erotic touch. Still kneeling before each other, Dionysus slid his hands between their bodies and skated the tips of his fingers over her aching breasts. She shivered and moaned, pressing herself against his hands. With his thumb and forefinger he lightly pinched her nipples, causing her to gasp. All around her, she heard echoes of the same, a seductive reminder that they were not alone.

As Dionysus continued caressing her breasts, she turned her head to look across at the gathered crowd of followers. Every eye was upon them, gazes unwavering. Many were idly fondling others as they watched, but they kept their worshipful focus unblinkingly aimed at Faith and her lover god. At that moment, he, too, looked out at the crowd.

"Watch as I take your queen," he told them, eliciting a sultry moan from the nymphs. Then he returned his focus to Faith. He circled one hand behind her head and brought her lips toward him, his touch no longer gentle. He ground his mouth against hers, branding her with the heat of his kiss. His tongue plunged between her parted lips, roughly possessing her. He was on fire, letting his followers know whom he claimed as queen. The roar of blood whooshed in Faith's ears as her heartbeat raced. She moaned into his mouth, feeling a gush of wetness slicken her thighs. Dionysus slid his hand between them.

"Wider," he growled. Excited by his forceful command, she granted his wish and spread her knees farther apart. As soon as she did so, Dionysus slid his hand between her parted thighs and sank two fingers deep into her pussy.

"Ah!" She cried out, breaking away from his kiss. For a moment she opened her eyes, enough to see the nymphs getting more aroused with each passing second. Many of them now had their clothes at least partially off, yet despite their eagerness for one another, they were more eager still to witness the consummation of their queen.

Dionysus ground his fingers against her, thrusting deeply. As he did so he made certain that his palm slapped repeatedly at her clit. She cried out, knees trembling as her orgasm built. In the distance she heard the nymph's low moans, as if they, too, shared her pleasure. Her hips swayed against Dionysus hand's and he responded by adding a third finger and stretching her wide. He swirled his tongue around her stiff, aching nipple before sucking it slowly between his lips. Faith wove her fingers through his silky hair as he did so, bringing his mouth more firmly against her breast.

"More," she gasped, letting her head fall back as she ground against him. She no longer cared who saw her, she was about to explode. Suddenly she felt a new invasion, as Dionysus' other hand roamed across her ass and then parted her cheeks, slipping just the tip of one finger inside.

She shattered, screaming out her release as wave after torrential wave of pleasure engulfed her. Riding out the throbbing pulses, she clung to Dionysus as if he were a lifeline amidst the violent storm of her climax. When at last the shudders calmed, Dionysus shifted position on the bed, guiding her down so she lay propped, half sitting, against the mountain of pillows. He knelt beside her, spreading tender kisses everywhere as she brought her breathing under control. Yet all the while he kept her aroused, teasing and pinching her still-swollen nipples.

"You're beautiful when you come," he murmured against her lips. "I want to see that again."

"Not yet," she replied, pushing against his chest. "First your people must see their king's pleasure."

She reached between their bodies to fist his cock. With her finger she spread the warm drop of pre-cum all around the thick head, moistening him. Then she commanded him the same way he'd done to her.

"Rise." Immediately he understood what she wanted. Going up on his knees, he moved toward Faith, grasping the headboard while positioning himself right before her eager lips. She slid the palms of her hands along his thighs, caressing the bulging muscle and sinewy flesh before bending forward to take his stiff cock into her warm, willing mouth.

He cried out as she took him, thrusting both hands into her hair to guide her head. She used her tongue to stroke his thick length while with one hand she caressed and cradled his balls, pleased by his low groan. Instinctively she knew what he liked, as if they had mated many times before. Perhaps, as she'd thought earlier, it was all tied in with her destiny.

He picked up a rhythm, slowly pulling his cock almost completely out of her mouth before sensuously sliding back in. She relaxed her throat, taking his thick length deeper as her other hand skimmed along the tightly bunched muscles of his ass. His heady musky scent perfumed the air around them, growing sharper and more concentrated as his arousal grew. She breathed in deeply as she continued to pleasure him, wanting to draw in Dionysus' scent, to surround herself with his manly fragrance.

She pressed her hands against his ass, bringing him closer to her as he swelled within her mouth. His balls tightened and she knew he was close. She lifted her gaze and saw his carnal pleasure reflected back at her. His eyes had gone black with lust, his lips were parted as he groaned low in his throat. He kept one hand cradled against the back of her head, holding her steady as his thrusts grew quicker. She readied herself for the warm gush of his seed, but just as she thought he would find his release, he withdrew from her lips.

Rivulets of sweat trickled down the sides of his face and his chest rose and fell with his ragged breaths. He bent down and positioned himself alongside Faith on the bed.

"You are so amazing, my stunning queen, like nothing I have ever experienced."

His attention was focused back on her breasts, murmuring soft words to her as he kissed and lathed her swollen nipples. Faith cried out, her breasts so sensitive that his caresses triggered low pulses throughout her body, especially in her groin. Her hips swayed against the bed, inviting him to join her.

"Take me," she begged. "I need you inside me."

"It is time," he agreed, lifting his head. Then, to her shock, Dionysus looked out at the spectators and snapped his fingers, as if giving some type of signal. Immediately six nymphs, three women and three men, reverentially climbed the stairs and approached the bed. As soon as they'd reached it, they removed their clothing.

Faith bolted upright. "What are they doing?" She had an odd urge — considering what had just been taking place — to hold the sheet up to her breasts and shield them.

"They are the chosen witnesses," Dionysus explained.

"There aren't enough witnesses already?"

"These six are my oldest followers, some older than I. By rights it is they who confirm to the others that the consummation has taken place and that you are my queen. Therefore, they are granted special seating at the event."

The chosen nymphs smiled upon Faith with beatific radiance. Then one of the men said, "We worship you already, our queen. Your crowning is a glorious occasion and we are honored to be a part of it."

Their obvious respect for her combined with the fact that these nymphs were as naked as she made Faith's embarrassment wane. She relaxed against the pillows. Dionysus, evidently convinced that her concerns had vanished, returned his attention to Faith.

"Now," he murmured, moving down the bed to position his head between her thighs, "where were we?" His tongue swiped at her wet folds. She moaned and arched against him, immediately desperate for more of his sensual seduction. He teased, drawing out her arousal, using the tip of his tongue to stroke her pussy and then circle around her clit, causing her hips to sway against the bed.

Dionysus placed a hand on either side of her thighs, spreading her legs as wide as they would go. "See how she flows!" he called out, and as Faith opened her eyes she saw the chosen nymphs crowd closer to the foot of the bed in order to gaze with adoration upon her wet pussy. Her cheeks burned, but she was at the same time so aroused that she no longer cared who saw. She only knew that she needed her lover god inside of her.

"Fuck me now!" she commanded, losing patience for the pomp

and ceremony. The nymphs circled the bed, two of them standing on either side and the remaining two staying at the foot. Dionysus crept forward, his thick cock jutting out. She felt cool hands circle her wrists, and to her surprise Faith realized that the nymphs were holding her down. For one moment she fought against their restraint, but as she looked at Dionysus she realized this was all some weird part of the ceremony. He smiled at her, dark lust shining in his eyes, then he turned to the male nymph standing beside him.

"Ensure I am ready for my queen," he said, his gaze never leaving Faith's. As she watched, the male nymph knelt, turning his face toward Dionysus, and in one smooth motion took the entire length of the king's enormous cock into his mouth.

Dionysus cried out, consumed with obvious pleasure. With one hand he steadied the nymph's head while he thrust into his mouth. A shard of jealousy stabbed Faith at seeing someone else pleasuring her king, but at the same time she was wildly aroused. Her hips slowly gyrated upon the bed and in response the male nymph attending her slid his hand down to her clit, stroking her lightly as she watched her lover being pleasured. Dionysus' nymph expertly fondled the king's balls as he sucked his swollen cock. After only a minute, he stopped what he was doing and stood, looking out upon the crowd.

"Our mistress is an expert in the art of love," he announced. "The king is well prepared, needing nothing further to begin."

A great cheer arose from the multitude. Dionysus smiled, but his attention never waved from Faith. He fisted his cock with one hand while the other caressed her spread thighs. Once more she arched her hips, needing him inside of her, and this time he complied with her demand. Positioning himself between her legs, he teased the opening of her pussy with the head of his thick cock. Then, in a single movement, he thrust his hips forward and buried himself inside of her.

"Ah!" She cried out, the combination of deep pleasure and

pain overwhelming her. Like the rest of him, Dionysus' dick was enormous and at first he did not move, giving her time to adjust to his size. As she relaxed around him, smooth hands and lips began caressing her everywhere. The nymphs had crawled atop the bed, keeping her pinned down by using their bodies to press her arms against the mattress while they kissed and stroked her face, breasts, and stomach. Her senses rocketed to overdrive, heartbeat slamming in her chest. Never before had she felt so flooded with sensation. Every nerve ending in her body crackled with desire. Helpless to do anything but succumb to the erotic journey, her jaw fell slack as she groaned in blissful agony.

Slowly Dionysus began to thrust, his stiff cock nearly sliding all the way out before he drove himself forward, deliciously pounding Faith's eager pussy. Each of her nipples was sucked by a different nymph; a man on her right side and a female on her left. Both nymphs were nearly as gorgeous as Dionysus himself, as if they'd all been pulled from elite modeling agencies. The female who sucked her nipple had full, supple lips and Faith realized she yearned for the woman's kiss. The nymph looked up, a sparkle in her arresting blue eyes, as if she'd heard Faith's thoughts. A seductive smile played about her mouth as she leaned forward to place her warm lips against Faith's.

Her kiss was moist and deeply erotic. She had lips as soft as rose petals. *A woman's kiss is different,* Faith thought in a rapturous haze. Her passion soared when the nymph slipped her tongue into Faith's mouth and she kissed her back in a heated frenzy. At the same time Dionysus picked up his pace, his thrusts becoming faster and harder as his arousal grew. She heard his ragged panting while she continued kissing the female nymph. Lips and tongues licked and nibbled at her breasts. Suddenly she felt a slick finger beginning to stroke her clit and she broke away from the kiss, groaning in ecstasy.

The scene before her was like nothing she'd ever experienced. Dionysus held her legs apart at the ankles, keeping her spread wide as he thrust. Each of her breasts was licked and sucked by a lustful nymph. A third one, a young man who mirrored the classical beauty in Renaissance paintings, was the one who fingered her clit, his magnificent touch about to send her once more over the edge. The other chosen witnesses, the third woman and remaining two men, gave their attention to Dionysus, stroking and kissing the perfect muscled flesh of his chest, back, and ass while he made love to her. His queen.

The music she'd heard earlier had returned, flutes and ceremonial drums, and mixed in with instruments were voices, hundreds of them. As she and Dionysus coupled the crowd of nymphs began to chant, low and hypnotic but growing louder and more frenzied as the sexual passion grew.

Her king's groans increased as he drove into her, his chest heaving as he thrust. His release was near, as was hers. The male nymph stroking her clit was in perfect harmony with her needs. He increased pressure, grinding his hand against her as her orgasm loomed. She burned with sexual heat, never more aroused in her entire life. Her eyes fluttered closed and she rocked against Dionysus, her scorched body meeting his every thrust.

The warm wet mouths of the nymphs continued to suck her nipples, their teeth lightly scraping the sensitive skin to drive soaring pulses of pleasure straight to her groin. She sobbed against the overwhelming passion flooding her body, desperate for the release hovering just moments away. The frenzied drumming grew louder and faster, rhythmic, heavy beats that echoed throughout the forest in perfect synch with their coupling. Layered in with the music were hundreds of breathy sighs and groans, a telltale indication of the activity surrounding them.

Faith let her head fall to the side and looked out upon a sumptuous array of lovemaking. Couples, trios, and groups all pleasured one another. Directly before the dais, a woman positioned on all fours took her lover's cock in her mouth while a second man thrust at her from behind. To the right a stunningly beautiful female nymph lay on her back, her head resting in a young man's lap as he fed her grapes while a second woman enthusiastically licked her pussy.

Mischievous laughter caught Faith's attention. A short distance away she spotted a group of male nymphs who had captured one of their own, blindfolded and handcuffed him to a tree, then took turns thrusting their stiff cocks into his eager ass. The nymph being pleasured groaned with erotic bliss as his partners plowed him. While she watched, Faith saw one of the nymphs who had already spilled his seed step over to the handcuffed nymph and begin sucking his cock.

Suddenly Dionysus' groans rose above all other sound. His pace turned frenetic, stretching her legs as wide as possible as he pistoned away, the swell of his thick cock filling her completely. Pinpricks of light flashed behind her closed eyes. She was so close. The male nymph rubbed harder, his knowing fingers going just where she wanted. She arched against him, giving herself one extra bit of pressure until at last she exploded with release, shuddering as fierce contractions racked her body. Second later, Dionysus' roar filled the forest.

"I make you my queen!" he cried, and as Faith gazed upon him she saw him tremble and throw his head back, his mouth falling open as he was consumed by the powerful orgasm. Without warning she herself was seized by a violent, second climax, this one ten times more forceful than the one she'd had only seconds before.

She screamed with pleasure, wildfire roaring through her body. At that same moment the forest reverberated with cries of rapture as the hundreds of mating nymphs found their release, collectively gripped in the seductive throes of climax. Faith thrashed against the pillows, her body shaking as if by an outside force. Suddenly a blinding streak of lightning lit up the forest, followed by fierce crashes of thunder, one boom more severe than the last, like the final triumphant notes at the culmination of a symphony. Faith cried out, sobbing as currents of the most sublime pleasure she'd ever known cascaded over her.

All at once, she felt her body alter, a seismic shift like a chrysalis emerging from its cocoon, transformed to a butterfly. She became hyperaware of her beating heart, the roar of blood in her veins, the sinuous strength of her muscles. Her limbs were smooth and supple, drenched in the limitless perfection of youth. With unequivocal certainty she knew her human existence was no more, replaced by eternal life. An absolute metamorphosis.

As their heated passion calmed, Dionysus collapsed upon the bed beside her. As they lay panting, the six nymphs chosen to witness the event climbed down from the bed to stand upon the dais, facing the crowd.

"It is done!" one of the male nymphs declared.

"La nostra regina! La nostra regina! Ti adorare!" Over and over the euphoric nymphs cried out their response. Inexplicably, though she'd never studied a foreign language, Faith understood every word. *Our queen! Our queen! We worship you!* And at that moment, she knew the truth. Her transformation was complete.

Dionysus rolled to the end of the bed and slid off. Turning, he held his hand toward Faith and helped her down. As she stepped onto the dais to greet her followers, she was infused with the most perfect sense of harmonious wellbeing, her body a vessel that would last forever.

Through eyes that were sharper and more clear, she looked out at the adoring crowd, smiling down upon them like a leader to her faithful flock. They waved to her from their places on the soft forest ground, their flawless skin still stained with the heated blush of passion. Already they venerated her, welcoming her into the fold with the profound certainly that she was meant to be their leader. Faith met their gazes, gripped by a deep and abiding sense of love. The feeling was so potent as to nearly be tangible. She also knew her feeling was not exclusively for the nymphs alone.

"Return to me." Perhaps once again reading her thoughts, Dionysus issued the quiet command from behind her. Faith looked back, struck by the beauty of his perfect, masculine frame casually reclining against the pillows. She smiled and climbed across the bed to lay beside her beautiful god, resting her head in the crook of his arm as he trailed fingers along her bare skin. With heartbreaking tenderness he dotted soft butterfly kisses across her face, his breath drifting over her like a warm summer breeze.

She sighed with contentment, tilting her head to one side as he gently caressed her cheek. She looked around through sated eyes, realizing to her amazement that the forest was suddenly teeming with gold. Glittering dust swirled in the air like a fantastical blizzard and showered everything in its wake: the nymphs, the animals, the forest trees and streams. Jubilant nymphs scooped up handfuls of the sparkling dust and tossed it back in the air, laughing and dancing as it drifted downward and covered their naked bodies.

Dionysus rose to a sitting position upon the bed, drawing Faith up beside him. "Bevete vino!" he shouted, drawing joyous cries from their followers. Like a crowd of drunken revelers they flocked to the stream, all suddenly in possession of shiny gold chalices. As Faith's gaze followed their path, she realized with a shock that the stream no longer ran crystal clear but was instead a deep blood red. Dionysus had converted the water to wine. The happy nymphs filled their cups from the magical stream, splashing and playing, the wine streaking rivulets of red through their gold-covered bodies, like rain on a dusty window.

Faith turned back toward Dionysus as he drew her closer to his side. "I thought you emitted gold only when aroused," she whispered.

"I produce gold when I am happy," he clarified, "whether that happiness is from desire for my queen" — he gently kissed her lips, then finished in a breathy whisper — "or when I am filled with love for her."

Her heart surged at his declaration, realizing she felt the same. Her gaze turned watery as her eyes filled with tears of happiness. With a gentle finger Dionysus reached out to swipe them away.

"My beautiful queen," he whispered. "You are now mine forever."

"And you are mine," she replied, desire for her mate stirring anew. Her gaze flicked downward, seeing evidence that she was not alone in her rising lust. She reached between their bodies, stroking his rigid cock as he sucked in a sharp breath.

"Tell me one thing before I take you," she demanded, already feeling empowered in her new role as his queen.

"Anything." His breath stirred. Beads of sweat were forming on his brow. He reached out to caress her breast, his touch not quite tender as he pinched her nipples. Faith moaned in response.

"Dana," she panted, needing to ensure her friend was unharmed and safe before she mounted Dionysus.

"Already free," he whispered. "As promised."

She straddled his thighs and then slowly impaled herself on his thick cock, gasping as she was deliciously stretched. Setting her palms atop his chest, she leaned forward, bringing her lips close to his ear.

"And now, so are you."

"Thanks to my beautiful queen." His breath was little more than a ragged whisper. In one smooth motion he flipped her onto her back and spread her legs wide. His eyes were stained ink black with lust as his sultry gaze seared its place on her heart.

"Mine forever," he growled, and then they spoke no more as Dionysus buried himself into his welcoming queen.

* * *

Three months later

All eyes in the small projection room were glued to the screen. The final shot was a wide pan of the abandoned psychiatric facility before the screen went dark and credits began to roll. It was without musical accompaniment as Faith felt that anything less than total silence would take away from the stark moodiness they'd achieved

in the film. When the last few feet of the sixteen millimeter film had played and the screen went black, the only sound in the room were Dana's sniffles.

Faith turned behind her. "Brings up the lights, would you, Cam?"

"Got it." Seconds later the room brightened.

"Absolutely brilliant, Faith," Dana said, wiping her teary eyes. "It's the best you've ever done."

"The best *we've* ever done," Faith corrected. She looked around at her faithful crew all gathered in the projection room for the viewing. "This never could've been done without you guys." She grabbed the champagne she'd brought along to celebrate. Easily untwisting the coiled metal around the top, she uncorked the bottle and raised it to the gathered group.

"To the best film crew anywhere," she said. "You guys rock."

She filled their glasses and they all clinked them together before drinking deeply.

"Damn, there really is something to the expensive stuff," Tyler said. He took another long sip and added, "I still can't believe we have the money for this."

"That and everything else," Dana added. "It's like Faith uncovered a gold mine or something."

Faith shrugged and raised her glass. "Here's to rich uncles."

"It's just so weird that your family never talked about him," Cam said, frowning. "But then you're the one he left all his money to when he died."

"Who cares?" Kelly laughed. "Besides, isn't there a saying about fortune smiling on the brave and frowning on the coward? If anyone is brave it's Faith, and she deserves every penny for it."

His twenty-something youthful exuberance still stirred fires of lust within her. An amused voice chuckled in her head. *If you want him, take him. Perhaps I'll even join you.* She smiled. God of ecstasy indeed. Dionysus had never met a sexual encounter he refused. And lately, nor had she. Never in her life had she felt more alive. It was all part of the frenzied, joyous, perpetual world

she now inhabited, and the showering of divine love from her perfect ancient god.